HALFHYDE AND THE FLAG CAPTAIN

HALFHYDE AND THE FLAG CAPTAIN

Philip McCutchan

ST. MARTIN'S PRESS
NEW YORK

Library of Congress Cataloging in Publication Data

McCutchan, Philip, 1920-
    Halfhyde and the flag captain.

    I. Title.
PR6063.A167H3   1981   823'.914   80-29075
ISBN 0-312-35684-6

ONE

As savage as ever, Cape Horn reared grim and grey to the northward, glimpsed through the spindrift blown by the westerlies off the tops of the rollers that threatened every moment to drop with smashing force on the quarterdecks of the vessels of the Detached Cruiser Squadron on passage from Puerto Montt in Chile to the British base in the Falkland Islands. Aboard the flagship, Her Majesty's cruiser *Halcyon*, Lieutenant St Vincent Halfhyde, taking a turn as Officer of the Watch though he was not in fact borne upon the ship's books, stared ahead towards the escorting sloops *Biddle* and *Delia*, keeping their station forty-five degrees on either bow: those small six-gun sloops-of-war were having the devil's own time of it down here at the world's bottom, and must be awash from stem to stern as they rose manfully to the crests and then for long moments disappeared down into the great sea-valleys.... Halfhyde turned as he heard himself addressed by a small, bird-like figure, oilskinned and sou'westered like everyone else on the compass platform and upper deck, and secured by a cat's-cradle of rope lashings to a high chair, not unlike a baby's, set in the fore part of the bridge.

'You called, sir?' Halfhyde approached: Rear-Admiral Daintree's voice was not a carrying one in a gale of wind.

A neat beard wagged from above the neck of the oilskin. 'Your thoughts, Mr Halfhyde. You have the aspect of Moses, facing death before he reached the Promised Land.'

'Death seems present enough, sir,' Halfhyde roared into the Rear-Admiral's ready ear, 'at least for those poor wretches aboard the escort!'

I

'Queen Victoria's service is not an easy one, Mr Halfhyde.'

'No, sir.'

'But her seamen have stout hearts – hearts of oak still, though our ships have been of blasted iron these many years,' Daintree said in an aggrieved tone. For a while he brooded, then said, 'All those ironclads, and not a sail among 'em!'

'I beg your pardon, sir?' Halfhyde asked politely.

'Golden Jubilee Review of the Fleet. I was present, you know.'

'Were you indeed, sir?'

'Yes. Diamond Jubilee's not so far off now and I dare say I may yet live to see the Fleet go farther downhill.' Admiral Daintree turned amid his many lashings and asked disagreeably, 'Where's my Flag Captain, Mr Halfhyde, do you know?'

'Captain Watkiss went below, sir—'

'Without permission! Kindly send your midshipman with my compliments, Mr Halfhyde. I wish words with my Flag Captain at once.'

'Aye, aye, sir.' Halfhyde raised an arm and beckoned to a plump youth who was putting as much distance as possible between Cape Horn and himself by shivering in the starboard wing of the bridge. 'Mr Perrin, if you please?'

'Aye, aye, sir!' The midshipman moved across, slowly climbing up hill for a space as the cruiser lurched to starboard, then running headlong as the roll projected him the other way.

'The Admiral's compliments to Captain Watkiss, Mr Perrin, and will he please come to the compass platform.'

'Yes, sir.' Mr Midshipman Perrin turned away towards the ladder, but was recalled by a bellow from Halfhyde.

'Tactfully, Mr Perrin, if you value your skin.'

'Oh, yes, sir!' Perrin vanished; the reminder had been, perhaps, unnecessary: Perrin had a wholesome regard for the uncertain temper of Captain Watkiss and a full awareness of the strength of arm of sub-lieutenants commanded by high authority to wield canes against the bottoms of midshipmen. Halfhyde returned to a contemplation of the surging waters, watching the great guns along the foredeck as they emerged from green seas, watching the sweep of the water along the fo'c'sle and the great salt gouts pouring from the hawse-pipes after purging the anchor-cables that drummed against the plating even though the slips and stoppers had been screwed down hard in expectation of appalling weather. Glancing aft, Halfhyde for a moment watched a curious procession making its gruesome way for'ard from the quarterdeck towards the waist: four armed privates of the Royal Marine Light Infantry gripping the arms of a pallid figure that was in the very evident throes of seasickness as it lurched and slid along the wet decks – the traitor Sir Russell Savory, finally apprehended aboard the old battleship *Meridian* in Puerto Montt before she had been handed over to the Chilean Navy, a gift from Her Majesty. Behind Savory was his captor, Detective Inspector Todhunter of the Metropolitan Police, his bowler hat flying from the end of its toggle as the dreadful westerlies raged around him. Mr Todhunter, drenched and windswept to the detriment of his blue serge suit, was a stickler for being dressed as befitted his position and standing in Scotland Yard and for giving his prisoner the laid-down exercise periods as would be expected by his chief superintendent in London. His chief super would not be impressed by reference to the exigencies of Cape Horn.

*   *   *

Captain Watkiss, despite the weather and the fact that he no longer held an independent command, was in a remarkably mild mood when Perrin knocked at the day-cabin door in his harbour quarters aft, whence the Flag Captain had proceeded to answer a call of nature in comfort.

'Ah, Mr Perrin! Good morning, Mr Perrin.'

'G-good morning, sir.'

'Well, out with it, what d'you want?' Captain Watkiss shot his starched shirt-cuffs until they extended below the four gold stripes on the sleeves of his monkey-jacket and obscured the lurid head of the tattooed snake whose body wound up his forearm. 'Don't stand there exchanging pleasantries, boy!'

'No, sir. The Admiral, sir. He would like to speak to you, sir.'

'Yes, very well, why didn't you say so – no, damn you, don't argue! I detest back answers, *detest* 'em.' Captain Watkiss took up his gold oak-leaved cap, placed it on his head, screwed his monocle into place, and stood on tiptoe to stare at his tub-shaped reflection in his looking-glass. Then, frowning, he removed the cap and replaced it with a sou'wester, and took a capacious oilskin from his wardrobe. 'Very well, Mr Perrin, thank you, you may return to the compass platform.'

'Yes, sir, thank you, sir—'

'You're more pimply than ever, Mr Perrin, most unhealthy-looking to be sure.' Captain Watkiss faced him squarely. 'What's the reason? Everything has a reason, that's fact, I said it. What's yours?'

'Sir, the – the ... we're very short of fresh vegetables, sir.'

'Oh, nonsense, that's got nothing to do with it, there's always lime-juice available, is there not, Mr Perrin? Drink some.'

'Yes, sir—'

'And don't neglect your exercise or I'll have you running up to the foretop and down again for a full watch.' Captain Watkiss prodded the midshipman's stomach with his telescope. 'And keep regular, that's most important. Black draught's wonderful stuff. What does the Admiral want of me?'

'I – I don't know, sir.'

Watkiss glared. 'Never say "I don't know" to a senior officer, Mr Perrin, you should have learned that at least by now. The correct answer is I don't know but I'll *find out*. However, on this occasion, I shall find out for myself.'

As Perrin retreated, the Flag Captain pushed through from his cabin, a thick, rotund figure looking oddly like a short-legged crow in its black oilskins, the monocle reflecting golden fire from the electric lights along the alleyway as Watkiss bounced his way for'ard to the compass platform. Reaching it after climbing many ladders somewhat breathlessly, he saluted the figure of his Admiral and announced his presence. 'You wished words with me, sir.'

'Ah yes, Watkiss. Dammit,' Daintree said irritably, 'I thought you were here already, if you understand me. Kindly do not leave the compass platform without permission in future.'

Watkiss reddened. 'Permission my backside, sir! With great respect, of course. I submit, sir, that I am not a blasted snotty still wet behind the ears—'

'No,' Daintree interrupted, 'you're my Flag Captain, and I have a right to your presence. As a senior officer, you should know better, but I shall nevertheless amend my stricture: in

4

future you'll kindly not leave the compass platform without informing me first—'

'My dear sir, I made an attempt to inform you, but you were asleep—'

'Fiddlesticks!'

'I repeat, sir, you were sound asleep and I decided not to waken you. I consider myself quite senior enough to make such a decision. I remind you, sir, that I have been accustomed to the command of my own ship, indeed of a flotilla—'

'And you feel constricted whilst acting as my Flag Captain?'

'You put it well, sir. Yes, I feel a certain constriction.' Watkiss retrieved his monocle, which had been torn from his eye by the weight of the wind, and screwed it back firmly. 'As Flag Captain, of course, I command the ship, I'm aware of that. But the command is not an independent one.'

'Quite.' Daintree's voice was frosty. 'Rest assured your purgatory will not last for long. When we reach Portsmouth, I shall exchange you for someone more congenial to me – I shall make my arrangements with the Admiralty.'

'I—'

'Thank you, Captain Watkiss, the matter is closed. I wish to speak to you about von Merkatz.'

'Von Merkatz, sir? I think the blasted Hun no longer concerns us, does he? The bugger took his squadron out of Puerto Montt before we left, did he not – and will be steaming fast to join his blasted Kaiser in Kiel!'

Daintree tapped the guardrail in front of his scraggy body. 'Perhaps, and perhaps not. He's wily, you know – a twister if ever there was one. Not to be trusted.'

'Why, in that, I concur, sir. Indeed I do! I dislike Huns, dislike 'em intensely. But what do you suspect, if I may ask?'

Admiral Daintree lifted his telescope in the air, extended it to its fullest extent, and sighted it like a rifle at some invisible enemy. 'Bang, bang, bang,' he said fiercely.

'I beg your pardon?' Watkiss asked.

'War, Watkiss!' Daintree said in much excitement. 'Von Merkatz wished to cut Savory out from under our noses. He may try again, and upon the high seas. Savory is still, it seems, of the utmost value to the Kaiser and the German government.

5

We could be steaming into an ambush, don't you see? Soon we shall be approaching Staten Island. Are we to go round the island to the eastward of Cape San Juan, or are we to go through the Le Maire Strait?'

Watkiss said, 'I fancy the wind and weather must decide that, sir.'

'And I fancy not! I fancy our assessment of the mind of Admiral von Merkatz must decide, Watkiss. Will he come at us with the guns of his squadron from northward of Cape San Juan, or will he lie in wait in the Le Maire Strait, springing out upon us like some wretch of a pickpocket intent upon his prey? Which?'

Watkiss shrugged. 'Which indeed, sir? You may well ask! It's six of one and half a dozen of the other in my opinion. Whichever route we chose may be the wrong one.'

Daintree pulled abstractedly at his beard. 'We shall confer at six bells. All persons concerned in the Savory case are to muster in my sea-cabin and I shall pick their brains.'

*   *   *

Below in the warrant officers' mess when the daily exercise of his prisoner was over, Detective Inspector Todhunter stared from a porthole towards Cape Horn, now beginning to recede somewhat towards the west. His view was bleak and misty, for now and again the dreadful waters rose to wash over the thick glass of the port and when they fell away again they left it dripping with salty smears. Mr Todhunter's mood was as bleak as the glass: he carried the overwhelming responsibility for the safe delivery to Britain of the traitor Savory, now thank goodness the prisoner Savory, and never mind the fact that above him stood Rear-Admiral Daintree and Captain Watkiss. He, Todhunter, epitomized the law of Great Britain here present in southern and violent seas, and as such he represented civil power and the Secretary of State for Home Affairs. He was feeling the worse since he had just suffered rudeness at the horny hands of Mr Mottram, late gunner of Her Majesty's battleship *Meridian* and who was now, like Todhunter and all the old battleship's company, taking passage back to Portsmouth. Mr Mottram, a man of action and little feeling, had told

6

him to 'wrap up' during a discourse about his great responsibilities.

'It's the Admiral wot bears the weight, Mr Tod'unter. Not you.'

Todhunter shook his head firmly. 'The Civil Power is superior to the military – or naval. That's laid down in the Constitution.'

'Not off Cape Stiff, or anywhere else at sea. If Savory drowns, say, it won't be your fault, will it?'

'I wasn't thinking of that, Mr Mottram. I was thinking of his escape. That may be unlikely, but it's a tremendous weight upon me I do declare.' Mr Todhunter brought out a large blue handkerchief and mopped at his face: the warrant officers' mess was very stuffy, a nasty cold fug being present, and much smoke from the off-watch warrant officers' filthy pipes, and a tang of gin, and a most alarming thunder from the deckhead as the seas dropped aboard and rushed hither and thither as though seeking out the prisoner Savory to snatch him from custody. . . . Mr Todhunter's stomach grew queasy and the sweat on his brow told him unmistakably that a return to the upper deck would be advisable always providing he stood to leeward. He groped in his pocket and brought out his panacea: Doctor Datchet's Demulcent Drops, the Remedy That Never Fails. Mr Todhunter called to a steward for a glass of water, placed two tablets in his mouth and drank them down, suffering Mr Mottram's sardonic look. As he got unsteadily to his feet, a seaman boy appeared in the doorway of the mess, his sou'wester beneath his arm, and addressed the flagship's boatswain, Mr Peabody.

'Mr Peabody, sir, permission to speak to Mr Tod'unter, sir?'

Mr Peabody waved an arm. 'Go ahead, lad.'

The boy entered and spoke to the Detective Inspector, bringing tidings that the Admiral wished his presence in his sea-cabin at six bells. Mr Todhunter nodded, and rushed for the fresh air. He had delayed a little too long in taking his remedy.

*   *   *

When the messenger from the compass platform reached the wardroom, Canon Rampling was lying at full stretch on a

7

leather settee like a bison taking a forenoon nap in unlikely surroundings. The canon, chaplain to Admiral Daintree's squadron and thus back aboard his own ship after an interesting experience under Captain Watkiss aboard the *Meridian*, was not in fact asleep but reading with a growing sense of boredom the obituaries in a copy of *The Times* that had been aboard the *Halcyon* since she had sailed from Portsmouth two years earlier. It was a miracle, the canon thought, that the fragile pages had held together for so long; but the newspaper's longevity was possibly due to the fact that it had only recently been discovered wrapped around a consignment of officers' toilet rolls brought up from the paymaster's stores soon after leaving Puerto Montt. Canon Rampling had already read it some four or five times from cover to cover and was glad enough to be interrupted by the summons to his Admiral's quarters. He had found life dull after the excitement of the overland chase in Chile, all the way from Puerto Montt to Valparaiso and back, to say nothing of the daily shipboard tantrums of Captain Watkiss which had always brought something unexpected. Aboard *Halcyon* he was back, when the weather permitted, to church services during which the ship's company sang lustily but without tune, and some members of his seafaring congregation could from time to time be heard uttering words different from those laid down in the Church Hymnal; soon he would be offering simple advice upon marital problems brought to husbands by the mail when the squadron reached port. Lifting himself from the comfort of the settee and proceeding to his cabin to cover his cassock with oilskins the better to negotiate the upper deck *en route* for the sea-cabin, Rampling pondered on his summons: Daintree was not of a religious turn of mind and the call was unlikely to be connected with God. Rampling's musings turned naturally to Sir Russell Savory, traitor to the Queen, mouldering in the cruiser's cells under the watchful eyes of the Master-at-Arms and the ship's corporals, plus Mr Todhunter, that Chief Superintendent-ridden sleuth. Savory would be much on Daintree's mind and was doubtless the reason for the services of God's deputy being required. Savory might well have a need of religion now.

*   *   *

The Admiral's sea-cabin was larger than that of the Flag Captain, but not much: Canon Rampling took up a good deal of the space, while Daintree fitted neatly into a corner, small and dapper, physically overwhelmed by his chaplain and to a lesser extent by Watkiss' rotundity. Mr Todhunter stood handily beneath a port, his face greenish and his walrus moustache drooping sadly. Admiral Daintree pulled out a turnip-shaped timepiece. As he studied its face, six bells clanged out from aft, the sound being brought for'ard by the storming westerlies blowing from astern.

'Time, Watkiss. Where's that fellow Petrie-Smith for God's sake?'

Captain Watkiss screwed in his monocle. 'I didn't send for him, sir. In my opinion he's not needed, and I dislike him intensely anyhow, damn diplomat masquerading as an assistant paymaster, balls—'

'Thank you, Captain Watkiss, in my opinion his presence *is* necessary, indeed vital, since he has the background knowledge, the diplomatic angle, and now we've cleared away from Chile there's no further need of the charade of the assistant paymaster.' Daintree stared hard at his Flag Captain. 'You've not put him to work, I trust?'

'No. I always avoid speaking to the fellow whenever I can,' Watkiss said with dignity, 'and I do not propose to speak to him now if you insist upon having him present.'

Daintree shifted irritably. 'Mr Halfhyde?'

'Sir?'

'Kindly send a messenger for Mr Petrie-Smith at once.'

'Aye, aye, sir.' Halfhyde pushed open the door of the sea-cabin, and wild, spray-filled wind swept in, dampening Mr Todhunter. The messenger found and despatched, Halfhyde returned; the atmosphere was not propitious. Daintree was looking huffy, Watkiss was red with anger, and Todhunter looked far from well. The only one fully at ease was Rampling, who asked cheerfully if Savory was in need of unction.

'Unction my backside!' Watkiss snapped, pre-empting the Admiral's answer. 'The man's not facing the death penalty, not yet anyway!'

Rampling glared. 'I did not suggest *extreme* unction, Captain Watkiss, merely unction, which is a different kettle of fish

9

and can be expressed as mere friendly sympathy, a stimulation of the spirit to enable it to face—'

'Yes, yes, yes. That's not what he needs. He needs flogging.' Watkiss sat back with his arms crossed above his stomach, a veritable blaze of gold stripes. 'A traitor to the Queen, by God, can anything be worse? I'd have the bugger hove to the fore truck all the way round the Horn, damned if I wouldn't!'

Daintree could be heard clearing his throat. 'Have you anything further to offer, Watkiss?'

'No, sir, I have not.'

'I'm most glad – most glad. We are not here to discuss unction in any event. Tactics – strategy – not unction.' Daintree closed his eyes so as not to see Captain Watkiss; Watkiss was a boor and a pervasive one: he was very difficult to ignore but the attempt had to be made if sanity was to prevail. Silence, an angry silence, took over until Mr Petrie-Smith of the Foreign Office, in which establishment he held the exalted rank of Senior Clerk, this being close in the hierarchy to the Permanent Under-Secretary of State, knocked and was bidden in the Admiral's piping voice to enter. Watkiss scowled at him briefly and then, with much ostentation, averted his face from the frock coat and black trousers now wet with seawater – some damn landlubbers never learned a thing – and the gold-rimmed pince-nez balanced on the bony nose. Petrie-Smith, bald as a billiard-ball and as thin as a starved horse, ignored Watkiss and stooped his long frame politely towards Admiral Daintree.

'In what way may I help, Admiral?' he enquired.

'Savory. Be seated, if you please.'

Petrie-Smith hesitated; the only seat left was on a settee next to Captain Watkiss. But as Daintree began to show impatience he sat, and Watkiss turned a little farther away so that the two were virtually back to back.

'Now then,' Daintree said. 'I'm a man of few words and I'll not waste time. However, since I'm comparatively fresh to the Savory case, I shall summarize so that someone can correct me if I am wrong.' He cleared his throat. 'Savory purloined blue-prints concerned with the British naval ship-construction pro-gramme with the intention of selling them to Germany along with a mass of detailed knowledge personally acquired during his years of service in the Directorate of Naval Construction at the Admiralty. Having fled the country, he was found in where was it—'

'Angola, sir,' Todhunter said. 'Whence unfortunately he was taken aboard Admiral von Merkatz' squadron – but subsequently arrested by me in spite of many difficulties. With the help of Mr Halfhyde, I must add.'

'Yes. He was sentenced to penal servitude for life, and then escaped, to be re-arrested by Todhunter recently in Chile, as we all know. Yes.' Daintree frowned. 'What is it, Flag Captain?'

'You put it too simply, sir. Savory was in Chile for a purpose, not just to hide, which one might infer from your summary. He—'

'I am aware of what he was there for, thank you, Watkiss—'

'But I shall state it nevertheless, sir, so that none of us is left in any doubt as to how *vital* it is that Savory does not fall into German hands,' Watkiss said frigidly over his turned shoulder; and then proceeded with his exposition. Savory's purpose, he said, was to assist the German Emperor's designs upon British trading facilities and concessions in South America. Savory, as a high official of the Admiralty before his fall from grace, had been a man of many contacts with other government departments, such as the Committee of Privy Council for Trade, which included the Commercial Intelligence Branch. He could have been of the utmost importance and use to Germany's schemes, Watkiss said with emphasis. 'And having lost him,' he added, 'von Merkatz will be in bad odour with his blasted Kaiser—'

'Indeed he will,' Daintree agreed, 'which is why I fear a German attack upon my squadron while we're still well inside South American waters, and I must decide what to do.'

'If attacked, sir?'

'Yes.'

'But good God above, my dear sir, the answer's surely quite plain? If attacked, we open fire and sink the bugger!'

Daintree nodded. 'Such would be my wish, most certainly, but it must depend upon the exact nature of the attack. Your views, Mr Petrie-Smith? I see from your face that you have some.'

'I have, Admiral.' The diplomat was looking scandalized. 'On no account must your ships open fire upon the Germans—'

'But—'

'For that way lies war, Admiral. Neither Her Majesty nor Her Majesty's Government will countenance war against Her Majesty's grandson, you have my word for it!'

There was a sniff from Captain Watkiss; Daintree, glancing at his Flag Captain sharply, said in a mild voice, 'Yes, well, no one desires war, of course, and that is why I referred to the *nature* of any attack, do you not see?'

'An attack's an attack,' Watkiss said flatly. 'It has no nature, and must be met with force and gunfire, by God!'

'But that does not necessarily follow, Watkiss. What I fear is something more subtle than von Merkatz actually opening upon us – he will wish no more than us to provoke war.'

'What will he provoke, then, may one ask, sir?'

Daintree blew out his cheeks. 'Dammit, I don't know yet! Suppose he were to waylay us in narrow waters such as the Le Maire Strait—'

'Go round Cape San Juan and he can't.'

'Yes, yes. But let us hypothesize, Watkiss. Von Merkatz could perhaps force us inshore, crowd my ships on to the rocks along the coast of Tierra del Fuego, risking collision even—'

'Rubbish, my dear sir, he'd not endanger his own ships!'

Daintree persisted. 'I believe he might, for the greater prize of Savory. Put us ashore, at the mercy of wind, weather and rocks – and at the German mercy also. A boarding-party to seize Savory ... it can be done, gentlemen! Now, if he should attempt that, should I resist him by gunfire, or should I not, that is the question?'

'Yes,' Watkiss said.

'Most certainly not,' Petrie-Smith stated, his words clearly carrying the stamp of Whitehall. 'War is started by he who opens first, the provocation having nothing to do with it. I am not a sailor, Admiral, but I must suggest that any such situation as you have described must be met by – ah – by good seamanship and discreet handling of your vessels, and by no other means. If I am pressed to put it into a single word, I would say this: retreat. Retreat from the situation at your best possible speed, Admiral, if you value your command.'

*　　*　　*

In the privacy of his own sea-cabin, Watkiss shook his telescope in the air, his face mottled. 'What an objectionable little bugger that Petrie-Smith is! A worm, like all diplomats and other shore-side loafers! Retreat my backside. I shall never retreat from the Hun!' He shook his telescope again.

Halfhyde coughed into his hand. 'The Admiral, sir. I believe he took Mr Petrie-Smith's words to heart.'

'Well, if Daintree retreats,' Watkiss said belligerently, 'I shall relieve him of his command and take over myself, damned if I won't! I'll get the blasted leech to pronounce him insane.'

'Risky, sir, very risky. The Fleet Surgeon's unlikely to compromise his own reputation—'

'You mean you don't think Daintree's mad?'

'Frankly, no, sir. And if you should give the Fleet Surgeon a direct order, it could misfire and rebound upon yourself.'

Captain Watkiss made a hissing noise of great anger, and stamped his foot hard upon the deck. 'I'll not have the name of the British Navy tarnished, by God! I'll not stomach retreat! We'd be the world's laughing-stock, buggering off from the first approach of a German man-o'-war!'

Halfhyde did his best to smooth troubled waters. 'The really important thing, sir, is Savory himself. If—'

'Oh, balls and bang me arse, Mr Halfhyde, what nonsense you talk sometimes. The important thing is the invincibility of the fleet – the fleet that never refuses battle.' Captain Watkiss bustled about his cabin so far as he was able, two steps one way, two the other. Then he halted, frowning and pulling at his chin. 'I wonder!'

'Yes, sir?'

'Savory. He may know a thing or two, may he not? He must have some notion of what von Merkatz is likely to do, I shouldn't wonder. Why should the man not be questioned, Mr Halfhyde?'

'If you remember, sir, that was considered, but Mr Petrie-Smith's view was that any questioning should be left until Savory had reached England.'

'Damn. Yes. Well, balls to Petrie-Smith, I am the Flag Captain and thus in command of the flagship!'

'Indeed you are, sir, but Admiral Daintree—'

'Daintree, Daintree!' Watkiss said witheringly. 'Daintree'

too old to have a proper command of anything, he's not far off being senile. That's between you and I, of course, my dear Halfhyde,' he hastened to add. 'As for me, I propose to have Savory questioned with a view to finding out whether von Merkatz intends chicanery, or whether he's all bombast and bluff, which is what I suspect to be the case. In short, Mr Halfhyde, I do not propose to have my ship turn away from a mere show of force that is not to be sustained in action. I may decide to steam straight through the German line if we should meet von Merkatz at sea. Be so good as to send a messenger to Canon Rampling. I wish him to report to me at once.'

TWO

The day was darkening now and Cape Horn was well astern as Daintree's squadron moved north-easterly towards Staten Island on track for the Falklands base. With the westerlies still behind them, the White Ensigns, the commissioning pennants and the flag of the Rear-Admiral streamed forward from the mastheads and peaks, fluttering madly to the gale-force wind. Green water still tumbled over the decks and hatch coamings, over the great guns and the boats securely griped-in to their davits. At four-hourly intervals the boatswain's pipes and the bugles of the Royal Marine Light Infantry sounded out for the change of the watch on deck and in the engine-rooms and boiler-rooms of the cruisers on passage. At intervals great sailing-ships were observed, windjammers with cargoes for Chile bravely beating into the roaring westerlies, trying for a shift of wind that would carry them round into the South Pacific, ships that lay under no more canvas than reefed top-sails as the gale tore across their decks and made weird music in their rigging.

On the compass platform of his flagship Admiral Daintree was helped clear of his lashings by the combined efforts of Mr Perrin and Lieutenant Lamphorn, also ex-*Meridian* and like Halfhyde taking a turn at the watchkeeping; Daintree, as his squadron temporarily moved away from the possible dangers of the land, intended taking a nap in his sea-cabin until such time as he would be forced to chose his route off Staten Island.

'Mr Lamphorn, I am to be called the moment you raise the western extremity of Staten Island.'

'Aye, aye, sir.'

'Or any of von Merkatz' ships, of course.'

'Yes, sir.'

Daintree jutted his beard in the light from the binnacle. 'Also if Captain Watkiss should come to the compass platform. Remember *I* command the squadron – not my Flag Captain. Forget that at your peril, Mr Lamphorn.'

Snapping his meagre jaw, Admiral Daintree stepped to the after end of the compass platform. Captain Watkiss appeared to believe that he was God and to have scant respect for his Admiral. Years of command (and it was most extraordinary that Watkiss should ever have been permitted such by his superiors at the Admiralty) seemed to have gone to his head, Daintree thought. Muttering, the Admiral left the compass platform. Lieutenant Lamphorn lifted his telescope and stared ahead, searching through the gloom for he knew not what: it would be some while yet before he raised Staten Island, and he scarcely expected to find the German squadron in open water. If von Merkatz intended nefarious deeds, then he would surely wait until he could use Staten Island's various rocky promontories as cover until the last moment.

He lowered his glass. 'Keep a good watch, Mr Perrin.'

'Aye, aye, sir.'

'Warn all lookouts, if you please.'

'I've done that already, sir.'

'Do it again, Mr Perrin.'

'Yessir!' Mr Midshipman Perrin called orders to the port and starboard lookouts and bawled along the wind to the man on watch in the foretop. Lamphorn paced the bridge, broodingly, his long face sallow against the black of his oilskin and sou'wes-ter, the latter neatly and securely tied beneath a bony chin, a knot which he felt at intervals in case it should come adrift. A conscientious man, he checked everything at least twice; still brooding, for something in his bones warned him of trouble ahead, he paced to the binnacle and had many words with the quartermaster down the voice-pipe to the wheelhouse in the conning-tower: the man was to watch his course most carefully and to guard against any tendency of the ship to carry port helm. The southern tip of South America was most treacherous and not an inch was to be made in that direction. Not an inch. And a spare hand was to be sent at once to double-check with the chief boatswain's mate that all was secure on deck: anchors and cables, boats' falls and gripes – although of course the seaboat's crew and lowerers must be ready to swing out the seaboat in an emergency and their readiness was to be checked upon as well – and all deadlights clamped shut and upper-deck hatches secured against the sea.

'Aye, aye, sir.' The quartermaster, a petty officer of much experience of the sea and officers, leaned his body backwards and removed his mouth from the voice-pipe. He addressed one of his helmsmen: 'Right, Lofty, you 'eard all that guff. Trot round and report back with some nice, 'ot cocoa from the galley but don't go an' upset the chief buffer by pokin' yer nose into 'is business – right?'

On the compass platform Lieutenant Lamphorn rose and fell on the balls of his feet, bending his knees in the process like a policeman on the beat. Another gaze around with his telescope: all seemed clear, except for the lights of a sailing-ship well away to the south-east, lights that came and went as the vessel rose to the heights of the greybeards or dropped down to lie invisible behind the enormous surges of water. As Lamphorn noted the time at two bells in the first watch, the sound of a G being blown upon a bugle reached him faintly from aft: the Commander, Executive Officer of the flagship, would be starting on his rounds with the Master-at-Arms behind a lantern, making sure all was well below, peering for sin and insecurity in every nook and cranny of the messdecks a-swing with hammocks and noisy with the snores of sleeping off-duty watchkeepers. With the Commander ensuring the ship's well-being below and he himself having already ensured its security on deck, Lieutenant Lamphorn felt the flagship was ready for any untoward occurrence.

*   *   *

Earlier that day a scene had taken place between the Flag Captain and the Admiral's chaplain, who had reported as ordered but flatly refused to question Savory.

'My dear sir, you're asking me to be a spy.'

Watkiss snapped, 'You weren't so mealy-mouthed a few weeks ago, Canon. It was I who accused you of being a spy against the blasted dagoes, was it not, and you appeared to accept the charge with equanimity.'

'As did you,' Rampling said loftily. 'The results of it, anyway.'

'Yes, for the purpose of my orders you were useful enough. But since you've spied once you can damn well spy again, can't you? In any case, it's not spying. It's a simple interrogation.'

'But not one ordered by the Admiral. I cannot go against my Admiral. I am not a disloyal man, Captain Watkiss. Besides, Savory's not my province,. he's Todhunter's. Why not ask Todhunter?'

'Todhunter's a policeman,' Watkiss said with contempt. 'What good would he be? Savory would immediately smell a rat! You, on the other hand, are a man of God and therefore—'

'Exactly – a man of God, who must remember his cloth. I reject your request, Captain, and must—'

'It's not a request, blast you, it's an order!'

Rampling stood up, smoothed down his cassock and reached for his oilskin. 'One I am bound to refuse to obey, sir. I take orders only from my Admiral. May I suggest—'

'Get out. Get out of my cabin at once, sir!'

'I wish only to—'

Watkiss bounded to his feet and raised his telescope. The monocle flew from his eye with spirit. He glared up at the canon's large square face, which held an impertinent grin. 'Get out, I say!'

The remainder of Watkiss' day was unsatisfactory and was spent between his sea-cabin and the compass platform and the business of seeing justice done at Captain's Defaulters, a somewhat lengthy affair since the proceedings had not been held since Daintree's squadron had arrived in Valparaiso; a number of misdemeanours were presented by the Commander, who in the interval had held his own lower court. Watkiss handed out stoppages of leave and pay, extra work in the dog watches and a couple of punishments-by-warrant in two more serious cases concerning drunkenness and the striking of a petty officer. Justice dispensed, Watkiss simmered down from his confrontation with the chaplain and put his now untrammelled mind to the question of the wretched prisoner in the cells. After much thought he decided to ignore the fellow and to follow the promptings of his own perspicacity: von Merkatz would use bluff and that was that. The bluff would be called if the Hun should manifest himself. This decided, Watkiss spent a good deal of time in studying the charts and busying himself with dividers and parallel rulers, a perusal of the Admiralty Sailing Directions for the area from which he assessed the tidal sets, and little sums scrawled in pencil on a signal pad. This done, he bided his time until after dark and at four bells in the first watch made his way below to his harbour quarters beneath the quarterdeck to satisfy himself that his servant was not making use of his sleeping-cabin while he himself pigged it in the sea-cabin. All was well. Climbing back towards the compass platform, he encountered Perrin emerging from the after screen by the wardroom.

'Ah, Mr Perrin. Rounds?'

'Yessir!' Perrin saluted hastily. Despatched by the Officer of the Watch to make one of the periodic rounds that took place throughout the night, he had taken the opportunity of visiting his hammock in the midshipmen's chest flat to extract a bar of chocolate from beneath his pillow. 'Rounds, sir.'

'Kindly do not repeat my words back at me, Mr Perrin, it's a wretched habit sometimes indulged in by the lower deck of which you are not a member.'

'Nossir!'

'Is the Admiral on the compass platform, Mr Perrin?'

'No, sir—'

'Where is he, pray?'

'Asleep, sir, in his sea-cabin, sir.'

'I see. And who has the watch?'

'Mr Lamphorn, sir.'

'Ah. Thank you, Mr Perrin, carry on with your duty. One moment.' Watkiss placed his monocle in his eye and stared at the midshipman. 'What is that round your neck, may I ask?'

'A – a scarf, sir.'

'So I see. But it is red and green, is it not, Mr Perrin?' The tone was deceptively mild, hiding the steel. 'Knitted, perhaps, by your mother?'

'No, sir. By my nanny, sir.'

Watkiss' eyes bulged. '*Nanny*? God give me strength! I never thought I'd live to hear it! A blasted nursemaid, perpetrating

...*take it off*, Mr Perrin, remove it this instant or I shall suffer a fit. Here.' Captain Watkiss reached out his hand, seized, and jerked. The scarf unwound from Perrin's neck, spinning him like a top as the woolly substance gripped. Red and green stripes, visible in the police light outside the after screen, swirled in the wind. Captain Watkiss let go the end and the dreadful garment vanished into the wastes of the sea. 'I am prepared to pass a scarf of dark blue wool, but nothing else, d'you hear me, Mr Perrin?'

'Y-yessir! I'm sorry, sir.'

'If you feel cold, so be it. Cold never hurt anyone, and it makes men.' Shocked beyond further speech, Captain Watkiss strode for'ard; mothers and nannies were dirty words off Cape Horn. A word in the ear of the Commander, who would pass it on to the sub of the gunroom, who would then produce his cane – that would be the thing! Still disbelieving what he had seen and heard, Watkiss reached the compass platform and confronted the Officer of the Watch.

'Good evening, Mr Lamphorn.'

'Good evening, sir.'

Watkiss pulled the collar of his oilskin around his ears. 'A nasty night. I'm not surprised the Admiral's turned in. Did you not see that garment Perrin was wearing, and I stress the *was*?'

'Er...?'

'A scarf, Mr Lamphorn, a monstrosity of many colours! I won't have it! Are you the Officer of the Watch, or are you not?' Watkiss shook his telescope.

'Y-yes, sir—'

'Well, I'm glad you know what you are, Mr Lamphorn, but you keep a blasted poor watch if you fail to notice when a damn snotty's out of the dress of the day. The Dress of the Day signal to the squadron this morning included no mention of blasted red and green scarves, did it, Mr Lamphorn?'

'I think not, sir. No.'

'Then use your eyes, Mr Lamphorn! I've remarked before that you're about as much use as a curate in a brothel. I remark it again now. What are the admiral's orders, Mr Lamphorn?'

'He's to be called,' Lamphorn answered nervously, 'as soon as Staten Island – the western end – is sighted, sir.'

'I see. Anything else?'

20

'He's also to be called if the German ships are sighted, sir, and—'

Watkiss nodded. 'I understand no decision's been reached yet as to our course past Staten Island. The Admiral's leaving it a trifle late, I fancy, since we shall soon be there – though I doubt if we shall see land unless a moon comes up. What say you, Mr Lamphorn?'

'Well, sir, I agree with you.'

Watkiss planted himself at the fore guardrail of the compass platform and stared belligerently ahead into the wind-blown dark. Lieutenant Lamphorn fidgeted in acute embarrassment: how could he tell the Flag Captain that he was under orders to report his unwelcome presence to the Admiral? The Flag Captain would slay him ... in due course Mr Perrin was heard returning from his rounds; he made his report to Lieutenant Lamphorn. The cruisers steamed on, *Cardiff* and *Hector* keeping station on the stern lights ahead of them while *Biddle* and *Delia* maintained their escorting positions by taking bearings of the flagship's port and starboard lights respectively. Lieutenant Lamphorn dithered, pulling at his chin, and at last, behind Captain Watkiss, gave an embarrassed cough and resolved his problem up to a point.

'Sir, if I may suggest it, should not the Admiral be called now?'

Watkiss glared. 'Why call the Admiral, pray?'

'Because, sir, as you said earlier, we can't be far off the Le Maire Strait and a decision is called for.'

'Really.'

'Sir—'

'Oh, hold your tongue, Mr Lamphorn, I am the Flag Captain and I have as much experience as Admiral Daintree. More, I fancy.'

'But it's my duty—'

'Balls to your concept of your duty, Mr Lamphorn, *I* am your duty and remember I've had cause to complain about you in the past. If I were you, I would not tempt me further,' Watkiss added somewhat ungrammatically. 'Do you understand me?'

Lamphorn wrung his hands. 'Sir, the Admiral—'

'One word more and you can consider yourself in arrest.' Captain Watkiss stamped his foot, and as he stamped it sudden light came from *Biddle* on the port bow. 'Yeoman! *Biddle*'s calling by Aldis. Read the signal, man!'

'Aye, aye, sir.' As the message came through, the yeoman of signals read it off for the Flag Captain's benefit: 'Admiral from *Biddle*, sir, I have observed lights ahead now extinguished and believe darkened ships to be present in the Le Maire Strait.'

'Good God!' Watkiss bounced up and down in a rage. 'Why has my foretop lookout not reported it, is he blind? Find out, Mr Perrin. Mr Lamphorn, telegraphs to half ahead both engines, the engineer officer to be told he may be required to regulate by revolutions. Douse all lights, order the rest of my squadron to do the same, and make my intentions known to all ships.'

'But sir! The Admiral—'

'The Admiral is not to be disturbed, Mr Lamphorn, and that is an order from your Flag Captain, who is quite capable of conducting the squadron.'

'Very well, sir, under protest. What intentions do you wish passed to the ships in company, sir?'

Captain Watkiss thumped the guardrail. 'First of all, Mr Lamphorn, balls to your protest, and secondly, my squadron is to be informed that they are to maintain their stations on me as best they can, and woe betide any Captain who fails to do so. They shall follow my movements, which will be directed towards the enemy ... towards the blasted Hun lurking in the Le Maire Strait, Mr Lamphorn! Mr Perrin?'

'Yessir?'

'My compliments to Mr Halfhyde and he is to report at once to the compass platform.'

'Aye, aye, sir!' Perrin sped down the ladder to the upper deck, and Watkiss moved squatly to the binnacle and the voice-pipe. 'Quartermaster! Boatswain's mates to go round the ship at the double and pipe the hands to clear for action and man the guns.'

'Aye, aye, sir,' the disembodied voice came up. 'Are the buglers to sound General Quarters, sir?'

'No, they're not,' Watkiss said promptly, not wishing to bring Daintree awake just yet. Slamming back the cover of the voice-pipe, he turned to face the enemy.

THREE

There was noise along the upper deck as the ship's company doubled to their action stations, and there were banging sounds from the main armament as the guns' crews closed up, but all this was largely lost in the continual tearing racket of the wind and therefore failed to penetrate the slumbers of Admiral Daintree in his sea-cabin; an elderly gentleman of frail constitution, he was dead tired and snoring loudly.

As Halfhyde reached the compass platform, Captain Watkiss was angrily chasing Lieutenant Lamphorn from his stance behind the binnacle. 'You're no damn use, are you, Mr Lamphorn, and don't answer me back. I'll take the ship myself.'

'Take her where, sir?' Halfhyde asked from the darkness, and the Flag Captain swung round, startled.

'Oh, it's you, Mr Halfhyde. You sound impertinent, and why didn't you get here quicker? Starboard five,' Watkiss added, down the voice-pipe.

As the cruiser's bows began their gentle swing to port under starboard helm, Halfhyde repeated his question, re-phrasing it to his Captain's satisfaction: 'Where are we heading, sir?'

'Into the Le Maire Strait, Mr Halfhyde, where else? I'm on the track of that damn Hun, don't you see?'

'I don't see the Hun—'

'No more do I at the moment, but he's been seen from *Biddle* and I'll soon have the bugger in my sights.' Watkiss bent to the azimuth circle on the standard compass and began taking bearings upon what appeared to be nothing, using the instrument as though it were a gunsight aimed at the enemy. 'The motto of the Whale Island gunnery school, Mr Halfhyde! If you wish for peace, prepare for war. That's what I'm doing.'

'And the Admiral, sir?'

Watkiss straightened. 'Everyone keeps talking about the Admiral. I wish they'd hold their blasted tongues. I see no reason to bother a sick man.'

Halfhyde raised his eyebrows. 'Sick, sir?'

'Tired, then. One should have consideration for one's elders.'

'But—'

'Kindly hold your tongue, Mr Halfhyde. Take over the ship, if you please, while I assume overall command.'

'Mr Lamphorn's the Officer of the Watch, sir.'

'Mr Lamphorn's a fool,' Watkiss said briefly, and Halfhyde shrugged. All this was Watkiss' funeral; not to obey the Admiral's night orders, not to call him when faced with what seemed to be an emergency, was asking for court martial, but Watkiss must be presumed to know this for himself. Whilst coming up the ladder, Halfhyde had heard a reference, loudly uttered by the Flag Captain, to 'my squadron'; this was quite in character but nonetheless outrageous. However, there it was: Captain Watkiss had somehow thought himself into the position of command, which he was accustomed to think of as being his right. Watkiss was Watkiss, and didn't change. The flagship moved on at half speed on the main engines, still coming slowly round to port with no further helm orders, or any other heading instructions, from the Flag Captain. Before she turned full circle back towards Cape Horn, Halfhyde checked the swing, staring ahead through his extended telescope and trying vainly to pick out the contours of the land which surely could not be far off now. Then, suddenly and only just in time, there was a small break in the overcast sky, the clouds parting to let through some moonlight, and Halfhyde picked up the entry to the Le Maire Strait between Staten Island and Tierra del Fuego, the world's most barren spot, grey and grim and unfriendly and with white tops gleaming under the moon along the rollers surging into the narrows. And something else, seen at the same moment by Captain Watkiss, who uttered a shout of triumph.

'There he is, the bugger, lying in wait! That's the blasted *Friedrich der Grosse* and the German cruisers, right before my guns!' Watkiss leaned over the guardrail and shouted down: 'You there, that man, captain of the gun!'

'Yessir?'

'Stand by to open fire. Lay and train on the German flagship.'

'Aye, aye, sir!'

Below the compass platform the gun-shields swung and the great barrels lifted against the vast outline of the German battleship. Halfhyde, swearing beneath his breath, left the binnacle and strode to his Captain's side. 'Captain, sir, you cannot open without the Admiral's order!'

Peevishly Watkiss said, 'Don't be impertinent, Mr Halfhyde, my order was only to stand by. Nothing else. Bring my squadron up to full speed, if you please, and set a course towards the German flag.'

'What do you intend to do, sir?'

'I may decide to ram.'

'You cannot ram and sink four ships without sinking yourself, sir!'

Watkiss shook his telescope violently in the air. 'Are all my officers lily-livered cowards, Mr Halfhyde? Do you wish to be laughed at by a blasted foreigner? Come away from the binnacle.'

'Sir—'

'An order, Mr Halfhyde. Come away, and join that fool Lamphorn in disgrace!' Captain Watkiss butted his body at Halfhyde, thick and heavy as a rum barrel, and took the vacated place at the binnacle. Glaring ahead with angry and determined eyes, he passed the order down the voice-pipe: 'Engines to full ahead, steady as you go.' Turning his head for a moment he addressed the Officer of the Watch. 'Mr Lamphorn, sound collision stations. Prepare to ram. The cable and side party to stand by the collision mat.'

'Aye, aye, sir.' The orders were passed hastily. With little more than half a mile to go before the two flagships would strike, the upper deck of the *Halcyon* came alive with seamen and petty officers, the latter bawling commands into the roaring wind while below more parties doubled to clamp down the watertight doors and the stokers and engine-room artificers prepared their minds for an unpleasant death if matters should go, as they must, awry. Into the tense atmosphere of the compass platform pattered Rear-Admiral Daintree, aroused at last from deep slumber.

'Good God, Flag Captain, what the devil is going on?'

'I am about to ram, sir.'

'Ram who?'

'Admiral von Merkatz, of course!' Watkiss snapped. 'Who else?'

'You'll do no such thing! You'll not sink my flagship under me, Watkiss! Why was I not called, may I enquire? You will put my engines full astern this moment, Flag Captain, d'you hear me?'

'To do that, my dear sir, would simply be to strip the holding-down bolts of the main engines. I shall not.'

'Then you are under arrest and will face court martial upon arrival in Portsmouth and will be shot like Admiral Byng. I shall give the engine orders myself.' Daintree's beard jutted towards the voice-pipe, but Watkiss lifted a hand and held the cover clamped shut.

'You are too late, my dear sir, which I was not. The court martial boot may be found upon the other foot. Look!' Watkiss, his voice triumphant, pointed ahead. 'The bugger won't face me! He's turning away, as I felt sure he would. All foreigners are damned cowards and so, I regret to say, are some British admirals.'

'What was that?' Daintree asked sharply.

'I was referring to Admiral Byng, who was shot for cowardice, though in fact *he* was wrongly charged.' Captain Watkiss was jumping up and down in victorious excitement now; the flagship moved on beneath the moon, still under full power, as the *Friedrich der Grosse* slid away to starboard. Beyond her could clearly be seen the remainder of the German squadron – the heavy cruisers *Kaiser Wilhelm*, *Nürnberg* and *Königsberg*, all three of them making haste to clear the British flagship's track. The escorting *Biddle* and *Delia* steamed past them like cheeky terriers, and cheers came back along the wind to be joined by more cheering from the flagship's upper deck. Captain Watkiss removed his sou'wester and waved it vigorously towards the *Friedrich der Grosse*, which appeared to be in some difficulty, with men running hither and thither, mainly towards the

26

battleship's after part. The reason became clear within moments: a nasty grinding crash was heard and *Halcyon*'s searchlight showed the German's crumpled bow, a bow that was pointing down into the boiling sea towards the submerged rocks that were gripping the broken plates like a vice.

Watkiss shook a fist towards the scene. 'A damn stupid thing to do, to turn away into danger! All blasted dagoes are fools.'

'Admiral von Merkatz is not a dago, Captain—'

'All foreigners are dagoes, sir – that's fact, I said it. Mr Lamphorn, you may resume your watch, but resume it carefully. I should think even you could cope now that our track ahead is clear.' Watkiss swung round on Daintree. 'I suggest we do not stand by, sir. The Hun has three cruisers to assist him.'

'True, but the tradition of the sea—'

'Oh, balls and bang me arse, my dear sir, tradition is all very well but is of less importance at this moment than Savory,' Watkiss said with impatience. 'I have saved the situation so far and do not propose to see it jeopardized again. If you should give the order to stand by to assist, I shall dissociate myself from it and shall see to it that my comments are noted in the log.'

Daintree's face was white with fury. 'You are an extremely tiresome officer, Watkiss. I find you offensive.'

'In that case, sir, I shall remove myself to my sea-cabin,' Watkiss snapped, and bounced away towards the after part of the compass platform, leaving his Admiral to seethe in frustration. Then he came back again, importantly. 'A suggestion, sir.'

'I require no suggestion from you, thank you, Watkiss.'

'Oh, very well, in that case I shall make a signal as from myself – from the Flag Captain to von Merkatz. Yeoman?'

'Sir?'

'Make to the Hun: Regret my steering jammed. I hope you are not unduly inconvenienced.'

'Aye, aye, sir. In English, sir?'

'If the blasted dagoes can't speak English like anyone else, that's their misfortune, not mine.'

Watkiss left the compass platform.

*   *   *

'A nice morning, Mr Halfhyde.' It was; the squadron, having come safely through the Le Maire Strait, was into fine weather with only a stiff breeze and plenty of sun as they began the run in towards the Falkland Islands and the security of the British base; and with that happily in mind, Detective Inspector Todhunter was in a relaxed mood. He essayed a witticism. 'Admiral Daintree was too dainty, I fancy, sir!'

Halfhyde stared. 'What?'

'Admiral ... well, never mind, Mr Halfhyde. What I meant to say was, it's thanks to Captain Watkiss that we escaped the attentions of the Germans.'

'It would appear so, Mr Todhunter, indeed. Yet there was an element of luck about it. I can only hope luck stays with us as far as Portsmouth.'

'You think there could be more trouble, Mr Halfhyde, do you?'

Halfhyde laughed, but without humour. 'If you were von Merkatz, would you not be feeling vengeful?'

Todhunter pursed his lips. 'Oh dear, yes, I would, I suppose. But he's stuck fast back there, is he not, Mr Halfhyde?'

'Come, come, my dear fellow, all he has to do is transfer his flag to another of his ships!'

Mr Todhunter's morning was spoiled. 'Yes. But no ship has been seen yet.'

'Yet!' Again Halfhyde laughed. 'The South Atlantic is still before us – we have many thousands of miles to steam to Portsmouth Dockyard, you know!'

'Then you don't believe we've seen the last of Admiral von Merkatz, Mr Halfhyde?' Todhunter pulled nervously at his chin and a hunted look passed across his sad face. 'It's more than my career's worth to lose that Savory. I don't know what my chief super would say, that I don't. Or rather, I do, and that's the trouble. My chief super's not an easy man, Mr Halfhyde.'

'Those in authority seldom are, but don't lose heart. The South Atlantic's a big area, and with luck we shall be like the needle in the haystack. And tomorrow in the afternoon watch we shall be in Port Stanley, Mr Todhunter, and absolutely safe for a while. That's something to look forward to, isn't it?'

'I suppose it is, yes. All I want is to see the Clarence Pier at Southsea, Mr Halfhyde, and then the train from Portsmouth

Hard to Waterloo station – with the prisoner Savory. Then I'll be happy. Not till. I –' Todhunter broke off, staring glassy-eyed towards the flagship's port quarter. 'Oh, my God, just look at that, sir!'

Halfhyde turned to follow the outstretched arm of the Detective Inspector. From the south-west a heavy pall of smoke was approaching – a ship, as yet hull-down but moving fast. Excusing himself, Halfhyde turned away and went at the double to the compass platform. Already identification of the onrushing ship had been made by the masthead lookout and as Halfhyde arrived this was being reported to Daintree.

'German first-class cruiser *Kaiser Wilhelm*, sir, wearing a vice-admiral's flag, sir.'

'Damn. Where's my Flag Captain?'

'Here.' As if by magic, Captain Watkiss had materialized at the head of the ladder, his monocle flashing in the bright sunlight. 'I take it von Merkatz has transferred his flag, sir. Well, we shall see.' Watkiss levelled his telescope.

'See what, Flag Captain?' Daintree asked.

'See what is to happen next, of course, my dear sir.'

'Nothing is to happen next,' Daintree said.

Watkiss' telescope came down and was snapped shut with an angry motion. 'Pray what do you mean by that, sir?'

'What I say. Nothing is to happen. Our countries are at peace – and no thanks to you, Watkiss. Besides, we are close enough to the Falklands to feel no fear—'

'*I* do not feel fear wherever I am, sir.'

Daintree sniffed. 'Be that as it may, I intend to enter the Falklands in peace, Watkiss, so long as Admiral von Merkatz makes no hostile move, which I firmly believe he will not.'

'I see. Then what, sir, do you suppose he *will* do?'

Daintree smiled, a somewhat superior smile. 'I imagine it likely enough he will enter the River Plate and report to his Embassy that the *Freidrich der Grosse* was hazarded by the stupid ship-handling of a British Flag Captain.'

'You, my dear sir, are the Admiral, are you not?'

Once more Daintree smiled and looked smug. 'Certainly. But it was not I who sent that signal. By your own action, my dear Watkiss, you've assumed the personal responsibility for the handling of the ship. I imagine von Merkatz will make much of that in his report to his Emperor, who will not be slow to submit representations to Whitehall.'

Captain Watkiss went a deep and dangerous red and seemed about to offer further comment; but refrained and, turning abruptly away, bounced down the ladder to the upper deck. He bustled aft angrily, muttering to himself, intending to submerge his bitter feelings in exercise: a few turns of the quarterdeck kept the bowels regular and the muscles in tone. Upon the quarterdeck he was astonished to find a scrawny figure, capless and wearing no more than a long-sleeved flannel vest with pin-striped trousers supported by braces of heavy canvas, a figure whom he recognized as that blasted man Tidy, Canon Rampling's servant, once rector's warden of the Canon's country parish in Yorkshire in the days before Rampling had entered Her Majesty's service.

Watkiss halted.

''Morning, Captain,' Tidy said.

'Come here at once, Tidy.'

'Doan't see why I should be ordered about. I'm not in t'navy, as thi well knows, Captain, not enlisted like—'

'Come here!' Watkiss roared. Slowly and warily, Tidy came, looking much put out. 'I'm not having blasted churchwardens on my quarterdeck, Tidy, especially when they're improperly dressed. Look at you!' Watkiss reached out with his telescope and jerked at the canvas braces. 'Damn disgrace and I won't have it. You're not an officer, and this is an officers' deck. Your place of exercise is the fo'c'sle. Go away.'

Tidy drew himself up, glaring. 'I'll report you to rector, that I will!' The churchwarden backed away from Watkiss' upraised telescope, and left the quarterdeck. He went trembling with indignation; Watkiss was impossible, a very rude man, and churchwardens were accustomed to respect, even from the squire, whose position, give or take a point or two, could no doubt be considered the equivalent of that of a post captain in the Royal Navy.

Not for the first time, Churchwarden Tidy regretted being inveigled by the rector, whom he still couldn't think of as a chaplain, into accompanying him as his seafaring servant. But the rector had been insistent, and he was hard to resist, and the clincher had been his pull with the Admiralty which had ensured Tidy's special status as a civilian embarked for particular service with his rector. Tidy sniffed and drew the back of a hand across his nose; he didn't like the sea or his ambiguous status afloat. Even the petty officers turned up their noses at him; the rector had tried to get him the entree to the petty officers' mess, but there had been objections since he was, in the petty officers' eyes, a mere steward, and they wouldn't mess with a steward. Hence the indignity of the compromise that had led to his being ordered to sling his hammock, not certainly in a broadside seaman's mess, but also not in the petty officers' mess; his station was in the flat outside it, which meant his body was bumped to kingdom come every time the petty officers changed night watches. They seemed to take a delight in doing it on purpose and Tidy, with clenched teeth, thought of a cuss that sounded like booger each time a bullet-like head nudged his bottom.... He went now, since he was a man of his word, to make his complaint to the rector in the latter's cabin. He found Canon Rampling doing physical jerks and clad only in his long pants; thick hair sprouted above the waist-band and muscled arms moved rhythmically to the great weight of dumb-bells. Up, down, up, right and left extend, back to the shoulders, up, down. The rector was bathed in sweat and seemed a shade breathless: he was not as young as he had been, and Tidy clicked his tongue and reminded him of this.

'I'd take it easy if I were you, rector. 'Tisn't reet when you get past t'forty mark.'

'Nonsense, my dear Tidy, God will tell me when to stop.'

'Aye, mebbe 'e will an' all, mebbe 'e won't like. I'd not chance it, rector.'

Whether or not God had spoken Tidy didn't know, but Rampling stopped and laid the dumb-bells on the deck of his cabin. 'Is there something you want?' he asked cheerfully.

'Aye, rector. It's that Captain Watkiss,' Tidy said in an aggrieved tone. 'Chucked me off t'deck, 'e did.'

'I'm afraid it's his deck, Mr Tidy.'

'Yes, well. An' that's another thing – calls me Tidy. No need to be rude, like.' Tidy paused. 'Reckon I've a good mind to resign when we get to Portsmouth...'

'When we get to Portsmouth,' Rampling said, 'we'll part company with Captain Watkiss, so take heart.' He reached out

31

a large hand and placed it on the churchwarden's shoulder, giving a friendly grip. 'The time will pass, and we're in God's hands. He will provide, be sure of that, my dear fellow.'

'But just in case he doesn't, like—'

'Yes, yes, I'll have a word with Captain Watkiss.'

*　　*　　*

Next afternoon, still under sunny skies and with a fair breeze blowing out the flags and ensigns, Admiral Daintree's Detached Cruiser Squadron entered Port Stanley in the British outpost of the Falkland Islands. A gun salute was fired from the base as the Admiral steamed past the land batteries, and aboard the cruisers the bugles sounded the Still and the boat-swains' calls echoed across the waters of the harbour. The vessels proceeded to the anchorage where the routine drill of arrival was smartly carried out: all together, the anchors smashed into the water as the engines were put astern to draw the hulls up with a bight of cable on the bottom, while simul-taneously the lower- and quarter-booms were sent out, and the steam picquet-boats, under the charge of midshipmen, were lowered by the watch. In command of the flagship's boat was, by the mischance of sickness and two injured legs among his fellows, Mr Midshipman Perrin ex-*Meridian*. As the boat took the water she was seen from the compass platform to swing round and yaw somewhat wildly to starboard, a fact noted by the keen eye of Captain Watkiss.

Watkiss leaned out from the starboard wing. 'That boat. That damn steam picquet-boat!'

Distractedly, Perrin looked up and hurriedly saluted. 'Yes-sir?'

'Mr blasted Midshipman Perrin, you're a disgrace to Her Majesty!'

'I – I'm sorry, sir—'

'What are you, Mr Perrin? Kindly inform me loudly *what you are!*'

'Yessir.' Perrin swallowed, then bawled out: 'A disgrace to Her Majesty, sir!'

'Yes. Exactly! Get your boat under control or I shall have your guts for garters.' Watkiss paused. 'Mr Perrin!'

'Yessir?'

'God give me strength. Break out your blasted White Ensign – you're under way, are you not, at any rate up to a point?'

'I'm awfully sorry, sir.'

'Bah!' The Flag Captain watched for a moment longer, then swung away in dudgeon. Taking the reports from the Officer of the Watch, he approached Daintree, who was sitting on his seat at the forward guardrail, hunched, in Watkiss' opinion, like an ailing sparrow. 'The flagship has her cable, sir. The remainder of the squadron is anchored.'

'Thank you, Flag Captain, thank you. I shall go below to my quarters and clean for the shore. Kindly have a signal made: I shall visit the Flag Officer in Charge in one hour's time.'

'Very good, sir, but will you not wait for his signal asking you to attend upon him?'

Daintree gave Watkiss a piercing look. 'He's junior to me in the Flag List. I do not attend upon the whims of my juniors, Flag Captain.'

Daintree turned his back and Watkiss scowled: he had asked for that, to be sure. He turned to the Executive Officer, who had just reported to the compass platform. 'Commander, you may fall out the hands from stations.'

'Aye, aye, sir.'

'And call away the Admiral's barge – the Admiral will be going ashore presently—'

'The barge is being painted and overhauled, sir,' the Commander said remindfully.

'Oh, damn, yes, so it is, so it is.' Captain Watkiss breathed hard down his nose. 'Then warn Mr Perrin that he'll be required to stand by to come alongside from the quarter-boom to embark the Admiral. Oh, and one more thing: no leave is to be piped until the Admiral returns aboard, if then. The engine-room may go to four hours' notice for steam in the meantime, but must be prepared, if ordered, to raise steam on all boilers when the Admiral returns. See to all that, if you please, and send down to tell my servant that I'm on my way to my quarters and wish a bath.'

Captain Watkiss went down the ladder and made his way aft to wallow in his bathtub, which would afterwards be hand-emptied, can by can, by his servant. Wallowing, he was reflecting upon the blasted Hun who had shadowed the squadron all

33

the way since first being sighted the day before, and was now lying off the port, when a knock came at his outer door and Canon Rampling entered the day-cabin, off which the Flag Captain's sleeping-cabin led.

From amidst steam Watkiss said to his attentive servant, who was soaping his back, 'The chaplain's in the offing. I can smell blasted parsons a mile off. Get rid of him.'

'Aye, aye, sir.' Soaping was suspended, but the order had come too late. A cassock loomed in the bathroom doorway and the large face of Canon Rampling became visible.

'My apologies, sir. I have caught you at an awkward moment.'

'Yes. Kindly go away.'

'A quick word first if I may. I have prayers to take, and the matter is brief but of some importance.' Rampling coughed discreetly. 'If your servant...'

Watkiss took the point: Savory, he fancied, was about to be discussed but not in front of servants. 'Off with you,' he said to his bath attendant. 'I'll call when I need you.' The man departed. 'Now, then, Canon. It's about Savory, I take it?'

'Er – no.'

'Oh, for God's sake. Then what, may I ask?'

'My man Tidy—'

'Your man Tidy? Do my blasted ears deceive me, Chaplain? Here am I, plagued by the presence of that damn Hun outside the port, plagued by all the responsibilities of command as well as of Savory – and you come in to bother me about your man Tidy!'

'I wish only—'

'Get out! Get out this instant! What damned impudence, who the devil do you think you are I'd like to know!' Both the Flag Captain's hands came clear of the bathwater; in one was a sponge, in the other a loofah. The loofah was waved angrily like a telescope, the sponge Captain Watkiss cast through the steam at Canon Rampling, who at once obeyed orders and left. The Flag Captain's ringing shout pursued him through the outer door and past the sentry of the Royal Marine Light Infantry on guard with his rifle in the lobby: 'I don't give a fish's tit for your man Tidy and if his blasted name's mentioned to me again, I'll have the bugger keel-hauled!'

34

FOUR

The steam picquet-boat was called away and Mr Perrin brought his command from the quarter-boom to the starboard quarterdeck ladder to embark the Rear-Admiral. Daintree halted upon the upper platform of the ladder as the pipes of the gangway staff shrilled out.

'Commander?'

'Yes, sir?'

Daintree jerked the point of his sword down towards Mr Perrin. 'I'm to have the spotty youth, am I?'

'I'm sorry, sir, he's all that's available for duty.'

'H'm. Not much use, is he? I don't want to founder on the way in or back again, y'know, Commander.'

'I feel sure Perrin will cope, sir.'

'Well, I can only hope so.' Daintree trod lightly down the ladder and stepped aboard to Mr Perrin's salute. He sat himself down in the cabin, the orders were given, the boat was borne off the flagship's side by the boathooks of the bowman and stern-sheetsman, and headed inshore towards a small and rather dirty jetty: the Falklands were bleak enough in all conscience and not much of a place to command; Daintree was glad to have a seagoing appointment, though at the moment he had many worries and all of them revolved around the wretched Savory and Admiral von Merkatz waiting, as it now seemed likely, to pounce once the squadron was at sea and *en route* for Portsmouth. Either pounce, or shadow somewhat blatantly, if the past twenty-four hours were anything to go by. It was an unpleasant feeling, and undignified, for an admiral, a British admiral, to be followed about the broad ocean by a German;

35

Daintree could well understand some of the fireworks that had been sputtering from his Flag Captain, though he was not going to admit it because he detested Watkiss and his wretched autocratic ways and couldn't wait to be rid of him. And what would shadowing do for von Merkatz anyway? It really appeared quite pointless; but then, no doubt the German had something up his sleeve.

But what? Learn that, and Daintree would know how to proceed. Or Watkiss would – or would think he did. Damn Watkiss ... a pity the wretched fellow had such excellent connections in high places! Two sisters, damn it all, one married to the Permanent Secretary to the Treasury, the other to the First Sea Lord, who was a dreadful man in his own right. Watkiss was allied to the nation's purse-strings as well as to the nation's fighting capacity.

You couldn't hope to beat that combination.

Daintree sighed and stared perkily across the waters; the sun was starting to go down now, and shadows were forming, making the Falklands base look even more stark and dreary, in line with his own thoughts and fears for the future. The steam picquet-boat came alongside the jetty and Daintree got to his feet, thankful to have arrived safely. On the jetty waited a guard commanded by a senior lieutenant, and behind it was a horse-drawn conveyance, a primitive one to be sure. Daintree turned to the midshipman.

'Thank you, whatsyername.' He paused. 'What *is* your name, boy?'

'Perrin, sir.'

'Ah. I'd watch those spots, Mr Perrin, if I were you.'

'Yessir!'

'Nasty looking. Could turn poisonous.'

'Oh, I don't think so, sir!'

'Don't argue with me, boy, I'm your admiral.' Daintree stepped on to the jetty, and the naval guard presented arms. Perrin's face was very red; naturally, he had an enormous respect for admirals and post captains of Her Majesty's fleet, but he wished they would not draw loud attention to his spots in front of ratings. However, Perrin was able to console himself with the thought that he had successfully brought his Admiral ashore, which was an achievement in the professional sense. It was not, he felt, entirely detracted from by the comforting presence of his leading hand, Leading-Seaman Gramper, who would have tactfully put him right had he looked like going wrong ... Leading-seaman Gramper chose this moment to ask permission to go below to the engine-room. Just to check.

'Check what, Gramper?'

'Bilges, sir.'

Perrin nodded formally. 'Very good, Gramper, you may go.'

'Thankee, sir.' Gramper, a sea-daddy of the old school, touched a finger to his cap. He went for'ard, dropped down the engine-room hatch, nodded at his opposite number, Leading-Stoker Bustard, and pulled out a quid of tobacco which he stuffed into his mouth and began to chew. Black saliva drooled from a corner of his mouth as he uttered. 'Poor little sod, eh!'

'Who, Gramps?'

'Why, that Perrin.'

'All midshipmen are poor little sods,' Bustard said.

'This one's afflicted. Pimples ... more'n most of the young gennelmen.'

Bustard flicked some cotton-waste over a gleaming brass instrument. 'Needs a woman.'

'Ar. So does all of us, eh!' Leading-Seaman Gramper hadn't had a woman since Valparaiso, but they were all in the same boat and there was nothing to be gained by moaning about it. There were no women in the Falklands, only sheep, not much cop. Not that they would be in port for long anyway ... Gramper sighed and said, 'Roll on Pompey. Commercial Road on a Saturday night, can't go wrong, eh?'

'Queen Street'll do me, mate. Not so far to bloody walk, is Queen Street.'

'Gar!' Gramper was contemptuous. 'All them barrack-stanchions from the 'ulks, they've sodded up the Queen Street tarts. Catch a dose, more likely than not. Barrack 'ulks, they're riddled with it.' So was all Portsmouth, but physical distance from his shipmates when on the fornication hunt gave a man a sense of greater safety, and that was important otherwise you worried yourself into the grave. And of course you couldn't do without it, stood to reason, though some of the holy joes did without that and without drink too. Leading-Seaman Gramper was not a holy joe, and had a more than passing acquaintance with all the bars in Pompey Town, plus Chatham and Devonport to a lesser extent. He pulled at his beard and stared down at his bare feet: toe-nails needed cutting, sod it – they'd go and trip him up and send him arse over bollocks like as not. He chewed on, brooding now about the human freight they were taking back to Pompey: that Savory, traitor to the Queen. Cor! Deserved all he got, did Savory – a *gentleman*, trying to flog naval secrets to the Germans, that took some beating. The good old Queen, now, she was all right and had enough to put up with without traitors to add to the load. All that money, all them jewels, all those palaces and castles – but never a man since His Royal Highness had hopped the twig. Leading-Seaman Gramper scratched reflectively beneath an arm ... the queen hadn't any pimples so far as he knew. Funny, that. It took a man different, but God alone knew why that should be. Poor little fat pimply Perrin, he had a hell of a life, always the butt of the Flag Captain, and he hadn't the look of one who'd ever get a woman easy like, except maybe one day for his rank. Leading-Seaman Gramper reflected upon his own luck. Sod rank, which he hadn't got: a bushy beard, a thick head of hair, a breezy swaggering manner, plus other things of course – they got the tarts better than rank did! Sometimes a man had to be sorry for officers, they had to think of rank before anything else, it was in their nature and part of their duty ... Time passed, and the two shipmates entered into a discussion of other topics of interest to the lower deck until a voice called from up topsides.

'Leading-Seaman Gramper?'

'Coming up, Mr Perrin, sir.' Gramper hoisted himself to his feet, bent his way through to the tiny stokehold, opened up the boiler with the aid of a long iron grab, and sent a stream of black juice into the fire, where the gob sizzled and spat for a moment before being consumed in steam. Then Gramper turned away and went nimbly up the ladder to the deck. Reaching the sternsheets he saw Daintree returning in his horse-drawn conveyance.

'Admiral weren't long, sir,' he remarked.

'No.'

Daintree disembarked from his carriage and stepped across

to the picquet-boat, where he was saluted aboard. 'Back to my flagship most speedily, if you please, Mr Perrin.'

'Aye, aye, sir.' Perrin passed the orders and the boat came off the jetty efficiently and headed across the harbour. There seemed to be something the matter with the Admiral, Perrin thought: he was chattering away to himself and he kept shifting about on the settee in the cabin, and alternately pulling at his beard and making little darting motions with a clenched fist, as though battering at some invisible enemy – once when he was doing this he caught the eye of Mr Perrin upon him and speedily changed the gesture to a beard-pull and then cleared his throat with much ado.

Something was in the air.

Back alongside, the Admiral was ceremoniously piped aboard and once upon the quarterdeck could be heard ordering the Flag Captain to have steam on the main engines for leaving harbour. Perrin took the picquet-boat to the quarter-boom where he made fast and then, behind his crew, went aboard via the boom to be met upon the quarterdeck by Sub-Lieutenant Parker-Price who, by virtue of being the flagship's senior sub-lieutenant, held the position of sub of the gunroom, the mess used by the sub-lieutenants and midshipmen.

'Well, young Perrin.'

'Yes?'

'Yes, *sir*.'

'Yes, sir.'

'Interrogatively, Perrin, as in your first utterance.'

Perrin swallowed. 'Yes, sir?'

'I see you have brought the Admiral back.' Mr Parker-Price, tall and immensely thin, loomed over the midshipman like a bean-pole. 'No troubles, I trust?'

'Oh, no, sir! None, sir!'

'You handled the boat efficiently, Perrin?'

'Oh, yes, sir! I think so, sir!'

Parker-Price sniffed. 'Damn *smug* for a snotty.' He seemed to ponder for a moment, then said, 'For smugness, Perrin, six of the best.'

Perrin stared. 'W-what ... sir?'

'I think you heard. To the gunroom immediately, Perrin, at the double.'

His face as red as his bottom would soon be, Mr Perrin scuttled down to the gunroom. Mr Parker-Price followed more slowly and with greater dignity. Mr Perrin was bent across the gunroom table, with his monkey-jacket lifted clear of his rump, and Parker-Price seized a thin, pliant cane and took a number of preliminary swishes in the air. When punishment was over, Mr Perrin's eyes held tears of rage and indignity. This was twice since Cape Horn: once for nanny's scarf, and now for doing his duty with efficiency. He wondered why he had ever gone to sea.

* * *

Conference was in the air again, this time in the spacious surroundings of the Admiral's quarters aft. Arranged in sumptuous chairs and settees, with gin served by the Admiral's petty officer steward, were the Flag Captain, the Commander, Lieutenant Halfhyde, Mr Petrie-Smith of the Foreign Office, and Detective Inspector Todhunter.

With all glasses charged except that Todhunter hadn't got one at all, Daintree raised his eyebrows. 'No gin, Todhunter?'

'I don't partake, sir.'

'Don't – er – partake?'

'Never, sir.' Todhunter was firm. Partaken he had in the past, but never so much as when he had become thoroughly inebriated upon whisky in the unlikely surroundings of the African jungle during his original pursuit of the traitor Savory: never again. It was not worth it; his chief super would be against it. And his late father had partaken, to the immense sorrow of his late mother. So, not even a very small quantity of gin. Mr Todhunter felt obliged to offer an excuse because the Admiral had seemed so astonished. 'I have a need, sir, to be circumspect in regard to my stomach.'

'Gin's good for it, but never mind. We have more urgent matters to discuss, gentlemen. Weighty news has reached me from the Flag Officer ashore.' Daintree paused, and glanced with dislike at his Flag Captain. 'Yesterday, it seems, a despatch was brought by cruiser from Cape Town, as a result of a cable received there from the Admiralty. My orders are changed. I am not to take my squadron to England.' There was another frigid glance towards Captain Watkiss, who would now remain as Flag Captain for somewhat longer.

'Where are we ordered to, may I ask?'

'Into the River Plate, Flag Captain, as I was on the very point of saying. Or rather, to lie off the mouth of the Plate and be ready to enter if required.'

Watkiss asked, 'Do you mean, if *ordered*, sir?'

'No, Flag Captain, I do not. I said if required, and if required was precisely what I meant. The decision to enter will be mine, and mine alone. A weighty matter indeed, as Mr Petrie-Smith will no doubt appreciate.'

'Indeed I do, Admiral – it is always a most serious matter to violate territorial waters, most serious – both the Argentine and Uruguay—'

'Dagoes the lot of them,' Captain Watkiss interrupted loudly. 'May I ask, sir, what the trouble is, since trouble I assume there to be if a British naval presence is likely to be required?'

'Buggers have arrested our Ambassador to Montevideo,' Daintree said with brevity.

'Which buggers, sir?'

'The Uruguayans, of course. Montevideo's in Uruguay, is it not? There's been some kind of revolution, I gather—'

'Revolutions are endemic to these blasted South American states,' Watkiss said angrily.

'And the new government has thrown our Ambassador into gaol, regarding him as friendly towards the previous government—'

'What about von Merkatz?' Watkiss asked. 'Is he to become involved as well, do you know?'

Daintree tut-tutted. 'I'm not in communication with the German Admiralty, Watkiss, nor am I privy to the mind of the Kaiser—'

'Nor am I,' Watkiss said truculently, 'but I can make a damn good guess: von Merkatz will see this as another blasted opportunity to make trouble for us and for the Queen. It stands out a mile, does it not? The blasted Huns have interests in both the Argentine and Uruguay, and—'

'Yes, yes, thank you, Flag Captain.' Daintree held up an admonitory and impatient hand and with some relief turned towards the Detective Inspector, who had been manifesting intense concern and dismay and was wriggling about in his chair as the naval gentlemen harangued each other. 'What is it, Todhunter?'

'The prisoner Savory, sir! What is to become of the prisoner Savory?'

'Why, he must come with us, must he not?'

'But it's my duty, sir, to deliver him to justice as soon as possible!' Mr Todhunter was almost wringing his hands. 'My chief super's not a man to accept excuses, sir.'

Daintree blew out his cheeks. 'I'm afraid your chief superintendent must bow to the exigencies of the service, my dear Todhunter. He can scarcely blame you. In any case, my orders are clear and must be obeyed. I am to leave for the River Plate as soon as my ships have steam.'

'But sir ... cannot the prisoner Savory remain here in Port Stanley, and I too, with a strong guard? Surely there is cell accommodation in the naval dockyard?'

Daintree nodded. 'Certainly, and I confess I raised the point with the Flag Officer. He refused to take Savory, who might well linger here for many months awaiting another passage to the United Kingdom. My ships are still under orders for Portsmouth as soon as matters are settled in the Plate, which may be speedily done, and are thus seen as the quickest means of bringing Savory to the justice of which you spoke, Todhunter.'

'But my chief super—'

'Oh, hold your tongue!' Captain Watkiss interrupted furiously. 'Do you expect the Admiral to be buggered about by some wretched—'

'Thank you, Flag Captain, I am well capable of making my own utterances.' Daintree turned again to the Detective Inspector. 'Rest assured that the Admiralty will have Savory much in mind, and your superiors will already have been informed that you are now subject to Her Majesty's naval requirements and under my orders. The responsibility is not yours, as I've said.'

Todhunter bowed his head. 'Thank you, sir. Thank you very much indeed, sir.'

'Try not to worry. Worry is worse for the stomach than gin.'

42

'Yes, sir, I believe that to be true. My late mother, sir, was a woman much given to worry and this led, according to the medical gentry, to indigestion and flatulence—'

'I'm sorry to hear that, Todhunter—'

'She became of a bilious disposition, sir, with a poor complexion...'

Watkiss bounced to his feet, telescope gripped in his fist like a constable's baton. 'Pray excuse me, Admiral. If the flagship's to go to sea, I have much to attend to and should not be delayed by discussions about flatulence.'

*   *   *

While the flagship's boilers were brought up to immediate notice for steam, along with those of the rest of the squadron, Captain Watkiss strode his quarterdeck with Halfhyde. He was still angry. 'Blasted policemen. Somehow one fails to associate them with mothers. Daintree's too weak for high command.'

'Why so, sir?'

'Why, did you say? Because admirals shouldn't allow time to be wasted on damn leech's twaddle, that's why! The sick are a blasted nuisance. Look at me for example. Never had a day's sickness in my whole life! Never needed the damn leech even for an ingrowing toenail! Wind and weather – Cape Horn – snow and ice – the tropics, China, the Mediterranean – even Scotland, and God knows that's bad enough. I survived them all, Halfhyde. Todhunter looks like death warmed up.'

'He was talking of his mother, sir, not himself.'

'Oh, don't argue, Mr Halfhyde, I detest being argued with. Heredity – there's a lot in it. Both my parents rode to hounds, grandparents too. Made men of 'em.' Captain Watkiss turned and stared seaward. After a moment he uttered an expletive and bounced energetically on the balls of his feet. 'The Hun, Mr Halfhyde! He's no longer there! The bugger's gone to sea. No doubt the chief yeoman will have reported to the Admiral – why didn't he blasted well report to me also, I'd like to know, I'll have his guts for garters, see if I don't! What d'you make of this, Mr Halfhyde?'

Halfhyde shrugged. 'One could make anything of it, sir, but speculation won't help us.'

43

'Oh? I call that a rude answer to my question.'

'I apologize, sir. I shall re-phrase it: any guess we could make might well be very wide of the mark.'

'H'm. Yes, yes, I see that, of course.' Watkiss sounded sage. 'What you say is quite true, certainly. We should be thankful he's gone, I suppose.' He frowned and went off at a tangent. 'The Admiral. Can't think why he wanted *you* at his conference. You're only a lieutenant of less than eight years' seniority, after all.'

'Quite, sir. The same thought had occurred to me. I was not required to contribute.'

'Sat like a blasted dummy.' Captain Watkiss raised a hand and scratched thoughtfully beneath his uplifted chin. 'Daintree's deep, you know. It's sometimes hard to tell what he's thinking, if you follow me. Personally, I prefer plain speech, call a spade a spade, don't you know. I've a suspicion he may have some particular task for you, and wanted you to be a party to whatever it is from the start. I – ' He broke off as the Officer of the Watch approached, the trailing loops of the empty sword-belt that denoted his status swaying against the frock-coat. 'Yes, Mr Forbes, what is it?'

Lieutenant Forbes saluted. 'The Engineer Officer reports steam upon the main engines, sir, and the engine-room ready to proceed.'

'He does, does he, Mr Forbes?'

'Yes, sir—'

Watkiss flourished his telescope and his face reddened. 'What blasted impertinence! Damned engineers, think themselves to be gentlemen and continually prove the opposite! I am the Flag Captain, Mr Forbes, I am not on the compass platform, and I do not receive reports in harbour at second hand. Send down to the engineer and tell him to make his report in person and make sure he's not covered in coal-dust.'

*   *   *

As Her Majesty's cruiser *Halcyon* stole out to sea, followed by the *Cardiff* and the *Hector*, with *Biddle* and *Delia* in their accustomed stations to port and starboard of the flagship's bow, the flagship's Master-at-Arms, MAA Pickering, sat ensconced in his

44

cabin with the former Master-at-Arms of the *Meridian*, MAA Titmuss. Masters-at-Arms of the British Navy were important persons, albeit of the lower deck, and as such were entitled to a cabin and a sword, neither of which, naturally, were of officers' pattern. The cabin was small, dank, and dark, having no ports but being situate almost dead centre in the ship; it was prone to both rats and cockroaches but it was a sight better than the broadside messes, or even the petty officers' mess, with all them swinging hammocks and a terrible stench of feet and body sweat in hot weather, enough to make anybody puke their guts up.

Tonight, the Master-at-Arms' cabin smelled strongly of rum, for Master-at-Arms Pickering had the duty of supervising the daily issue of grog to the lower deck ratings. Certain attributes of sleight-of-hand usually enabled any good Master-at-Arms to reserve a proportion for his own use, and tonight as on other nights of late Pickering was sharing it, having found a friend in a friendless world: Masters-at-Arms were commonly the most loathed persons aboard any of Her Majesty's ships of war, since they headed the ship's police.

'Your good 'ealth, Mr Titmuss,' MAA Pickering said.

'Good 'ealth, Mr Pickering.'

They smacked their lips; *Halcyon*'s rum was good, and though rum was supposed to be standard throughout the fleet, Masters-at-Arms prided themselves on being able to notice differences; a lot depended upon how much the particular shoreside paymaster had surreptitiously watered it down to his own profit. But this was first-class, and they quaffed. There was little need of speech, and indeed, as both would have put it, there was sod-all to talk about anyway.

'Good 'ealth again, Mr Titmuss.'

'Likewise, Mr Pickering. When I gets me ship again, you can call on yours truly.'

'Ar.' Mr Pickering belched, a spirited blast. Soon, sod-all to talk about or not, rum had loosened tongues and the topic was the inevitable one: bloody Todhunter and bloody Savory, the latter set uneasily between the opposing goalers of civil power and Royal Navy. 'Stone the crows, that Tod'unter, fair gets on a man's tits ... no pun intended, Mr Titmuss, o'course.'

'No offence taken.' Mr Titmuss waved a hand.

45

'Little piss-quick! All bowler 'at an' Gladstone bag. Bloody shoreside peelers, think they're God. Dunno what things is coming to, sod me if I do.' MAA Pickering glowered. '*My* ship, this is, not Tod'unter's. *My* cells. Know what?'

'What?'

Pickering leaned forward across the table between them, and smote it with a beefy hand. 'Little bastard comes down again 's afternoon, poking and nosing, prying in corners, opening up that Savory's peep-'ole to make sure 'e's there still, asking questions till me throat gets sore with answering. Kept on quoting 'is bloody chief super at me. Well, I ask you! We, Mr Titmuss, are the 'eads of the ship's police, right – well, you *was* an' will be again. What I mean is this: as 'ead o' ship's police, I rank like I was a commissioner or whatever the bloody civilians call them. Tod'unter, 'e won't 'ave that.' Pickering took some more rum. 'Detective Inspector my granny's arse. Needs taking down a peg.'

'That's right,' MAA Titmuss agreed righteously.

'Good mind to do it.'

'How?'

'Eh?'

'How, Mr Pickering?'

MAA Pickering pulled at a protuberant lower lip. 'Dunno yet. It'll come. See if it don't. What about them Germans?'

Titmuss belched and said, 'I don't reckon much to 'em, not really.'

'I'm not so sure. Huns is Huns, all said an' done.'

'Well, that's true.'

'Bastards.'

'Yes.'

'*Scheming* bastards.'

'Yes.'

'So they'll need watching, Mr Titmuss. When we gets to the Plate, they'll need watching, you mark my words. Don't reckon they'll do much at sea 'cos they can't, not really.' Mr Pickering ruminated over a little more rum. 'Get that Savory safe to Pompey, and I reckon I could stand in line for Warrant Master-at-Arms. I've got the time in, just a question of a recommend from the perishing Admiral, or that Watkiss. That Watkiss now! Rum 'un, ain't 'e?'

46

Titmuss winked. 'Not asking me to be disloyal, are you, Mr Pickering?'

'Ar. I reckoned it might be like that.' Pickering nodded and ruminated some more. 'Lieutenant-at-Arms ... one day! Cor! That'd make my Fanny sit up, all right!'

'Mrs Pickering?'

The Master-at-Arms scratched his face. 'Not sure really. I married 'er when me first died ... or I thought she died, while I was on a commission up the Straits. Found out after, she'd run off with a gunner's mate from Whaley, rotten bastard. That's strictly between you an' me, I 'ope I need 'ardly add.'

'O' course.'

Pickering glared at the bottle of rum. 'Bloody booze, makes a man say what he didn't ought. 'Ave another, Mr Titmuss?'

'Thanks.' Titmuss held out his glass, and both were refilled somewhat splashily.

'Then I'll go and check that Savory before perishing Tod'unter comes down again. Make sure 'e's bin to the 'eads while I'm at it.' MAA Pickering clicked his tongue. 'Some people'd never believe what some bloody defaulters on cell punishment gets up to, they wouldn't really. I was a ship's corporal in the Pompey barrick 'ulks once. Bugger kept shouting out 'e wanted to go to the 'eads, and I didn't budge, thought 'e was just out to rile me like.'

'And 'e wasn't?'

'No. When I collects up 'is oakum in the morning, 'e'd shit in it.'

*   *   *

The Detached Cruiser Squadron proceeded under starry skies through a smooth and placid sea, making good speed north-north-westerly for the River Plate and the salvation of the British Ambassador, whose release was to be demanded. Shortly after clearing away from Port Stanley, Mr Petrie-Smith had sought another private interview with Rear-Admiral Daintree in order to impress upon him how vital it was to play matters easily and not provoke anyone to combat. Things could be, he pontificated, on a knife-edge.

'Your theme song, I fancy, Mr Petrie-Smith.'

'My duty, Admiral. The world's peace is important.'

'And not so fragile it's likely to be shattered by a fracas upon a South American river.'

Petrie-Smith wagged a finger, a gesture that Daintree didn't take to. 'I would not wager upon that if I were you, Admiral—'

'You're *not* me. I'm in command of this squadron, and I shall handle it how I wish and the devil take the Foreign Office.'

'But really, Admiral—'

'Good night, Mr Petrie-Smith, I am tired and not as young as I was. I intend to turn into my bunk.'

With a bad grace, Petrie-Smith left the sea-cabin, banging the door behind him. Undressing down to his combinations only, since at any moment at sea a call might come in an emergency, Rear-Admiral Daintree pondered upon the immediate future. Now was perhaps his chance to bring himself to the attention of Their Lordships of the Admiralty. He was getting on in years, was old for the rank of rear-admiral, and to retire as a vice-admiral would be nicer and would augment his pension when he went on the Retired List. His best foot would be thrust forward and never mind Petrie-Smith and his old maid's outlook. Of course, as ever, there were snags and the most thorny was his Flag Captain. If anybody could make a dog's dinner of an operation and a rear-admiral's promotion prospects, then it was the good Watkiss. All the same, Daintree, was not down-hearted; there were various ways of handling tricky situations and before going to sleep he carried out a careful study of the Admiralty Sailing Directions for the River Plate and its contiguous coasts.

FIVE

Master-at-Arms Pickering, less than sober, swore roundly at his senior ship's corporal. 'I've a good mind to take you before the Officer o' the Watch, 'ave you shoved in the report. Sod could 'ave kicked the ruddy bucket, an' then there would I be, eh?'

'Sorry, Master.'

Pickering smouldered. He placed his eye once more against the peep-hole in the stout cell door. The prisoner Savory was seen clearly in the police light, lying not on the metal shelf that did duty as a bunk, but on the deck, doubled up and in obvious pain – a pain in the gut, the Master-at-Arms supposed. He was groaning, so he was alive, which was something, but he, the Master-at-Arms, should have been called earlier. Bringing a bunch of keys from a pocket, Pickering unlocked the door and marched in.

'What's all this then?'

Savory groaned but made no answer. Pickering bent and started to lift the prisoner back to his hard bunk. Savory gave an agonized scream and Pickering, sweating, laid him back on the deck and then turned upon the ship's corporal. 'Go an' get the Surgeon,' he ordered, vacating the cell as he spoke. 'An' ask Master-at-Arms Titmuss to kindly step this way. I'll stay 'ere till the Surgeon comes, all right?'

This ship's corporal departed speedily, boots clumping along the deck and up many ladders; the cell accommodation was low in the ship, below the waterline in fact, a dank and smelly place. MAA Pickering sweated again and wiped his brow as the rum emerged from his pores; to lose a prisoner by death was almost as unprofessional as losing one by escape, and the sooner the Surgeon took the responsibility the better. The first person to arrive was Master-at-Arms Titmuss, breathing hard with his exertions.

'Ah, Mr Titmuss.' MAA Pickering explained the situation; MAA Titmuss stared through the peep-hole at Savory, who for reasons of security and a certain rigidity of mind prevalent among Masters-at-Arms had been locked in again.

'Gawd,' Titmuss said. 'Looks bad, I reckon, Mr Pickering.'

'Yer. Surgeon's on 'is way,' Pickering said. 'Point is, someone 'as to report to the Captain. Or Officer o' the Watch, any 'ow.'

'You, I reckon, Mr Pickering.'

'Should be, yes. On the other 'and, see, *you* was the Master first responsible—'

'Aboard the *Meridian* I was, that's right.'

MAA Pickering stroked his chin. 'Still are, up to a point.'

'Oh no, no, Mr Pickering, it wouldn't be right for me to shove me nose in, not aboard your ship.'

'Not shove your nose in. Just make the report, like, to the compass platform.' MAA Pickering was well aware that he stank of rum and that the wind blowing over the compass platform was unlikely to disperse it all; it wasn't worth the risk. 'Do me a favour, eh? Go an' – ' He broke off: echoing footsteps were heard approaching and a moment later a mess jacket appeared with scarlet cloth between the gold stripes of rank upon the sleeves – three gold stripes, the Fleet Surgeon in person. MAA Pickering hastened forward with his report and diagnosis.

'Swinging the lead, very likely, sir. Or maybe it's the stench, sir. Paint an' bilgewater an' tar, sir.'

'And rum.'

Pickering's eyebrows went up. 'Rum, sir? Why, I—'

'Open up the cell, Master, and let me see my patient.'

'Aye, aye, sir.'

*   *   *

On the compass platform, Sub-Lieutenant Parker-Price, Officer of the Watch, became aware of a rising smell of spirits as a heavy step was heard upon the ladder from the upper deck. A person came up and stepped carefully around to leeward of the binnacle. 'Officer o' the Watch, sir?'

'Yes. Who might you be?'

'Name of Titmuss, sir. Late Master-at-Arms o' the *Meridian*, sir.'

Parker-Price gave an acid, tight-lipped smile. 'I happen to be a little deaf on that side, Master. Go round to the other side, if you please. The windward side.'

'Sir?'

'I think you heard me. Do as I say at once.'

'Yessir.' MAA Titmuss swore beneath his breath, cursing the very name of MAA Pickering who had stooped so low as to pull seniority on him and given a direct order, such as could not be disobeyed – not with the bloody Fleet Surgeon standing there as a witness, ears a-cockbill. And Titmuss was accompanied by an aroma that was equal to that of Pickering himself – and the Officer of the Watch, the bastard, had already smelled it. MAA Titmuss stepped with reluctance to windward, and Parker-Price lifted his nose ostentatiously and sniffed.

'Drink, Master. You're drunk, man!'

'Begging your pardon, sir, I am not drunk, sir. A tot, sir, taken late in the—'

'Don't argue with me, Master-at-Arms, I say you're drunk as a fiddler's bitch.'

'No, sir, with respect and not presuming to argue, sir, just a tot, sir—' MAA Titmuss broke off as an interruption came from just aft of the compass platform. A figure appeared, bearded and with dishevelled white hair blowing around its face: the Rear-Admiral himself, in nightshirt and dressing-gown.

'Mr Parker-Price?'

'Sir?' Parker-Price snapped to attention.

'What's all this? Who's drunk?'

'This person, sir.'

'Oh. Who's he?'

Once again MAA Titmuss identified himself.

'From the *Meridian*? What are you doing here at this hour?'

'Sir, a report, sir.' Rum fumes swept the compass platform. 'The prisoner Savory, sir. Sick, sir.'

'Savory? Sick?' Daintree waved an arm somewhat wildly

51

towards the Officer of the Watch. 'Oh, damn you, Mr Parker-Price, why was I not told earlier? There you stand, blethering about a man being drunk, while a vital prisoner lies sick in his cell! What's your excuse?'

'Sir, I—'

'Oh, nonsense. When you've been in the service a little longer, you'll learn, I trust, to organize yourself and your priorities. Send for my Flag Captain at once, and for that policeman.'

'Very good, sir,' Parker-Price said surlily.

'Mr Parker-Price, no one knows better than I that my orders are very good. Kindly give the proper response immediately.'

'Aye, aye, sir.' Mr Parker-Price's clenched teeth could almost be heard in his reply.

Daintree addressed MAA Titmuss. 'Now, Master-at-Arms, what is the nature of the prisoner's illness?'

'I don't know, sir.'

'Don't know?' Daintree stared closely. 'Has not the Surgeon arrived at the sickbed?'

'Yessir, Fleet Surgeon, sir. He said summat—'

'What did he say?'

'Pie rexier, I think, sir, of unknown origin.'

'Yes, yes. That means he doesn't know either, like all leeches, they don't even understand rheumatics, let alone anything else. Oh, dear, oh, dear! This is most serious.' A gust of wind whipped the Admiral's dressing-gown up over his face; he clawed it away angrily. 'Where the devil is – oh, there you are Fleet Surgeon, and about time. Your report instantly, if you please.'

'In regard to Sir Russell Savory?'

'Plain Savory. Her Majesty has seen fit – dammit, the fellow's a traitor, is he not, and a traitor cannot be—'

'A traitor he may be, but he's also a very sick man.'

'Ah yes.' Daintree nodded. 'What of, Fleet Surgeon?'

'Well, sir.' The Fleet Surgeon, a stringy man with a long face like that of a horse, gave a cough; it was many years ago that he had qualified and his practice had been frugal since. Diagnosis was never easy. 'I have yet to make tests, sir. But he has a high temperature, and palpation suggests extreme tenderness of the abdomen.'

52

'Suggests?' Daintree asked acutely. 'Cannot you be sure, you're paid enough?'

'I fear an inflammation of the appendix,' the Fleet Surgeon answered, not committing himself too far.

'Yes, I see.' Daintree blew out his cheeks. 'Well, that's not particularly serious, is it?'

'It can be fatal, sir.'

Daintree jumped. 'Fatal, by God! He's not to die, Fleet Surgeon, you shall see to that.'

'I shall do my best, sir.'

'Yes, do. What do you propose by way of treatment?'

'First, leeches will be applied to the abdomen in the hope that they'll suck out the poison. Then he'll be poulticed.'

'If the leeches fail to suck?' Daintree asked keenly.

'Exactly, sir.'

'Medicine? Patients are always given medicine, physic, surely?'

'In appropriate cases, sir, yes. In this case I shall administer black draught to clear out the bowels.'

'Yes, good idea, that,' Daintree said approvingly. 'A good clear-out never fails, never. I suggest—' Daintree broke off as a figure came across the compass platform towards him. 'Now what is it, Mr Parker-Price? Not another complaint about drink, I trust?'

'No, sir. Admiral von Merkatz, sir, upon the starboard quarter.'

*   *   *

Leeches were adhered to Savory's stomach, black lumps that slowly swelled with his polluted blood while a sick-berth petty officer watched with a professional eye. With him stood a number of interested parties: Captain Watkiss, Detective Inspector Todhunter, MAA Titmuss on sick-berth guard, and the Fleet Surgeon, the latter now out of his expensive mess dress and clad in the blood-stiffened frock coat and striped trousers that he wore for amputations. All of them had anxious expressions, and not a word was said until the Flag Captain gave tongue upon seeing the sick-berth petty officer perform an unhygienic act.

53

'Fleet Surgeon, do you normally allow your po-bosun to pick his blasted nose over the patient?'

'Hodges!' the Fleet Surgeon snapped, looking up.

'Sorry, sir.'

Captain Watkiss was not propitiated. 'Haven't you ever heard of hygiene? This place is filthy.'

'Newfangled nonsense. Good, honest dirt never hurt anyone, Flag Captain. There's this fellow Lister, but he'll not last.'

'Nor will Savory at this rate! Can't you hasten those damn leeches?'

The Fleet Surgeon gave an audible sigh. '*I* am in charge of the surgery and sick bay, Flag Captain, not you.'

'Don't be impertinent or I shall have you placed in arrest.' Captain Watkiss stabbed with a finger. 'That leech there. It looks sick.'

'That's the idea,' the Fleet Surgeon said. 'It sucks, and then is sick. Hodges!'

'Aye, aye, sir.' The sick berth petty officer took up a pair of rusty iron tweezers and seized the afflicted leech, jerking it away from its hold upon Savory and placing it upon a pan of salt. After a moment, Savory's blood and some pus were ejected and Watkiss felt quite ill himself. Like chestnuts before a Christmas fire coming to the point of being cooked, each leech in turn indicated repletion and was removed to the salt pan, where it regurgitated.

'Is he any better, sir?' Detective Inspector Todhunter enquired anxiously after study of the results.

The Fleet Surgeon shrugged, and took up a thermometer which he thrust into the patient's mouth. At the same time he felt for the pulse; removing the thermometer he examined it, pursed his lips a little, shook the mercury down and laid the glass beside the salt pan and its horrible occupants. Then he palpated the stomach again before pronouncing. He said, 'Little change, I fear.'

'Use a poultice!' Watkiss snapped, brandishing his telescope over the inert form that looked close to death.

'All in good time, Flag Captain.'

'I never heard of a blasted doctor that didn't poultice from the start,' Captain Watkiss said truculently. 'God knows where

54

you learned your trade, Fleet Surgeon, I don't! I said, use a poultice, did you not hear? I meant *use it now*.'

'I think,' the Fleet Surgeon said equably, 'that you're disturbing my patient. I shall ask you to leave – all of you.'

'Damn you to hell, you—'

'If you refuse to go, Flag Captain, I shall wash my hands of the patient and leave you to save him, since you are so much better a doctor than I. At the same time I shall inform the Admiral quite unequivocally that you are placing my patient's life in jeopardy.'

'You – you ...' Words failed Captain Watkiss; he seethed, then said, 'Very well, then, have it your own way, blast you, but if you should fail to save your patient in my absence the full facts will be reported to Their Lordships at the very first opportunity. Refusal to poultice, by God! Doctor my backside. *Leeches!*' He bounced to the door, followed by a hand-wringing Detective Inspector. Looking back just before he left, Watkiss saw the po-bosun using his tweezers again and replacing the leeches upon Savory. He went petulantly along the alleyways with Todhunter, almost too angry for speech. But not quite; he had a lot to unload. 'Medical men!' he said with extreme bitterness. 'What a useless lot to be sure!'

'I've known some good ones, sir,' Todhunter said unwisely. 'My old mother—'

'Fiddlesticks!'

'Varicose veins, like. Out before you could say Jack Robinson, just a flick of the knife, sir. And police surgeons too, sir. Always diagnose death very quick indeed, sir—'

'Oh, hold your tongue, Todhunter, what a stupid thing to say.'

'Sorry, I'm sure, sir.'

*   *   *

'The German,' Daintree said next morning. 'He's still there.' He pointed; von Merkatz had shifted and was now off the port bow.

'I can see that for myself, sir,' Watkiss snapped. He breathed heavily for a moment or two. 'What's the bugger up to, I'd like to know! It's almost as though he smells death – like a vulture –

55

and is waiting to pick up the corpse.' He paused, then shook his telescope towards the German. 'Waiting, by God! That's it, isn't it?'

'What is, Flag Captain?'

'Why, he's waiting – to pick up Savory! Not dead, but alive! I wouldn't be surprised if all this was some sort of pre-arranged plot – a plot, my dear sir, to get Savory out of his cell and into surroundings from which he can escape by – by jumping overboard and being picked up. In short, the fellow's been malingering, and with a purpose ... it wouldn't take much pretending to fool the Fleet Surgeon into thinking a man to be sick.'

Daintree laughed. 'Nonsense, Flag Captain. Savory wouldn't have a hope of jumping overboard – he'd not get past Titmuss.'

'On the contrary, it's only too easily done, especially once he's convalescing. Exercise on the upper deck, which the blasted leech – Fleet Surgeon – is certain to recommend before long. Well, his recommendations won't be accepted, that's all about it.'

Daintree demurred. 'There is a human responsibility towards the sick.'

'Sick my arse!' Watkiss said energetically. 'I've already made the point he's malingering!'

'That's nonsense too. Whatever you say, he wouldn't be able to fool my Fleet Surgeon.'

'Fleet Surgeon's an ass,' Watkiss responded dismissingly. 'Won't poultice. As like as not Savory'll die anyway.'

'Whilst malingering, Flag Captain?'

'Oh, hold your ... I think you misquote me, sir, possibly deliberately. I meet with nothing but frustration aboard your flagship, sir, as I shall report to Their Lordships upon my return to the United Kingdom. In my experience it's highly unusual for an Admiral to argue continually with his Flag Captain to the detriment of the good order and discipline of his blasted squadron. I shall report that too.'

Daintree said icily, 'You have a tortuous mind, Flag Captain, like a serpent.' He seemed about to add more when the Fleet Surgeon appeared up the ladder. 'Good morning, Doctor. How's the patient?'

'Better, sir.'

'As I suspected!' Watkiss snapped.

Daintree brightened. 'Oh, excellent, most excellent! I'm very glad indeed. What's the – what's the – er—'

'Prognosis, sir. Fair. I believe I shall save him.'

Watkiss bustled across. 'You poulticed, of course, as I advised?'

'No. The leeches did the trick. The leeches and the clearing action of the black draught. Savory has responded very positively, I'm glad to say, and is now out of pain.'

'Good,' Daintree said. 'I'd like a report of progress each watch, if you please, Doctor.'

'You shall have it, sir. Of course, I promise nothing – it's possible his condition could deteriorate, but I'm hopeful we shall get him to Montevideo.'

'To Montevideo?' Watkiss repeated with a dangerous look in his eye. 'For what purpose?'

'I propose he be landed, Flag Captain.'

'The devil you do! I say he shall *not* be landed!'

Daintree said, 'The Fleet Surgeon's advice must be heeded, Flag Captain—'

'Heeded, yes. And then rejected. Dammit, you're the Admiral, my dear sir!' Captain Watkiss bounced up and down furiously. 'I'll not have you landing Savory smack into the blasted arms of von Merkatz! I'll not have it, I say! I won't permit it! I commanded the *Meridian* – I was responsible for Savory's capture and I'll not have him put on a blasted plate and handed over like a damn penny in a church collection!'

'You talk impertinence, Flag Captain—'

'And you talk drivel, sir.'

'Get off my compass platform!' Daintree, his face white, made shooing motions with his hands. 'Go away at once!'

'Nothing would give me greater pleasure, sir,' Captain Watkiss said with dignity, and flounced down the ladder. At the bottom was Halfhyde, about to ascend.

'Good morning, sir.' Halfhyde saluted the Flag Captain.

'Where are you going, Mr Halfhyde?'

'To the compass platform, sir.'

'I wouldn't go up there if I were you, Mr Halfhyde.' The Flag Captain's voice rose loudly. 'It's the abode of lunatics.' Brandishing his telescope, he made his way aft: the quarterdeck, and

57

his daily exercise, beckoned. Disregarding the Flag Captain's advice, Halfhyde proceeded up to the compass platform, where the Admiral was not in the best of tempers, and merely grunted when Halfhyde saluted him. Then he waved a hand in the direction of the German cruiser.

'Confounded nuisance,' he said. 'I don't like the proximity, Mr Halfhyde. It adds to the hazards of the sea.'

'I have no doubt Admiral von Merkatz will stand clear, sir.'

'Possibly. I hope so! Meanwhile, I'm projecting my mind ahead.'

'Yes, sir?'

'It's obvious von Merkatz is standing by on account of that wretched fellow Savory. My Flag Captain suggested that he might try to take Savory off, but that's ridiculous, of course. How the devil could von Merkatz know Savory was going to develop an inflammation of the whatever-it-is?'

'I agree, sir.'

'I'm glad somebody does,' Daintree said huffily.

'However, I see dangers, sir. Suppose Savory should decide to take advantage of the situation, and try to make a break over the side?'

'That's what Captain Watkiss suggested, but it's rubbish.' Daintree paused. 'Isn't it?'

'Well, sir, I think he should be closely guarded until he's returned to the cells – just in case.' Halfhyde coughed. 'I think a break is unlikely, but what would your orders be if it should take place?'

'You mean if Savory actually plunges overboard and swims?'

'Yes, sir.'

'I'd call away the seaboat, Mr Halfhyde, and have him pursued, of course. I'll guarantee to have my seaboat in the water before the German's!'

'Yes, indeed, sir. And the question of opening fire?'

Daintree stared, wide-eyed. 'Shoot him, you mean?'

'Shoot *towards* him at all events, sir, if only to keep the Germans away.'

'Yes. Well, we shall see. I dislike the idea of opening upon a fellow Englishman, but the fellow's a traitor when all's said and done.' Daintree looked broodingly across the water at the

58

German cruiser and the great flaunting ensign of the Kaiser blowing out along the wind above the grey menace of the guns and torpedo-tubes. The moment of decision might come at any time now, and the whole affair would be very tricky indeed; the German Emperor was a hot-tempered ruler, very spirited, and was said ever to be seeking an excuse to take on the British Navy in war. He appeared to have little love for his imperious grandmother in Windsor Castle, much less for his Uncle Edward, Prince of Wales. The lot of a British admiral was not always a happy one, and anxiety tugged hard at the heart-strings of Rear-Admiral Daintree. The old Queen, God bless her, was no coward, nor were her sailors and soldiers, but workaday England had no wish for war, at any rate not over a damn traitor who might be better shot dead before any clash of arms with the naval might of Germany could come. The admiral who failed to do what might be regarded as his duty, and settle the matter cheaply by the expenditure of one killing round of small-arms ammunition, could be held much to blame should the great guns start to roar over land and sea and the military and naval youth of Britain be committed to blood and flame. It was a high responsibility, but it might not happen after all. Daintree turned once again to Halfhyde as his squadron, under German eyes, forged on towards the River Plate.

'Mr Halfhyde, we *must* project ahead.'

'Sir?'

'The Plate! I have a feeling von Merkatz means to stay with us, and will anchor outside the river with us. It's at the Plate that the trouble will come.'

'In what guise do you see it coming, sir?'

'I don't know! That's my difficulty. He'll wait till our defences are down, probably.'

'You mean when – if – we enter the river itself, and steam into Montevideo?'

'Yes! That's it! We'll be slap inside a port where even the new authorities are likely to be friendly towards Germany. All sorts of things can happen, can't they?'

'Perhaps so, sir, but we may be sure the Admiralty will have taken that into account, and evidently they believe we can cope.'

'Yes. But certain subterfuges may become necessary.'

'Indeed, sir?'

The Admiral was silent for a few moments before uttering again. 'You have a reputation, Mr Halfhyde, for handling what one might call special missions,' he said. 'I shall bear that in mind, and may have a use for you.'

'Can you be more precise, sir?'

'No, I can't at this moment, but be sure I shall tell you in good time.'

*   *   *

Detective Inspector Todhunter, for the first time since childhood, had started biting his fingernails. So near and yet so far – Savory as it were under hatches, but many a long sea mile to Portsmouth Town and the railway station – and that wretched German ship hanging about all ready to commit a felony. The trouble was, of course, that the prisoner Savory was in actual fact no longer under hatches but very much above them, all nice and comfy in his sickbed. A watch was being kept on the sick bay door and in addition to an armed sentry, a watchkeeping rota of responsible persons had been formed to take charge: Mr Todhunter and Masters-at-Arms Pickering and Titmuss. Neither Pickering nor Titmuss had considered it compatible with their status to take watches, but the Flag Captain had given the order and that was that. Currently, it was Mr Todhunter's watch and whilst biting his fingernails he pondered upon his chief superintendent in far-off Scotland Yard and wondered to what precise lengths his superior officer would go to in order to retain Savory in custody. Chief Superintendent Portlock was something of an enigma and more than something of a snob: he tended, and of course he was not alone in this, to go easy on gentry. It was, after all, the gentry who employed the police force to stand between them and the common people and to protect their lives and property against assault; but Chief Superintendent Portlock went beyond this admirable concept and quite often actually stretched the Law in favour of the gentry. Now, Savory was a knight: Sir Russell Savory. That meant gentry, or it should; but there were snags. From sundry observations made in the past by that Captain Watkiss, Todhunter had understood Sir Russell Savory to be not quite a gentleman but rather a person of humble origin who had made good (before making bad, that was). In short, an upstart. That could complicate matters *vis-à-vis* Chief Super Portlock, whose attitude would be unpredictable but would be made known, should Todhunter err, in no uncertain fashion in due course. To mention just one thing: perhaps he, Todhunter, officially in full charge of his prisoner and never mind Captain Watkiss or the Masters-at-Arms, should have insisted that Savory be treated for his unfortunate complaint in his cell rather than be virtually freed. In the case of gentry, of course, that would have been wrong; but if Savory was a mere upstart, then Todhunter had been guilty of over-soft handling. If as a result of this Savory should somehow manage to get away from custody, then the fat would be well and truly in the fire, gentry or not, for class would have been overridden by worse considerations. Mr Todhunter bit furiously until relieved from his duty by Master-at-Arms Titmuss at eight bells in the forenoon watch.

Titmuss jerked a thumb towards the door of the sick bay. ''Ow's 'is nibs, eh?'

'I've not enquired, Mr Titmuss.'

'Should 'ave. I 'ave to enter 'is condition in me report.' Titmuss clicked his tongue, and brought a pencil from behind his ear. 'Watches, Mr Tod'unter, are 'anded over proper in 'Er Majesty's ships of war, stuff me if they ain't. Go on in and ask.'

Mr Todhunter felt inclined to complain, but thought better of it. Titmuss had an immovable look about him, like a bull sculpted in granite. Breathing hard down his nose, Mr Todhunter entered the sick bay and made his enquiries of the sick berth petty officer. Duly informed, he emerged and MAA Titmuss, producing a notebook, sucked at the lead of his pencil and stood expectant.

'The prisoner's condition is improving,' Todhunter reported. 'Temperature one degree above normal, bowels responding to medication, swelling greatly reduced—'

'Pain?'

'No pain now, Mr Titmuss.'

'No pain now, temperature falling, likewise stomach swelling, 'as shat.' MAA Titmuss finished the labour of writing and closed his notebook. 'All right, Mr Tod'unter, watch 'anded over and report accepted and you needn't 'ang about.'

'Don't you think he might be returned to his cell, Mr Titmuss?'

'That's up to the Captain,' Titmuss said, 'on the advice o' the Fleet Surgeon.'

*　　*　　*

Two days later it happened, if not quite as predicted by the Flag Captain and feared by Todhunter: Savory was allowed on deck, at the insistence of the Fleet Surgeon. Savory might be a prisoner, a convict recaptured on the run, but he was a human being and doctors, by virtue of the Hippocratic oath, dealt in human beings. Fresh air and gentle exercise he must have, then after a day or so the decision would be taken as to whether or not he was to be returned to cell accommodation and the stench of paint and bilgewater and other things. Savory was led to the quarterdeck by two armed seamen with MAA Titmuss in rear and Todhunter lurking unofficially in the background, his bowler hat firmly secured by its toggle against a blustery wind. The sea looked inhospitable, Todhunter thought, all white horses and nasty waves, and the flagship was surging about, disturbing his stomach and making walking in a straight line difficult. As Savory was brought through the after screen on to the quarterdeck, Captain Watkiss was observed walking towards the stern. When he turned to bounce forward again, he appeared to explode. His arms waved like a windmill and he roared out, 'You there! Those men! Todhunter! Titmuss! Get that man off my quarterdeck instantly!'

Todhunter, his police instincts coming to the surface in pursuance of his duty, advanced bravely and started to utter. 'Captain, it was my understanding that you approved the doctor's—'

'Yes!' Watkiss screeched. 'Yes! But not on the quarterdeck! The quarterdeck is *my* deck and I won't have it sullied, damned if I will! Blasted ratings, blasted prisoners ... bah!' The telescope just missed the brim of the bowler hat. 'Get him clear! Take the bugger to the fo'c'sle!'

Todhunter gave a despairing sigh and turned; and then, having turned, he almost had a fit. Savory had gone. Todhunter doubled forward and caught up the procession beyond the after screen door; MAA Titmuss had wasted no time in obeying the Flag Captain's loudly uttered orders. Proceeding forward, they all emerged on to the fo'c'sle, where the motion was much, much worse and the wind seemed stronger, battering at Mr Todhunter and sending the bowler hat to the end of its toggle, where it blew and danced like some black puppet on a string, and tugged and tugged at Mr Todhunter's lapel where its ringbolt anchored it. Under the eyes of Admiral Daintree and the personnel on the compass platform, the prisoner Savory took his exercise. But not under their eyes alone: on the flag deck the chief yeoman of signals stared through a telescope and reported to the compass platform that interest was being taken by the officers on the German flagship's bridge. And within a matter of minutes the *Kaiser Wilhelm* was seen to be altering course a little inwards, as though approaching the British flag for a closer look, or worse.

Halfhyde, Officer of the Watch, drew the Admiral's attention to the enemy movements. 'I suggest Savory be taken below at once, sir.'

'I think not, Mr Halfhyde. I wish to estimate von Merkatz' intentions. He may show his hand, and can then be dealt with. The moment danger develops, then Savory can be taken below in safety. I shall not be panicked.'

'May I ask, sir, how you propose to *deal* with the German as you say?'

Daintree tapped a hand irritably on the forward guardrail. 'I don't know yet.'

'But surely—'

'Patience, Mr Halfhyde, patience! Patience is a virtue.' The squadron continued on its course, all eyes now upon the party walking the fo'c'sle and upon the German cruiser. Slowly, the *Kaiser Wilhelm* closed towards the British flagship's bow, her decks seemingly lined with men who could just be watching with interest or could be standing by to grapple a swimmer aboard. Halfhyde was filled with anxiety and alarm for an old man's obstinate stupidity: Daintree was running it much too fine, and without point so far as Halfhyde could see. Then suddenly the Admiral appeared to see the danger for himself. 'The German's putting my ship in hazard!' he cried out. 'Wheel hard a-port, Mr Halfhyde!'

Halfhyde bent immediately to the voice-pipe and passed the emergency order down. Almost at once, the flagship answered her helm and began a massive swing away to starboard; doing so, she gave a heavy lurch as she came flat across the wind and sea, and her fo'c'sle heaved horribly, causing havoc on the slippery decking. Savory was seen to pitch forward towards the port guardrails and MAA Titmuss came to grief as his feet caught a bottlescrew slip on the anchor-cable. He cannoned heavily into the armed seamen just as Mr Todhunter, running willy-nilly downhill as the deck sloped wickedly, went flat and slithered towards the deep and windswept ocean until his crutch struck a stanchion and held him open-legged and half over the side, uttering sharp cries of agony. In the middle of all this, Savory was seen to have vanished and at the same moment as his loss registered on the compass platform Mr Perrin, Midshipman of the Watch, reported the *Kaiser Wilhelm* sending away her seaboat.

SIX

'Firing parties, Mr Halfhyde! Marksmen to the fo'c'sle immediately!'

'Aye, aye, sir. Are they to shoot to kill?'

'Not, I think, to kill. Only to keep the Germans at bay.' Daintree turned as more disturbance smote the compass platform. 'Ah, Flag Captain—'

'You may well say "ah", my dear sir. You've made a balls of it! You've lost my prisoner – I repeat, *my prisoner* – by your damn stupid manoeuvre! Are you aware that Savory seems to have gone overboard – no doubt involuntarily, cast by your blasted incompetent ship-handling, sir?'

'You – you—'

'And now, if he cannot be retrieved in time, he must be shot. What about the seaboat's crew and lowerers of the watch? I've heard no pipe.'

'Damn!' Daintree said, going a deep red. 'Mr Halfhyde, away seaboat's crew and lowerers!'

'I've already passed the order, sir.' Halfhyde, leaning dangerously out over the port guardrails, reported the seaboat going down on the falls and ready to slip. Captain Watkiss' ears had evidently failed him, or the wind had carried the boatswain's calls away from him. Slipped, the seaboat pulled manfully ahead as the gunner's mates doubled around the decks detailing the firing party. Rifles were hastily released from the chain guard, which was unlocked by the Royal Marine Light Infantry sentry outside the Admiral's and Flag Captain's quarters aft. Armed men doubled to the fo'c'sle, where Mr Todhunter had been released from the guardrail and

65

withdrawn to safety inboard and was now rubbing his crutch and looking pale and agonized. In the meantime the cutter from the *Kaiser Wilhelm* was approaching with astonishing rapidity, giving clear evidence of German efficiency and seamanship, and making straight for a head that was bobbing about in the turbulence off the port bow of the British flagship. The Commander was now upon the fo'c'sle and, with a lieutenant, was waving his arms and shouting to the German boat to stand clear. Captain Watkiss chose this moment to have the flagship's main and secondary armament manned.

'Sound for action,' he ordered, placing his monocle in his eye and glaring towards the *Kaiser Wilhelm* and its wretched Admiral's flag. 'Yeoman, warn the rest of the squadron to stand by to open upon the Hun.'

'Aye, aye, sir.'

Daintree spun round. 'Flag Captain, you shall do no such thing with my ships. I countermand the order. Bugler!'

'One moment, sir.' Captain Watkiss thrust his stomach forward and lifted an arm to push the bugler aside. 'I am merely taking precautions, that is all. I may not open, but the threat should have an excellent effect.'

'You should have asked my permission first. I am the Admiral.'

'No time,' Watkiss snapped. 'Now then, where's that blasted seaboat? Mr Halfhyde?'

'The cox'n is having difficulties, sir – he's come broadside to the sea—'

'Damn boat's crew not sufficiently exercised before I took over as Flag Captain,' Watkiss stated. 'I'll have the Commander's balls for breakfast if the blasted Hun gets to Savory first, damned if I don't!' He bounced up and down in a fury. 'Just look! The Hun's almost there!' Thrusting himself to the forward guardrail, he yelled down to the fo'c'sle. 'Commander!'

The Executive Officer turned his head. 'Yes, sir?'

'What the devil are you waiting for? Open fire with your marksmen! Pepper the sea around the blasted Hun, but cause a war at your peril.' There was something in Captain Watkiss' tone that suggested that if anyone was going to cause a war, it must be himself. 'Mr Halfhyde, where's the seaboat now, *my* seaboat?'

66

'Coming up, sir.'

'Commander!'

An angry face looked round again. 'Yes, sir?'

'My seaboat's crew, Commander. Tell 'em to stand by to ram the Hun.'

'What about the man overboard, sir?'

Watkiss brandished his telescope. 'Can't you think of anything for yourself? Savory's the first priority, of course, you fool.' A moment later, as the *Kaiser Wilhelm*'s boat came within range, the rifles opened. Sharp cracks came back to the compass platform, but in the confused seas the smack of the bullets could not be seen. More important, the rifle fire apparently had little effect upon the German seamen, who continued pulling towards the bobbing head which was now making towards a lifebuoy cast from the flagship's deck. As Watkiss studied the scene balefully, the British seaboat, now evidently under control, came into his field of vision, also heading for the hapless swimmer and threatening, at last, to put itself between him and the marauding Germans. But the Germans were dedicated men, acting like automatons under the spur of their Admiral's heel, and a superhuman effort brought them up to the swimmer first, and the moment his top half was with difficulty grappled aboard, they had swung round to head back for the *Kaiser Wilhelm* – which by this time had moved in a good deal closer, so that the armed men along her decks could be clearly seen as they prepared to do battle with the British rifles. The latter were still firing, though only to pepper the waves; Captain Watkiss was once again about to pre-empt his Admiral's order, and shout to the Commander to shoot to kill – for the blasted enemy had now revealed himself finally as such, the kidnapping bugger – when he lifted his telescope for what might be a final look at Savory.

'It's that blasted man Titmuss!' he exploded. 'It's not Savory! *Where the devil is Savory?*'

*   *   *

'No, I am not the prisoner Savory.' MAA Titmuss, wet, cold and scared, squeezed seawater from his uniform trousers and tried to appear official. 'Name o' Titmuss, Master-at-Arms o' the flagship,' he added untruthfully; a white lie he considered it to be in the circumstances, and these bloody Germans didn't speak enough English, stupid sods, for a full explanation. 'Ship's police. *Police*, see?'

'*Ja?*'

'Yes – yar.' So that had penetrated, and the Lord be praised. But the boat was still pulling for the *Kaiser Wilhelm*, with the *Halcyon*'s boat well behind, and MAA Titmuss had no wish to be taken aboard the German cruiser and become a pawn, some sort of hostage, likely enough, for the prisoner Savory. There could be nothing more unprofessional than for a Master-at-Arms to become a hostage for his own prisoner, and his promotion prospects would vanish for ever; it wasn't fair. MAA Pickering, who was really responsible for Savory, should be here in his place. Just because a swing of the bloody ship had made him go arse over tip into the hogwash! However, it couldn't be denied that the Germans had rescued him, and although a British rescue had only been fathoms away, it might be as well to express gratitude, and he did so.

'I reckon I'm grateful,' he said to the boat's coxswain. 'You picking me up, like. Thanks. No doubt you'll be putting me aboard my ship now? Me own ship, like. Eh?'

Hope faded; the Hun hadn't understood a word, not a bloody word. There was a grin and a stream of German, that was all.

The British seaboat was well astern now, and also, and luckily for himself, he was out of the effective range of the rifles, or nearly so; the odd bullet was zipping into the water, and one struck the boat's gunwale, but without much force behind it, as though it was tired at the end of its journey. That firing, now; it meant the British had opened first, and the Germans might make much of that, bloody squareheads, and they might treat him as a prisoner-of-war and intern him in the Fatherland, a nasty prospect. Wildly, MAA Titmuss looked round the heaving waters of the South Atlantic. If he went back overboard – if he could manage it before he was grabbed – he would very likely be hauled back again before the *Halcyon*'s seaboat could reach him. Then he might be charged by the Germans with attempting to escape whilst a prisoner-of-war, and he might be shot. You never knew with foreigners, they had funny minds. Then all of a sudden something came to MAA Titmuss and he recalled his early days in the navy, which he had joined as a boy seaman and had risen to the rating of leading-seaman before opting to transfer to the ship's police. The basic seaman in Titmuss took over and he acted immediately.

He rose to his feet and projected his tubby body like a squat torpedo through the nearest rowers, shoving them violently aside, until he had reached the midship section, where he crouched down. Over his head bedlam was let loose, the air was filled with shouted orders, and something very hard smote MAA Titmuss on the shoulder; he was so fat it didn't hurt much, and anyway it didn't matter now because he had got where he wanted. He pulled and levered while the Germans tore at him with hands and feet, and out came the bung. Water gushed into MAA Titmuss' stomach, and the boat began to fill fast, at once losing her way through the water. There were shouts of triumph as the *Halcyon*'s seaboat swept up alongside and from amidst the waterlogged Huns MAA Titmuss emerged like a whale to be received back on to British sovereign territory.

*　　*　　*

For some long minutes after Titmuss had been identified in the German boat, the British flagship's compass platform had been an uncomfortable place, with everyone present coming under the lash of the Flag Captain's tongue and fresh orders being issued every second, orders that sent boats away wholesale and had the entire ship's company, with the exception of the watchkeepers currently on duty, scurrying round the decks with toothcombs, looking for Savory. The air was heavy with threat: reports to Their Lordships, punishments by warrant, plus keel-hauling and mastheading and even flogging; though such latter punishments had been erased from Queen's Regulations these many years past, they lived on in the mind of Captain Watkiss. Panic was brought to a happy end by the upsurge of MAA Pickering, sober, to the compass platform, where he saluted the Flag Captain.

'The prisoner Savory, sir.'

'Yes, yes!'

'Below in cells, sir. I didn't ask the doctor first, sir—'

'Quite right! Below, is he? Well, thank God! Where did you find him, Master-at-Arms?'

'Well, sir, in the seamen's 'eads, sir. 'E'd 'ad a dose o' the black draught just previous to exercise, sir. The excitement, sir, and the fall 'e 'ad, like, it acted like a primer, sir. Blew the charge as you might say, sir.'

'Yes, I see.' Captain Watkiss hauled in his monocle and placed it in his eye. 'You say he fell. Where, precisely?'

'Down on to the port gun-sponson for'ard, sir. 'E creeped in through the gunport, sir. Reckon 'e was dead lucky, sir. *An*' no injuries, sir.'

'I wonder why he didn't take the opportunity to escape?'

MAA Pickering shrugged. 'Dunno, sir. Scared stiff o' the look of the sea, sir, shouldn't wonder.'

'Yes, perhaps. Thank you, Master-at-Arms. All's well that ends well and I shall say no more. But if you hazard your prisoner again, by God, I shall strip you of your crown and laurel and have you in cells in his place!'

'Yessir, thank you, sir.' MAA Pickering saluted and turned away. Within a couple of minutes Watkiss' telescope had picked up the fracas aboard the *Kaiser Wilhelm*'s seaboat and excitement reigned again. The result of the fracas brought loud cheering from the *Halcyon*'s company as their seaboat was seen to be returning while the German one sank, and the Flag Captain dug his telescope into the back-bone of the yeoman of the watch.

'Yeoman, as soon as my seaboat is safely secured to the falls, make to the blasted Hun, Flag Captain to Admiral von Merkatz: your villainous action will be reported fully to Their Lordships at the earliest possible moment.'

'Aye, aye, sir.' The yeoman paused. 'Boat coming off from the German now, sir, to pick up their men.'

'Very good. Mr Halfhyde, if that boat just reported should pursue my seaboat, fire is to be opened upon it.'

'I suggest caution at this point, sir.'

Watkiss glared. 'Caution my bottom! Why caution?'

'Because the seaboat has a good start, sir, and is certain to be safe now in any event, so—'

'In which case it wouldn't be necessary to open fire! Sometimes, Mr Halfhyde, you talk balderdash and I find you a blasted nuisance.' Captain Watkiss turned his back and strutted to the other side of the compass platform, from where a minute or two later he craned his neck to watch the returned seaboat hooked on to the falls. He shouted across to the yeoman of signals to send his message. This was done. The German response was, he considered, a rude one. Admiral von Merkatz indicated that he intended informing his Emperor that his chivalrous attempt to render assistance had resulted in the savage sinking of his seaboat and the hazarding of lives. More would be heard of it.

'How typically Hun,' Captain Watkiss said distantly. He proceeded to his sea-cabin feeling that he had handled matters well; Daintree had scarcely uttered, but silence gave consent and he could not now claim to have been overridden, nor could he accuse Watkiss of insubordination. Anyway, he had better not! Watkiss blew out his breath; Daintree was much too senile for command, as he had reflected earlier. He had no gall, no bite. A younger man was needed: himself, for example. He must report as much to Their Lordships ... and then there was Titmuss. Titmuss must be dealt with. It was unseemly, and indeed unheard of, for a Master-at-Arms to fall into the sea. He should be charged ... after all, in Her Majesty's Foot Guards, any wretched guardsman who fainted on parade was charged afterwards with the crime of falling out without permission. It needed some thought.

*   *   *

As the *Kaiser Wilhelm* hauled off towards the north-west, though remaining in company, Rear-Admiral Daintree left the compass platform and went to his sea-cabin where, separated from Captain Watkiss merely by a thin bulkhead, he sat at his desk and with trembling hands started to write a report for Their Lordships, a report of recent events that would be passed to Whitehall by the Commander-in-Chief at Portsmouth upon his squadron's return to home waters. It was a terse report, for Daintree was no literary man, and his comments were itemized and numbered in the proper service manner.

1 My Flag Captain abrogates to himself matters that are mine.
2 My Flag Captain imagines himself to be the Admiral, an appointment for which he is not fitted.

3 My Flag Captain is rude, disobedient and autocratic.
4 I request the soonest possible removal of my Flag Captain and the appointment of an officer of more amenable disposition.
5 I cannot under any circumstances stand my Flag Captain and ask that this submission be treated as most urgent. [underlined]

*   *   *

Mr Todhunter had reported to the sick bay, where he was forced to submit his crutch to an undignified examination, not by the Fleet Surgeon, not by a doctor at all, but by the po-bosun, an unqualified person but one who said he knew all about crutches and their adjacent parts.

'VD, Mr Tod'unter.'

'Oh.' Mr Todhunter hoped that the po-bosun washed his hands between patients.

There was a cackle. 'Not that you 'ave it.'

Todhunter felt it beneath his dignity to respond to that, which was an abominably coarse thing to say. An even coarser thing was said when the petty officer remarked that his performance would remain unimpaired and no damage had been done. 'You'll be sore for a day or two, that's all. I'll put some liniment on and bandage up. It'll be inconvenient and there'll be times when you'll 'ave to remove the bandage, as you'll no doubt realize, Mr Tod'unter, but that's the extent of it.'

'I shan't be able to get into my hammock.'

'Yes, you will, o' course you will. The usual swing up of the leg and up you go.'

'That's the trouble. I'll not be able to swing my leg!'

The po-bosun scratched reflectively at his head and seemed, as he stared at Mr Todhunter's crutch, to be visualizing it in bandages. Then he said, 'Well, you may be right at that, I dunno. I'll 'ave a word with the doctor ... see if you can be accommodated in 'ere till it's better.'

'Thank you very much,' Mr Todhunter said. Later, as he hobbled about the sick bay, a doctor, still not the Fleet Surgeon but a mere assistant surgeon, came down and looked at him and gave permission for his use of a sick-berth cot. Pleased, Mr Todhunter took the opportunity of using an instrument table in order to continue his lengthy report for Chief Superintendent Portlock. It was like a book already, for Detective Inspector Todhunter was a meticulous policeman who believed in writing everything down. One day, he might publish his memoirs. He was engaged in his task, and polishing a phrase here and there, when an almighty crash came from what he thought of automatically as upstairs and his pen scratched right across the paper in a most alarming fashion.

SEVEN

It was a day for reports: another, this time to Her Majesty's Secretary of State for Foreign Affairs, was being compiled by Mr Petrie-Smith in a corner of the wardroom when he, also, was electrified by the enormous blast from the deck, a sound that he recognized instantly as gunfire. Small pieces of white-painted cork insulation fell from the deckhead around Mr Petrie-Smith, like the offerings of seagulls. His whisky glass appeared to rise into the air, then vanished over the edge of the table he was using to write his report. God alone could tell what ineptitudes the naval officers were getting up to now; Mr Petrie-Smith hastened to find out, shoving his papers back into his despatch-case with a trembling hand. If ever he reached England safely, he would beg the Minister never to put him in contact with the navy again; it was too much. He had already written a good deal about the navy in his report; now there would doubtless be more to add.

He went up the ladder to the quarterdeck and scanned the seas. He smelled gunsmoke, very strongly. Wafts of it were sweeping down from amidships on the port side. Also to port, Vice-Admiral von Merkatz' flagship loomed, fortunately still afloat, close enough for Mr Petrie-Smith to see clearly that men were running along her decks and scrambling behind the various gun-shields and into the gun turrets. Mr Petrie-Smith went very pale and gave a gulp of fear but faced his duty bravely. He proceeded to the compass platform to remonstrate. Upon his arrival he immediately entered a pitched battle between the Rear-Admiral and the Flag Captain. (Or rather, not entered but hovered unremarked and disregarded on the fringe.)

'Ask Mr Lamphorn,' Daintree was saying with spirit.

'Oh, balls to Mr Lamphorn, sir, you are the Admiral and why should I bandy words with a blasted lieutenant of less than eight years' seniority, may I ask?'

'Because you appear not to believe me,' Daintree snapped. 'I repeat, ask Mr Lamphorn!'

'Oh, very well, very well. Mr Lamphorn?'

'Yes, sir.'

'God give me strength. Be more explicit.'

Mr Lamphorn's adam's-apple shot up and down a scrawny neck. 'The Admiral is right, sir. The German veered towards us somewhat dangerously—'

'In your opinion, Mr Lamphorn. I've never known you have an opinion before.'

'In *my* opinion!' Daintree said.

'I see, my dear sir. So you ordered retaliation?'

'I ordered a shot across his bows, Flag Captain. I think the effect has been good. Von Merkatz veered away again, as you can see.'

Watkiss grunted. 'I think you are sailing close to the wind, sir. Metaphorically.'

'I don't see why.'

'You don't see why? Well, I do. We are approaching the Plate, are we not?'

'What's that got to do with it, Flag Captain?'

'Everything, my dear sir, everything! In the Plate, in Montevideo – in both the Argentine and in Uruguay – the blasted Hun will be among friends, he will be entering what one might reasonably call a prepared position! Do you not see, for God's sake? He will make representations to his Ambassador and to the national authorities in the port and we're likely to find ourselves blasted well interned or something—'

'Oh, what nonsense, Flag Captain, how you do exaggerate—'

'Exaggerate my bottom, sir! What have you done? I'll tell you: you've opened fire upon a German warship, that's what you've done,' Watkiss said in total disregard of his own manning of the guns in the Le Maire Strait, 'and laid yourself open

75

to all manner of retaliation and blame. Just think what von Merkatz is going to make of *that!* Attack upon the high seas—'

'What about your own stupid attempt to ram, Flag Captain? What about that?'

'That,' Captain Watkiss said with dignity, 'is a red herring. I did *not* attempt to ram. My steering failed me, as I indicated in my signal to the Hun.'

'A tissue of lies, as you know well. What about the firing at the seaboat's crew?'

Watkiss smiled. 'Your order, my dear sir, not mine.'

'It was not! You gave the order—'

'You gave it first.'

'You threatened to open with my main armament—'

'A threat only, sir. One not put into effect. It is you who have now opened fire, and the results may be catastrophic – catastrophic, I say!' Captain Watkiss shook his telescope. 'With respect, sir, you are a nitwit. *What are you?* You will—' He checked himself just in time; admirals were admirals. Going a deep purple, and with his sky-blue eyes standing out like doorknobs, Captain Watkiss turned his back upon Daintree in order to leave the compass platform, and cannoned into Mr Petrie-Smith. 'What are you doing here?' he demanded.

'I merely—'

'Get off the compass platform at once.' Captain Watkiss gave the diplomat a push towards the ladder. 'There's enough trouble without the blasted Foreign Office taking part.'

Mr Petrie-Smith gave way; there was nothing more to be said. Captain Watkiss had said it all, and now there was any amount of ammunition for his report. Admiral von Merkatz had already started some acid signalling.

*　　*　　*

For the second time within a few weeks, Canon Rampling was faced with the possibility that he might have to set foot upon the soil of a Roman Catholic country; and while, as a broad-minded parson, he had no hard feelings, no really hard feelings, about Roman Catholics, he never relished the cut-off sensation that afflicted him when surrounded by persons of a different persuasion – he wouldn't say faith in the case of Roman Catholics since they were Christians after all. His spiritual home was the see of York still, even though he was now within the ambit of a very different sea; and though foreign cathedrals, especially those of France and Spain, were beautiful and impressive, none quite came up, in his view, to York Minster; and on a lesser scale to the parish church of St James in Wherp-in-Swaledale in the North Riding of Yorkshire, where for many years he had held the incumbency until his decision to serve in Her Majesty's Navy, than which no greater contrast could be imagined.

Canon Rampling brought out his watch: Mr Tidy was late. But not very late; no sooner had the watch gone back into the Canon's pocket than there came a knock at the cabin door and Tidy entered.

'Good morning, Reverend.'

'Good morning, Mr Tidy. The hassocks, if you please.'

'Aye.' Tidy, who before being appointed rector's warden of Wherp-in-Swaledale had in fact served in the office of verger, and now in a sense combined the two appointments, opened the Canon's wardrobe and brought out two maroon hassocks, placing them reverently by the bunk. Rampling lowered his bulky frame to its knees upon one hassock, leaning his elbows on the bunk and sinking his face into his palms. Tidy beside him did likewise; there was a subdued clang as his boot hit the chamber-pot beneath the bunkside table.

'Pardon,' Tidy said.

'We shall ask Our Lord's blessing and mercy upon us and upon those sorely afflicted in Uruguay. Or is it the Argentine?

'Uruguay, that's if you mean ambassador like.'

'Yes, of course, how stupid of me.' Canon Rampling uttered prayers sonorously and followed up the special intercessionary one with the Lord's Prayer and then one for Her Majesty the Queen and the Prince of Wales, mentioning the latter's scandal-prone name with a certain gloomy resignation. Remaining sunken-headed for a few more respectful moments, he then heaved himself back upon his feet and said, rubbing his hands briskly together, 'I'd like you to check the communion set, Mr Tidy, if you please. The travelling one. It's not been used for a while, has it?'

'No, it's not. Aye, I'll root through it, like. One in ship's chapel's not been used much either, 'cept by you and me and that loony sailor.' There was sourness in Tidy's voice; sailors were an irreligious bunch mostly, and Her Majesty's ships of war had been a great shock. Back in Wherp-in-Swaledale, everyone attended church on Sundays or rector asked why not. Aboard ship, though certainly, when the weather permitted, the sailors were fallen in and inspected and then mustered for open-air matins on Sundays, the atmosphere was different and the little chapel in the bowels of the ship was but poorly attended, as was Holy Communion. Just the loony; it was a sad reflection upon squire – that there Captain Watkiss – who was to blame for not setting a proper example to the parishioners. That Watkiss' only concession to God was to insist on taking Sunday matins himself and booting the reverend Canon out of his pulpit like; never once had he gone the whole hog and attended communion. What they would have done without the loony sailor, Mr Tidy simply didn't know.

Mr Tidy went along to the Paymaster's office and had the safe opened up and the travelling communion set brought out for checking. All was in order, though a little of the wine had evaporated through the cork, which had seen better days. There was enough, though. Mr Tidy went back to the Canon's cabin to report, and found the parson with his dumb-bells again, taking exercise. The Canon said, 'I may need to take communion to our ambassador, Mr Tidy.'

'In gaol, like?'

'Well, we don't know yet. He may be under house arrest, which I shall find more pleasant.' Rampling frowned, parted his combinations and scratched at his stomach. 'The trouble is, will I be allowed to go ashore?'

'Who's to stop you?' Tidy asked indignantly, though he knew the answer well enough. He gave it: 'That there Captain Watkiss. You ought to tell him what's what, Reverend. Tell him there's a higher authority, like.'

Rampling shook his head. 'You evidently don't know the navy yet, Mr Tidy, do you? That there Captain Watkiss as you call him ... he has no higher authority than himself as regards the conduct of a ship and its company. Captain Watkiss is not slow to point out that *he* is God.'

'What's that make the Admiral, then?'

Rampling lifted his eyes beyond the deckhead to heaven, but gave no actual answer. The naval hierarchy was indeed complex.

*   *   *

Next day at first light the Detached Cruiser Squadron, with the *Kaiser Wilhelm* in attendance still, had raised the entry to the Plate and the order was passed to all ships to stand by to reduce speed and then to follow the Admiral's motions. Greenery was in distant view now, the lush green of the thick jungle country behind Montevideo and the Argentine coast opposite. Strange smells were wafted out to the squadron by an offshore breeze, mainly of cow dung, of beef still upon the hoof.

'Unpleasant,' Daintree observed, sniffing.

'Very, sir. Like the blasted dagoes themselves. I fail to see why everyone can't be *British*.'

'What a stupid thing to say, Flag Captain.'

'Only if taken literally, my dear sir!' Watkiss snapped angrily, making darting gestures with his telescope. 'I meant to convey that there's no blasted reason why everyone can't adopt British standards of cleanliness and honesty.'

'Yes, yes. Damn that German!' Daintree was much on edge. He moved hither and thither about the compass platform, getting in the way of Mr Lamphorn and everyone else, looking down at his decks as the seamen moved about at the double and the cable and side party mustered on the fo'c'sle for the business of anchoring. He examined the chart laid out upon the chart table in the rear of the compass platform, drew a superfluity of lines with a pencil and parallel rulers, stared up at the sky, stared out towards the approaching shore and down at the dirty waters of the Plate. He muttered to himself for a while, then settled himself into his chair by the forward guardrail, seeming content at last. He spoke over his shoulder to Captain Watkiss.

'Your ship, Flag Captain.'

'I beg your pardon, sir?'

'I said, your ship. You shall take her to her anchorage. I shall not interfere.'

79

'That is understood, my dear sir.' Watkiss was tart. 'It is normal routine, is it not?'

'I wish,' Daintree said, 'you would not query everything I say.'

'I was not querying it, sir. I was agreeing with it.'

'Then cease doing so!'

Captain Watkiss lifted his hands as though in supplication to a superior God. The cruisers moved inwards; now the fine buildings of the great city of Montevideo lay in view ahead, while on the port bow reared the ugly slaughterhouses and other unpleasant places of the Argentine. Soon speed was reduced aboard the flagship and the reduction was passed by speed-flags to the escorts and to the *Cardiff* and the *Hector*. The escorting sloops had now moved into single line ahead and were leading the squadron in, *Biddle* being in the van. The *Kaiser Wilhelm* had altered her unofficial and threatening station, and had dropped to the rear of the line, a fact seized upon by Captain Watkiss.

'We British are acknowledged to be the best in the world,' he announced. 'That's fact, I said it.'

'What?'

'The Hun, sir, the Hun! He intends to follow us in, not lead.' Watkiss added, 'That's unusual for a blasted arrogant Hun. I'd have expected the bugger to push his way past. Obviously doesn't trust his own pilotage.'

There was no response from the Admiral, and Watkiss paced the compass platform, puffing out his chest and stomach. There was plenty of sun now, and its rays glinted on Watkiss' stripes of rank, on the gold oak-leaves upon the fringe of his cap-peak, on the rim of his monocle. Watkiss moved to the chart table and studied the chart, then approached Mr Lamphorn from the rear.

'Mr Lamphorn!'

Lamphorn jumped. 'Yes, sir?'

'Watch your heading, Mr Lamphorn. Watch your cross bearings. I shall wish to know precisely and to the split second when your bearings come on for anchoring.'

'Aye, aye, sir.'

Lamphorn bent to the azimuth circle on the compass and started taking bearings as ordered. There was as yet no real need to, but Captain Watkiss liked bearings, so bearings he would have. The taking of them looked efficient, and Mr Lamphorn, when in due course he passed the momentous barrier of eight years' seniority in his rank, much wished to be recommended for the coveted half stripe between his two thicker ones that would denote his extra status as a senior lieutenant. Not only did he take bearings, but he kept the Midshipman of the Watch on the hop by continually announcing facts of wind and weather and soundings – which were being taken by the leadsmen in the chains on either side of the bow – for entry in the Deck Log. This also sounded efficient, but there was no pleasing Captain Watkiss.

'Mr Lamphorn!'

'Sir?'

'Stop fussing. The wind doesn't shift every two blasted seconds.'

'No, sir.'

'You're like a blasted hen with a clutch of eggs.'

'Yes, sir.'

Onwards, inwards ... the estuary was wide, but after days and weeks of the great rolling waters at the world's southern end the squadron felt closed in as the arms of the land reached out towards the ships. With the engine sounds reduced by the slower speed, there was a degree of silence that somehow emphasized the change: ears grow accustomed to wind and ship noises. Watkiss moved to the chart again, then to the binnacle. A shove of an arm dislodged Mr Lamphorn, and Watkiss took a bearing of a promontory, another of a landmark on the opposite shore.

'As I thought,' he said. 'Come back, Mr Lamphorn. Wheel five degrees to starboard.'

Daintree came to life. 'What's that, Flag Captain?'

'You said you intended not to interfere, my dear sir.'

Daintree nodded, 'Yes, quite right. But have a care for my squadron.'

'I can read a chart as well as you can,' Watkiss said rudely. 'Mr Lamphorn, kindly look sharp and pass my helm order down, if you please.'

'Aye, aye, sir.'

'And signal the ships astern – come on, are you asleep, or

what, Mr Lamphorn?' His orders duly carried out, Captain Watkiss bounced forward and laid his stomach against the guardrail. He called down. 'First Lieutenant!'

The addressed officer looked up from his position in the eyes of the ship. 'Yes, sir?'

'Stand by for anchoring.'

'Stand by, sir!'

Captain Watkiss reached a hand behind his body and at the same moment snapped, 'Starboard anchor.' The chief yeoman of signals obediently thrust a green anchor flag into the outstretched hand, which grasped it tightly and held it aloft above the guardrails. In the right hand of the First Lieutenant another green flag was now held similarly aloft, and all hands on the fo'c'sle awaited Captain Watkiss' next order, which would come in mime: down would come the green flag on the compass platform, down would come the green flag in the hand of the First Lieutenant, and the eagle-eyed carpenter's mate at the capstan, which was already out of gear, would take off the brake and down would go the anchor on its slip-freed cable to hold the flagship steady. But the expected movement failed to come; an altercation was taking place upon the compass platform and a moment later Captain Watkiss bawled down to the fo'c'sle.

'First Lieutenant, disregard my motions.' The green flag was lowered. 'Mr Lamphorn has made his customary balls-up.' The squat figure of the Flag Captain bounced fuming to the centre of the compass platform and attacked the luckless Lamphorn. 'What the devil do you mean, Mr Lamphorn, by saying the bearings are opening?'

'They – they are, sir! The alteration of course, sir – I believe it was wrong.'

'Oh, balls and bang me arse, Mr Lamphorn, of course it wasn't wrong, and this is no time for blasted impertinence.' Captain Watkiss squinted along the azimuth circle. 'Oh, very well, have it your own way, port ten.' Nothing happened; he glared. 'Well, get on with it, then!'

'I thought you—'

'Thinking is stinking. Never think. Know. *Port ten!*'

'Aye, aye, sir. Port ten,' Mr Lamphorn said down the voice-pipe to the quartermaster. Captain Watkiss strutted back to the forward guardrail and once again raised his green flag.

'First Lieutenant!'

'Yes, sir?'

'Mr Lamphorn permitting, we shall anchor in a moment.'

'Aye, aye, sir.'

Captain Watkiss simmered, and his upraised arm began to ache as moments passed into minutes. By this time all hands on the fo'c'sle were edgy; if he, Captain Watkiss, should lower his confounded aching arm, the First Lieutenant might anchor the ship before time; and to issue another negative before lowering it would smack of indecision. God damn Mr Lamphorn, who should never have been allowed to pass for sub-lieutenant, let alone lieutenant. What a dreadful officer. Captain Watkiss turned a little and glanced over his shoulder. That blasted Hun was coming up now, looking as though he meant to steam past after all and enter Montevideo – just like a Hun, to try to get his oar in first and steal an advantage. Watkiss fumed. *Cardiff* and *Hector* were nicely in station, a trifle close perhaps, but that was due to Lamphorn's incompetence. The Flag Captain turned back to face front. *Biddle* and *Delia* had started to make signals back to the Flag and there was an urgent look about them, though as yet the yeoman hadn't read them off. And he never did. As the winking lamps sent their messages there was an almighty crump, the flagship stopped abruptly, and Captain Watkiss pitched forward, his stomach cushioning the cruel bite of the steel guardrail; then he toppled over. As the personnel on compass platform and fo'c'sle went flat on their faces, except for Admiral Daintree who after a forwards and backwards bounce was held between his chair and the rail, Captain Watkiss deftly seized a stanchion and thereafter dangled with his trousers at half mast over the shield of 'A' gun at the after end of the foredeck. There was a clang as his telescope hit the gun-shield and ricocheted overboard. This was followed by the sound of tearing metal as the *Cardiff* smashed into the Admiral's stern-walk aft, now stationary. Captain Watkiss closed his eyes and thought murderous thoughts as he prepared himself for a long drop down to the gun-shield. Then he heard hurried footsteps on the ladder to the compass platform, followed by a voice telling him to hold on: help was at hand.

'Is that you, Mr Halfhyde?'

'It is, sir.'

'Haul me up at once.'

Hands reached down, two pairs of hands, and the Flag Captain was heaved with some difficulty over the guardrail and set upon his feet. 'What the devil has that blasted fool Lamphorn done to my ship?' he shouted. 'By God, I'll have him in irons, I'll have him court-martialled and drummed out of the service, I'll have him ...' Watkiss' voice reduced in volume as he saw Daintree slumped in his chair. 'What's the matter with the Admiral?'

'Knocked out, sir,' Halfhyde said. 'I fancy his head hit a stanchion.'

'Bring him round, then. Fetch water somebody! Get the Fleet Surgeon here at the double. Mr Halfhyde, send to the Commander and tell him I want a damage report instantly.' Watkiss stared aft. 'Where's the *Hector*?'

'Collision for'ard, sir. She hit *Cardiff*'s stern.'

'Oh, my God.' For a moment Captain Watkiss placed his hands over his face, then uncovered again. 'Where's the blasted Hun, Mr Halfhyde?'

'Gone ahead, sir, to enter Montevideo.'

'You're sure?'

'Very sure, sir. Admiral von Merkatz signalled his condolences as he passed us by, and indicated his intention to enter and forward reports to the German Admiralty.'

EIGHT

There was a very large lump on Admiral Daintree's forehead and upon this his gilded cap rested uneasily and with a certain lack of authority. His face was pale and his legs felt weak but the Fleet Surgeon had administered sal volatile and put ointment on the lump so that Daintree was more or less operational and able to adjudicate in the alarming argument that seethed around him. In his view the fault for the multiple collisions was not Lieutenant Lamphorn's but his Flag Captain's; and he said so.

'Oh, rubbish, my dear sir, what a thing to say to your Flag Captain.'

'As Flag Captain, you're worse than—'

'Have a care, sir.' Watkiss' voice rose again. 'There are junior officers and ratings within earshot—'

'I don't give a—'

'And I do not propose to be insulted by you, sir, and I care not a fish's tit if you're the Admiral or a boy seaman. Let that be understood.' Captain Watkiss breathed deeply, his face purple, the more so as he had no telescope to shake. 'If you refuse to accept Mr Lamphorn as the culprit, then I suggest you look upon yourself in that light!'

Daintree gaped. 'I?'

'Yes, you, sir! All those blasted lines you drew upon the chart! The thing looks like a cat's cradle! You rendered navigation and ship-handling utterly impossible, and that is what I shall report to Their Lordships – that you made the chart useless and dangerous whilst I was attempting to bring the flagship to an anchor!' Captain Watkiss turned upon his heel to leave the compass platform in dudgeon, and was thereupon confronted by the Executive Officer, whose uniform was streaked with rust and fragments of dislodged paint. 'Well, Commander – the damage?'

'Potentially serious, sir—'

'Commander, I ask not for your prognosis, but for your factual report. *What is the damage?*'

'Bows buried in the sea bottom, sir, stern-walk sliced in half, Admiral's quarters open to the fresh air. The ship is seaworthy—'

'Thank God!'

'That is, we'll not sink. But we can't go to sea, sir, or I believe not. I fear the screws and rudder may be damaged—'

'Put a man down at once.'

'We have no divers, sir.'

'Then the carpenter shall hold his blasted breath, what a helpless lot my officers are to be sure! See to it at once!'

'If you give the order, sir—'

'Give the order, of course I give the order, don't be so blasted namby-pamby. This is one of Her Majesty's ships of war, not a kindergarten, Commander, even if Mr Lamphorn, from whom God preserve me in the future, may give the opposite impression.' Watkiss started to push past, then paused. 'Clamps.'

'Clamps, sir?'

'If the carpenter needs both hands free, tell him to squeeze a clamp tight upon his nose.'

*　　　*　　　*

Vice-Admiral Paulus von Merkatz, very soon after his flagship had been made fast in the harbour of Montevideo, had proceeded ashore in his full-dress uniform with cocked hat and sword to wait upon the Port Admiral and the Uruguayan military commander in the area; he found both Admiral Saldana and General Montañéz extremely friendly as befitted them not only as appointees of a new regime but also as supplicants for German trade, money and possibly military and naval equipment. For their part, the Uruguayans could be most helpful to the Fatherland. The Fatherland was expansive, was moving towards glory and the eclipse of Great Britain and her

Empire, and trade was valuable wherever it could be found. Vice-Admiral von Merkatz, who was a Prussian of the old school, disliked trade and felt deprecatory towards his role whilst at the same time admitting its importance as back-up to the military and naval machine that was being so ably forged in the furnaces and shipyards and arsenals of the Fatherland. In any case, once he had put the preliminaries in train, the trades-people would take over and leave him to his prime task, which was the policing of the shipping routes to the new areas of German influence and ensuring the total safety of German merchant ships when they plied those routes.

'The man Savory,' von Merkatz said when the moment was right. 'As I dare say you're aware, Sir Russell Savory is held aboard the British flagship – the cruiser *Halcyon*.'

There were nods, and arms waved beneath fawning smiles. Uruguayans were greasy people – like the Chileans with whom von Merkatz had so recently dealt, not to his advantage. He went on smoothly, concealing his dislike of men who wore gaudy, tasselled uniforms and curled their hair, 'He is valuable to my Emperor, which also you may know.'

'There have been whispers, rumours, yes.'

'Possibly he will be valuable to you also, gentlemen.'

'How is this?' General Montañéz asked, looking crafty.

'Your assistance in seeing that Savory is removed into *my* keeping from that of the British Admiral could be rewarded. I make no promises, but my influence with my Emperor is of no mean account, gentlemen.'

'And the nature of the reward, Admiral?'

Von Merkatz said, 'Your revolutionary government wishes to build up trade with Germany and no doubt you will wish to stand well with your government and help it consolidate its position now that it has won power. A word in the ear of my Emperor ...' He said no more; it would be unwise to be too forthcoming – it always was, with the inhabitants of South America. The possible military and naval assistance which he had in mind could wait to act as a prod if co-operation should prove slow.

'I understand,' Admiral Saldana said. 'I shall be in touch with our civil authorities, with our government ministers.' He cast a quick sideways glance at General Montañéz. 'As this

man Savory is aboard a ship, any action – should it be authorized by my government, of course – will be a naval commit-
ment.'

'Quite. And you will, perhaps, be making suggestions as to
how—'

'I shall perhaps be making suggestions, yes.' The reply was a
shade off-putting, almost a silencer. The Uruguayans were
good at bargaining, and von Merkatz understood perfectly.
Saldana went on, 'There is the British Ambassador – you know
this?'

'Yes.'

'That is why the British ships have come. And you?'

'I?'

'You have not come in any sense at all to add German
diplomatic pressure for the British Ambassador's release,
Admiral von Merkatz?'

'Certainly not,' von Merkatz said tartly and in much surprise. 'That is a domestic matter – or at any rate one between
you and the British Government. Queen Victoria's ambassador is of no concern to me whatsoever, nor to my Emperor. You
may do what you wish with him!'

'But suppose pressure should come upon yourself, from
Germany?'

'It will not, I assure you.'

Admiral Saldana, who smelled very strongly of garlic, leaned
forward, his dark face devilish. 'The grandmother – Queen
Victoria – is old but powerful. Your Emperor, Kaiser Wilhelm
– he is but the young grandson who stands in much awe of
Grandmama England as I believe he calls her. He—'

'Not in his own country. In Germany he is not the grandson
but the Emperor. When staying at Windsor Castle, at Osborne,
or at Balmoral, he retires for the night when told. This has
caused immense resentment. Do you understand, gentlemen?'

The Uruguayan officers nodded and chuckled and spoke,
rudely, in their own tongue for a moment. Von Merkatz
believed he could follow the gist: Queen Victoria was to get her
come-uppance from her grandson, and her ambassador was to
be left to suffer, so far as Germany was concerned, for the
autocratic ways of Grandmama England ... von Merkatz,
taking his leave to return to his flagship, felt that in some way as

yet undisclosed, the gaoled Ambassador from London might be used to his advantage in the extraction of Savory from the British squadron. The loss of Savory was a black mark against him, but all was not yet lost . . . a look of rage passed across the German Admiral's face when he thought of his proper flagship, the great battleship *Freidrich der Grosse*, still fast upon the cheerless rocks of Staten Island with his two other ships lying off in the Le Maire Strait to recover men and stores and equipment. Fury filled his heart, for blame would be sure to come to him from his Kaiser, and the rage was only partly assuaged by the stupid fate of the British squadron. Nevertheless, assuage a little it did; it had been most pleasant to steam past and cock a snook at stupid British inefficiency and lack of seamanship! The last thing von Merkatz had done before leaving the Uruguayan officers had been to make an official statement and complaint for handing to the German Embassy that the British had, whilst at sea, opened fire upon him and his substitute flagship; and he had hinted to the Uruguayans that any assistance rendered to the culprits now held fast in the thick mud outside in the estuary would be regarded by the Fatherland as an unfriendly act.

*   *   *

Captain Watkiss had drawn a replacement telescope from the paymaster's stores, not such a fine one as the one he had lost, but it would have to do. He flourished it towards Halfhyde.

'This is a pretty kettle of blasted fish, Mr Halfhyde! Can't damn well move!' At risk of his life and urged on personally by the Flag Captain with the direst threats, the hapless carpenter had clamped his nose and dived; after several attempts he had surfaced finally to report the rudder bent like a safety-pin and wrapped around the screws, resulting in a number of stripped blades. The *Halcyon* would not move again without proper divers and dockyard assistance that the blasted Uruguayans might not be willing to give. Even Captain Watkiss had to acknowledge that men could not be sent down with clamps upon their noses to carry out a long and heavy repair, a repair that in fact would need total replacement of the parts concerned. 'Blasted dagoes! Why can't they dredge their damn

89

rivers properly I'd like to know – it's a disgrace. Their Lordships may well demand compensation, I should think. And just look at *Cardiff* and *Hector*!'

From the Flag Captain's day-cabin the cruisers in company could not be seen but Halfhyde had read the reports sent by signal from each ship preliminary to the hastily-convened conference of Captains, Executive Officers, engineers, boatswains and carpenters from all the ships: the damage to *Cardiff*'s bows was such that she would have been able to make only slow headway through the water had she been able to move at all; but she could not. She had suffered damage similar to that sustained by the flagship, having been hit in a similar spot aft by the onsurge of *Hector* astern – and *Hector*'s shattered bow was admitting water past a broken collision bulkhead, rendering her well down by the head. Only *Biddle* and *Delia* were now seaworthy. Admiral Daintree's command was much reduced and up topsides, as Watkiss and Halfhyde conferred, Daintree was able to reflect sadly upon this as he stared down from what was left of his quarterdeck to the remains of his day-cabin into which the nose of *Cardiff* was still rudely thrust. More notations would now be made in his report upon his Flag Captain, who could surely never be employed at sea again. The man was a total disaster, utterly inept, and no ship was to be considered safe in his hands.... As Daintree stared bleakly across to *Cardiff*'s embedded fo'c'sle, where hordes of seamen plus carpenter's mates were rushing hither and thither under the panic-sounding shouts of their officers, Daintree was approached by his chaplain offering words of comfort.

'A sad business, sir.'

'Indeed it is, padre, indeed it is, most tragic.'

'Yet we must be thankful that no lives were lost.'

'Yes. Thank God.'

'His mercy is for ever sure.'

'Yes.' Daintree's affirmative was somewhat savage: he was still thinking about his Flag Captain, who seemed well able to inhibit the best intentions of God.

Canon Rampling continued on a note of intonation, 'Those who go down to the sea in ships—'

'Yes, yes.'

'And have their business in great waters—'

'Quite yes.'

Rampling coughed. 'These things are sent to try us, sir. We must not weaken. We must rise above them.'

'I'm not weakening, padre. I'm just damned angry, that's all!'

'Yes, that is understandable,' Rampling said briskly, rubbing his hands together in a washing motion. 'Very understandable indeed, but we must not allow ourselves to be ruled by anger, must we?'

'I am *not*—'

'God,' the chaplain said, 'moves in a mysterious way His wonders to perform—'

Daintree lost patience. 'There's nothing wonderful about a raving lunatic, padre. I refer to my Flag Captain, you understand. The fellow should be placed in restraint really.'

'Aha,' Rampling said non-committally. 'It's not for me to say, of course. But should you not be reflecting upon the word "wonders", sir?'

Daintree stared. 'Why, for heaven's sake?'

'Our Lord's intentions are not always revealed immediately in His acts. Sometimes He causes doubt and confusion, for we are but human beings—'

'Well, He's certainly caused confusion this time! Look at my squadron!' Admiral Daintree waved his arms towards the mess. 'Do you mean to tell me there's sanity behind all that?'

'It is possible, sir. Even likely.'

'Rubbish!'

'I venture to say it is not rubbish, sir, but rather could be an act of providence, of divine intervention.' Canon Rampling raised an authoritative hand as the interruptions began. 'If you will bear with me a moment longer, sir, I may be able to offer solace—'

'Solace my foot.'

'But consider, sir: are we in Uruguayan or Argentinian territorial waters, or are we not?'

'Not. We're just outside.'

'Therefore we do not come within any foreign jurisdiction, but are free. We shall not be required to leave within the statutory period, so—'

'We are not capable of doing so anyway,' Daintree said. 'But the provision applies only to belligerents in a neutral port in time of war, padre, and would be inappropriate to our current situation.'

'I see. But surely foreign warships cannot as it were violate territorial waters – permission is needed for entry, is it not?'

'Yes! I was under orders to enter only in extreme urgency, and I have not entered!' Daintree explained. 'Pray come to your point, padre.'

'Very well, sir. It is this. We are upon the high seas, and are in distress – in need of assistance. Had we entered territorial waters, the situation would have been very different. We would have stood guilty of a violation, and the shore authorities might well have detained us pending recriminations between governments, in which case the position *vis-à-vis* the man Savory might have become fraught with difficulty. But as it is, you see, we are in the position of supplicants, and neither the Argentinians nor the Uruguayans will wish to upset Her Majesty by denying us succour – such that will speed us upon our journey home to England.'

Daintree nodded in thought. 'Yes. You have a point, perhaps. I shall bear it in mind. But I confess I don't see how God comes into it.'

Rampling began again, patiently. 'I have said, sir, that God moves—'

'Yes, yes, but I'm bound to say I find His ways extremely clumsy.'

*   *   *

Mr Petrie-Smith's long and angular body was almost twisted into a knot, and the sweat of tension streaked his face. Naval officers were possessed of the most rigid minds he had ever encountered, and this time they could not, it seemed, be moved beyond Savory. Mr Petrie-Smith was perfectly willing to admit the vital importance of not allowing Savory to fall into German hands, or South American hands either come to that; but there were other considerations now, to wit, Lord Horace Vane, Her Majesty's Ambassador to Uruguay. Mr Petrie-Smith tried again.

'He must be considered, Admiral. Your orders are to ensure his safety.'

'Not at the risk of exposing my prisoner. Do you not agree, Todhunter?'

'I do most earnestly, sir,' Mr Todhunter said, sweating as badly as Petrie-Smith. As well as all the awful worry, there was a very close atmosphere in the Admiral's sea-cabin, to which Daintree had been forced back by the spoliation of his quarters aft, and the space was very cramped, much of it taken up by the general podginess of the Flag Captain. 'Whatever happens, sir, the prisoner Savory must not be put into jeopardy.'

'Quite. Mr Petrie-Smith, how would you propose to help the Ambassador, without jeopardizing Savory?'

'But Savory—'

'Kindly answer the Admiral's question, Petrie-Smith.' This was the Flag Captain, growing impatient. 'We haven't got all day.'

'I don't care for your tone, Captain Watkiss.'

'Oh, balls to my tone. Answer the question.' Watkiss sat with arms folded across his stomach, glaring through the port, looking at no one: none of them were worth looking at in his opinion.

Petrie-Smith compressed his already thin lips but gave in. He addressed Daintree. 'I see no conflict at all between the two. In any case, it is early yet for any final decision, which must surely be made in the light of developments—'

'Blasted Foreign Office talk, all meaningless.'

Daintree shifted in his chair. 'Flag Captain, kindly allow Mr Petrie-Smith to speak. Mr Petrie-Smith, pray continue.'

'Thank you, Admiral. In the first instance, I suggest you send a message to the port authorities for onward transmission to the President of Uruguay—'

'Certainly I shall make a signal, yes.'

'And ask for the release of Lord Horace.'

'Simply that?'

'Yes, at this stage, Admiral, that will be sufficient, I believe.'

'Well, I'm quite prepared to do that. And ask for assistance at the same time, don't you agree, Flag Captain?'

'For what it's worth.'

Daintree lifted his eyebrows. 'You believe it is not? My chaplain believes they'll respond.'

'Your chaplain may believe what he blasted well likes, my dear sir, and since when did he transfer to the Executive Branch of the Fleet I'd like to know! Man's an idiot. Those buggers'll leave us here to rot more than likely, and come out in their blasted canoes to laugh at us!'

Daintree shook his head. 'Oh no, no. I scarcely think so, Flag Captain. They'll not want us out here as a threat, or potential threat, which we'll be so long as they keep our Ambassador in gaol.'

'Threat my bottom!' Captain Watkiss said loudly, moving his body in such anger that Mr Todhunter was thrust to the end of the settee. 'Threat! My dear sir, with *Cardiff* jammed up your backside, and *Hector* tight up *Cardiff*'s, and all three upon the blasted mud, the only effect of a broadside would be to sink the blasted lot of us!' Suddenly, he got to his feet, his eyes seeming to bulge from his face. 'By God, the buggers, they've not wasted much time!'

'What is it, Flag Captain?'

Watkiss pointed his telescope through the Admiral's port. At the same moment a desperate rush of feet was heard, followed by an urgent knock on the door, and Mr Perrin entered, to find all heads crowding the scuttle. He made his report to the assembled bottoms, loudly. 'Sir, there are gunboats coming off towards us, gunboats from the shore, sir!'

'It's a blasted armada!' Captain Watkiss said truculently. 'A blasted armada crammed with soldiers!' He rounded upon Mr Perrin. 'Kindly explain why you didn't report a damned sight sooner, boy!'

Mr Midshipman Perrin was about to stutter some kind of excuse for flagrant slackness when an outburst of firing was heard and bullets smacked against the bulkheads of the sea-cabin. Mr Todhunter flew backwards as though hit, and collapsed on the settee; Petrie-Smith of the Foreign Office put his clasped hands over his head, protectively. Without reference to his Admiral, the Flag Captain shouted at Halfhyde.

'Mr Halfhyde, we are under fire! Sound for action, if you please. Mr Perrin, signal the rest of the squadron accordingly, and pass the word for the chief gunner's mate. He is to prepare to repel boarders.'

94

NINE

The troop-crammed boats, no less than a dozen of them and all under steam, swept on towards the stranded British squadron. The firing was kept up, though the rifles were apparently not shooting to kill. There were no casualties as the guns' crews closed up; the bullets bounced harmlessly off the steel bulkheads and gun-shields, and the only harm done was from ricochets, the results of which were at once attended to by the Fleet Surgeon and his team.

Captain Watkiss waved his telescope from the compass platform. 'Yellow-bellies, that's what they are. No stomach for a fight, don't want to provoke us.'

'I wouldn't bank on that, Flag Captain.'

'I don't propose to bank on it, my dear sir.' Watkiss bounced to the wing and bawled down at the chief gunner's mate. 'Chief Petty Officer Bunce, hold your fire until orders reach you, but when the word comes, let the buggers have it hot and strong. Don't spare a single man.'

'Aye, aye, sir.' Chief Petty Officer Bunce, who looked like a pirate of old, spat on his hands and rubbed the palms together. The fire would be accurate, the slaughter and blood intense. Armed with a shining cutlass as befitted his rank, Bunce ran a thumb along its edge. It would cleave through a neck nicely when wielded by his strong right arm. On the compass platform, Captain Watkiss was exultant. The natives were about to be shown a thing or two and have it brought home to them firmly that British ships could not be attacked upon the high seas with impunity; and Watkiss started by dealing firmly with

Mr Petrie-Smith, who had ventured to urge a degree of caution in the handling of the situation.

'What an idiot. How, may I ask, do you return rifle fire cautiously?'

'Their fire is so far harmless, Captain, and this must be borne in mind.'

'Bear it in mind, then, but don't bother me, it's your blasted mind, is it not?'

'But—'

'Go away at once or I'll order you to be shot yourself.'

Mr Petrie-Smith gave it up. He had done his best; now it was upon the navy's head. He retreated, in case a stray bullet should not prove harmless. His bowels felt watery, for he saw disaster ahead: it was possible the Secretary of State would cast blame upon him for this clash of arms since he represented the civil authority of Great Britain and under no circumstances should an official of the Foreign Office become associated with aggression. It could end his career if matters should go too badly wrong; and it wasn't fair, for who could be expected to deal sanely with Captain Watkiss? Mr Petrie-Smith made his cautious way along the safe side of the flagship and went below, rather fast, as a South American bullet pinged off a boat's davit. Along the decks the chief gunner's mate's party stood resolute behind their rifles and bayonets, ready for the repulsion of dago boarders, hairy and smelly men who would foul a British warship's holystoned decks. Watchful eyes peered from above beards, ears were strained for the order from the compass platform and that there Watkiss, who was a pompous enough old bastard certainly, and the bane of any sailorman's life most of the time, but who had a reputation for being fearless and ferocious in action, which was what counted.

The enemy came closer: now the boats were no more than a cable's length off the flagship's side. The Flag Captain gripped a megaphone in his right hand, the telescope now shifted to the left. The buggers were near enough; the time had come to warn them fairly of the consequences if they should come closer. Captain Watkiss lifted the megaphone and bawled out his message, or started to.

'Remain where you are, or I shall—' He broke off, his face a study in fury as he felt Halfhyde's hand on his arm. 'How dare you, Mr Halfhyde, you should know better than to lay hands upon a senior officer, and—'

'A moment, sir. I advise no threats, and advise it strongly. Our position has altered.'

'What the devil do you mean, altered? How can it?'

'I've just checked our anchor bearings, sir. You put us aground a little way *inside* Uruguayan territorial waters – not *outside* them.'

Watkiss' jaw sagged, the mouth remaining open.

'Which means the Uruguayans are entitled to board us, sir. We are in violation of their waters. We must not return their fire now, or we shall be arrested without a doubt.' Halfhyde paused. 'This puts Savory's fate in some question, certainly, but if we were to be arrested, he would undoubtedly be removed on a word from Admiral von Merkatz.'

'That swine! What do you suggest, Mr Halfhyde?'

'As I have said, sir, we must hold our fire, and after that we must play it very carefully.'

'Allow the dagoes aboard, d'you mean?'

'I think we have no alternative, sir.'

With dignity, Watkiss said, 'I shall put it to the Admiral; he must decide.' He crossed the compass platform towards Daintree and acquainted him with the situation. 'I propose not to seek action,' he said stiffly. 'We are in no position to engage.'

'Position appears to be the right choice of word, Flag Captain, does it not? May I remind you that it was none other than yourself who put us here?'

Watkiss reddened. 'Your blasted lines on the chart, sir!'

'Nonsense, but this is no time for argument, Flag Captain. Yes, I agree, you will cease fire immediately—'

'I haven't opened yet!' Watkiss snapped.

'Then refrain from doing so. Invite the Uruguayan commander aboard, and I shall parley. See to that at once, if you please.'

Captain Watkiss whirled about, face truculent. A parley, of course, was now inevitable but parleys were undignified affairs for British naval officers to take part in and when conducted with dagoes they were doomed to failure in any event, since dagoes never kept their word. Watkiss bounced to the starboard wing and called down.

'Chief Gunner's Mate!'

The piratical face looked up and a hand flew in salute to the cap peak. 'Sir?'

'There has been a change of tactics. You'll not open fire after all. Let the Uruguayans come aboard.'

The face was incredulous. 'Come aboard, sir, did you say?'

'Yes! I understand your feelings, Bunce, but it can't be helped. Your party will not now repel boarders but will form a guard of blasted honour, God help us all. The buggers are to be accorded every respect.'

*   *   *

A polite message had been bawled through the megaphone by Captain Watkiss, asking the Uruguayan boats to close the flagship's starboard accommodation-ladder, which would be lowered to receive them. The troop commander and two of his officers would be most welcome aboard, the Flag Captain yelled through clenched teeth, but the remainder must stay in the boats and lie off. The message passed, Captain Watkiss flung the megaphone across the compass platform as if punishing it for being a vehicle of virtual surrender. The Officer of the Watch was despatched to the starboard ladder where with his gangway staff of a Corporal of Marines, a quartermaster, two boatswain's mates and four side-boys he would receive the dagoes whilst the Flag Captain stood a little way back ready to greet and salute the guests before escorting them to his Admiral, who would still be using his sea-cabin.

The boats approached, belching filthy clouds of black smoke from unkempt funnels. Upon the bridge of the leading one a mangy cat roamed, its tail high in the air. Aft a Uruguayan seaman relieved himself over the side, grinning cheekily when he saw the British officer's eye upon him, and waving with his free hand. As the dreadful vessel came alongside, it crumped into the bottom platform of the ladder; there was a nasty creaking and grinding and the whole structure shook.

'Jesus Christ,' Captain Watkiss said. Yells in some totally unintelligible lingo came from the dago vessel. The grinding and shaking stopped; ropes were cast up and made fast to the quarterdeck bollards by the side-boys. Then up the ladder came the troop commander and his aides. Captain Watkiss glared, but saluted. The men were filthy; their apparel was, he supposed, military in a sense but struck him as being basically comic-opera as well as dirty and dishevelled. Each man's breast was covered from right to left and from left to right in cartridge-stuffed leather bandoliers and each had a revolver thrust into a holster at his right side.

Having saluted, the Flag Captain grunted; he could find nothing else to say.

'You are Admiral?' the troop commander asked.

'No. I am the Flag Captain. And you?'

'Me, I am Colonel Villanueva. With me, Colonel Oribe and Colonel Alonso.' Colonel Villanueva gave a big smile. 'Most happy to meet, Bag Captain—'

'*Flag* Captain.'

'Ah yes. Most happy to meet,' Villanueva repeated. He stared at the wreckage aft. 'Ships of Queen Victoria once very smart and ship-shape, no?'

'Yes,' Watkiss snapped, half lifting his new telescope. 'Now, I—'

'Are under arrest, all ships.'

Watkiss gaped. 'Oh, balls, you can't apprehend British ships!'

'Can and do. My English tongue perhaps not good. I spell: A, R, E, S, T. You understand?' Smiling still, Colonel Villanueva went to the side of the quarterdeck, leaned over and jabbered. There was much arm-waving, and before Captain Watkiss could react a surge of dago soldiers came up the ladder, waving rifles and revolvers and all talking at once. The gangway staff found themselves completely overwhelmed. The Officer of the Watch was thrust back against the after screen with a rusty bayonet at his throat; the Corporal of Marines and the others were rounded up and held in a circle of rifles. Colonel Villanueva stuck his revolver into Captain Watkiss' stomach and went on smiling. More and more men came up the gangway, a veritable swarm, backed up by soldiers from the other boats that now came alongside the first one to discharge their complement across its decks and pile aboard the flagship. Under more officers many of them made their way to the stern and leaped nimbly aboard the embedded bows of the *Cardiff* and ran aft; no doubt, Captain Watkiss supposed, some of them would continue towards the *Cardiff*'s stern and descend upon the *Hector*. It looked like a total take-over.

'This will be reported to Her Majesty's Government!' Captain Watkiss raved. 'Ships will be sent – battle squadrons – British regiments – Montevideo will be blown to smithereens, blast you!'

The smile was not to be shifted. 'See Admiral,' Colonel Villanueva said. 'Now, at once, pronto!' He shoved hard with his revolver. 'You are not boss man.'

*   *   *

Comic-opera they might be, but they had seized full control, a bloodless victory. The British ships, helpless already, were now even more helpless. Smelly men sunned themselves, a-sprawl on the immaculate paint of the gun-shields, on the holystoned quarterdeck, on the fo'c'sle. The cat sprang across from its own ship and prowled the flagship's decks, head down, tail still upright like a mast, eyes blazing. When Chief Petty Officer Bunce saw the animal scratching away at some coir matting as though preparing a site for revolting purposes he gave it a kick up its rear, and it raced away, spitting, to conceal itself somewhere below in the wardroom flat. Uruguayans, human ones, had penetrated down there as well, and Colonel Oribe had encountered Canon Rampling upon his knees and hassock in his cabin, making his supplications to God. When the cabin door burst open he rose, cut off in mid-prayer.

'What—'

'Your pardon.' Colonel Oribe had now seen the clerical collar; priests were to be respected, at least until they had revealed their faith or lack of it. 'Priest of Holy Rome, representative of Christ's Vicar-General on earth?'

'Of the Archbishop of Canterbury.'

'Ah, so. *Heretico!*' The door slammed, and Rampling gave a shrug. He wondered why the man had bothered to come in at all; he returned to prayer, thankfully. God was steadfast in a bewildering world, about the only thing that was. That fellow who had burst in was most probably seeking Savory. Canon Rampling uttered prayers for Savory; all men, even traitors, were entitled to intercession. On the other hand, did Savory really wish intercession of this kind? From Canon Rampling's understanding, Savory had been keen to join the Germans under Admiral von Merkatz, and von Merkatz was currently in Montevideo. He had very possibly despatched the soldiers to remove Savory from British custody into his own. That stood to reason; Canon Rampling gave a grimace and altered his prayer-line. God was adjured to give the matter further thought and allocate Savory to the fate He found most suitable for him, which in Rampling's own view, respectfully put, was in British hands, not German. Whilst all this was in progress Colonel Oribe, whose mission the clergyman had divined correctly enough, had found, not Savory but MAA Pickering accompanied once again by a strong smell of rum, and clad in the full glory of his frock-coat and sword. This he had donned when he had heard word of the Uruguayan boarding: if captured, his status must be made obvious to all. Seated in his cabin, he stared at the intruder.

'Beg pardon,' he said stertorously. 'I 'aven't asked you to come in to the best o' my knowledge an' belief.'

'You are who?'

'Name o' Mr Pickering, Master-at-Arms o' the flagship. An' you if I may make so bold?'

'Me, I am Colonel Oribe.'

MAA Pickering rose to his feet unsteadily; his stomach impacted against his cabin table and shifted it a little. He put his cap on and saluted. Officers were officers, never mind the nationality. 'Good morning, sir,' he said formally. 'Can I 'elp?'

'Savory.'

MAA Pickering lifted a pudgy hand and scratched the back of his neck beneath his cap. 'Savory, eh. Dunno like.'

'Near here live ze cells. I was told so. Savory is in the cells?'

'That's right, sir. My prisoner like. Locked up.'

'He is to be unlocked up.'

'Dunno about that. Got a chit, 'ave you?'

'Chit?'

'Aboard one of 'Er Majesty's ships, you need a chit. Need a chit for everything, see?'

'But now is different—'

'Oh no, no, no, nothing's different,' MAA Pickering said chidingly. 'Oh dear me, no! I 'ave to keep me own yardarm square, like. No chit, no 'and-over. You give me a chit from the Admiral, or from the Flag Captain, or from the Commander, you can 'ave the prisoner. Not unless.'

Colonel Oribe brought out his revolver. 'I think you are a much stupid man,' he said.

'Stupid I may be, sir, to the likes o' you, but I knows me duty and what's more I fuckin' *does* it. No chit, no Savory and that's final.' MAA Pickering sat down with a thump and stared with dignity towards Colonel Oribe. Then he raised his voice, which was a loud one; he had been a Chief Stoker before transferring to the police branch, and his voice had carried with authority across many a clanging boiler-room as the shovels and the red-hot coals flew to the heave and lurch of North Atlantic gales, or typhoons and hurricanes elsewhere. He shouted for his ship's corporals to hasten to his assistance, and as he shouted Colonel Oribe advanced with the hammer of his revolver thumbed back for firing.

Once before, some years ago, the then Chief Stoker Pickering had become involved in a brawl in a Malta bar which had the convenience of an on-site brothel upstairs. Chief Stoker Pickering, who had been descending the stairs at the time, had put on speed and had taken refuge behind a table against a large Malt seen to be coming his way with a bloodstained knife. Chief Stoker Pickering had then lifted up the table and flung it at the Malt, who had collapsed in a heap on the floor. It had been a simple manoeuvre but an effective one, and MAA Pickering now did it again. The cabin table was a heftier one than the one in the bar, but MAA Pickering was heftier, or heavier, than he had been at that time, and the table did more than flatten Colonel Oribe: it caused him, just as Ship's Corporal Judd appeared in the doorway, to fire his revolver. When MAA Pickering lifted the table clear, Colonel Oribe lay dead, for the impact of the table had forced his gun-hand up, and the muzzle into his mouth, and he had blown his head off, more or less.

'Bloody 'ell,' Corporal Judd said, staring down in awe.

'That's fucked it,' MAA Pickering said briefly. 'Give me an 'and, Judd.'

'What you going to do with 'im, Master?'

'Shove 'im in a cell like Savory an' chuck the perishin' key overboard.'

* * *

'I fail to see,' Admiral Daintree said, 'how you can have any reason to arrest my squadron, Colonel Villanueva.'

'Violation, Admiral. Our sea.' Villanueva looked smug and certain. 'This is an offence to our sovereignty, and you know this, I think.'

Daintree made a dismissive gesture. 'A small enough offence to be sure, Colonel, and accidental. An error of navigation on the part of my Flag Captain with no malice behind it, I assure you. Thank you, Flag Captain, that will be enough. No further interruptions, if you please, and that's an order. Colonel, I must ask you to negate this arrest and, indeed, to give us dockyard assistance so that we can leave your waters at the earliest opportunity. A reasonable enough request, I think?'

'No. I shall not grant.'

'Then kindly tell me why, if you please.'

Villanueva smiled. 'I do not please.'

'Then you admit,' Watkiss snapped before Daintree could react, 'that your excuse is damn feeble and you have no real reason at all!' He turned angrily as he felt the brush of Mr Petrie-Smith's lips against his ear. 'Oh, damn you, Petrie-Smith, what is it now?' He listened. 'What? Oh, stuff-and-nonsense, diplomacy! Diplomacy my arse! Balls to diplomacy, it's only another name for cowardice. If I wish to mention von Merkatz I shall do so, so kindly hold your tongue.' As Mr Petrie-Smith lifted anguished eyes towards his Maker, Captain Watkiss continued threateningly. 'Colonel, if indeed you are one, Villanueva, I suggest that blasted Hu – German, Admiral von Merkatz, is behind this! Am I right or am I wrong? Answer me at once.'

'Uruguay is sovereign, Captain.'

'Possibly, but that's no answer. You may as well be honest, since we've all seen von Merkatz enter Montevideo, seen him with our own eyes. Well?'

Villanueva sucked in his cheeks and pursed his lips. What

the British had seen could not, obviously, be denied. Neither could what they had done back in the Le Maire Strait, and the boot could be placed upon the other foot quite neatly. He said, smiling again, 'So. Admiral von Merkatz is in our port, yes. He is a cross man, and naturally—'

'Why naturally?'

'You forced his great battle-flagship on to the rocks, Captain.'

'No, I didn't. That was his fault. However, I see the game well enough now, thank you! You won't get away with it, you know! Her Majesty—'

'*You* will not get away, Captain. Your ships—' Villanueva lifted his hands and brought them together, then made an insulting gesture with two fingers. 'I need not say more. Our mud is thick and clinging and much will have entered the holes you made, no? You must accept arrest. You can do no other.' He paused meaningly. 'There is another thing also.'

There was a tense silence in the sea-cabin; all present knew exactly what the 'other thing' would prove to be, and Mr Todhunter looked as though he might burst into tears at any moment. It was too bad, to have his prize snatched away from him at this stage, but it began to have the look of inevitability now. He had been beaten by the Germans after all, and his career in the Metropolitan Police Force would be at a very sticky end. Strong feeling got the better of him and he blurted out, 'You'll not have him, Colonel Villanueva. You'll not! He's mine, and that's what he is, and I'm a Detective Inspector of the Metropolitan Police, headquarters at Scotland Yard. Chief Superintendent Portlock, he'll make representations to the very highest quarters in the land, you mark my words. You can't monkey around with Chief Superintendent Portlock and get away with it, oh no.'

Mr Todhunter subsided; the tense hush returned, with all eyes on Todhunter. Villanueva was smiling again, and looking sardonic; Todhunter put his head in his hands. He'd blown the gaff, silly duffer that he was, oh dear, oh dear. That Villanueva, he hadn't been sure, nor really had von Merkatz. Not really; that day when Mr Titmuss had fallen into the sea, it could all have been a blind, with a man dressed up as Savory taking exercise – the Germans never did get a close look at him, all they'd got was Mr Titmuss all said and done. Savory could have been landed in the Falkland Islands.

But now, of course, there was no doubt left.

Oh, what a fool!

* * *

'Right,' said MAA Pickering, breathing hard. The body of Colonel Oribe, by some miracle, had been carried to the cells without the manoeuvre being spotted by any of the dagoes. True, the Master-at-Arms' cabin was fairly adjacent to the cells, that being his special territory, but MAA Pickering felt the good hand of providence somewhere along the way. He slammed the door shut and locked it, then wiped his streaming face and handed the cell keys to the ship's corporal.

'Upper deck,' he said briefly. 'Nippy but nonchalant. Take the spare set too – I'll get 'em from me cabin, should 'ave thought o' that. Come along.' They went back to the cabin, where MAA Pickering handed over the spare set from a locked cupboard, and Judd departed with both sets for the upper deck, adjured once more to nonchalance. Ten minutes later he was back, by which time MAA Pickering was about to hasten out of the cabin in a ferment. He and Judd met in the doorway. Judd reported, 'All serene, Master. No trouble at all.'

'All serene my fanny! Know what?'

'What?'

'Never thought ... Savory's locked in an' all. We'll never get at 'im to feed 'im now, not without a charge o' bloody dynamite that'll blow 'is nibs up with it.'

* * *

Up in the Admiral's sea-cabin, a kind of agreement was in the air. To some extent both sides were stymied. Daintree's squadron could not move, arrest or not, without assistance from the Uruguayans; and Villanueva, who was an intelligent man, saw clearly enough the dangers and difficulties that could arise through too hard a tweaking of the lion's tail. That lion had teeth and had never shrunk from using them to take very big bites out of the world's map, leaving raw and permanent red behind. And every altercation could be resolved by compromise, by a little give and take to show one's basic reasonableness. The British, however, would not give in on Savory: on that point they were like the rocks of Staten Island. For Villanueva's part, Admiral von Merkatz would have to fight his own battles in that respect; it was clear that to bring him Savory would mean much trouble with Queen Victoria – physically it could be done, of course, for the Uruguayans were aboard in quite enough force, but would it be wise? Villanueva was a mere colonel; his newly-installed President might not wish too much force. The revolution was over. There had to be consultation at a high level, and in the meantime he would leave a number of his men aboard. In return for climbing down, temporarily at any rate, on the question of Savory, Villanueva proposed a concession on the part of the British: no pressure in regard to Lord Horace Vane, who was now officially admitted to be accommodated in the town gaol of Montevideo.

'Agreed,' Captain Watkiss said at once.

'*I* have to agree, Flag Captain,' Daintree said with sourness. 'I'm not sure that I do, yet.' He turned to Villanueva. 'Why does your government want Lord Horace, Colonel?'

Villanueva spread his hands. 'He favours our opponents and has committed crimes against the state of Uruguay by giving succour to them. For this he must pay. This our people expect and must have.'

'Sheer revenge, illegal under International Law and proper diplomatic practice,' Daintree said. 'It needs well thinking about, does it not, Mr Petrie-Smith?'

'Most certainly it does,' Petrie-Smith said with ice in his tone. 'Lord Horace cannot be left in a Uruguayan gaol, Admiral, he's our Ambassador and a peer—'

'*Courtesy* peer,' Captain Watkiss broke in. 'Not entitled to a seat in the House of Lords, is he?'

'No. But he's a member of the Foreign Service,' Petrie-Smith said indignantly. 'A colleague. We should not abandon him, Admiral.'

'No, no, it would be an appalling thing to do,' Daintree agreed. 'Colonel Villanueva—'

'Appalling my bottom!' Captain Watkiss rose to his feet, thrusting his stomach out like a laden lighter and shaking his telescope. 'Lord Horace Vane is of no blasted significance when set against that bugger Savory and no one can deny that. It's fact, I said it. What does Lord Horace know, for God's sake, other than how to construe blasted Latin, and Greek too for all I know, together with any other popinjay's knowledge of blasted protocol and which damn woman sits where at dinner and who says Your Majesty and who says Ma'am ... bah! Ten a penny. Savory's unique and so is his particular knowledge, and that's a fact too. I'll not part with Savory to the Germans and I know Todhunter will agree with me. What?'

Mr Todhunter clasped his hands together almost reverently. God had indeed arrived from an unexpected source. 'Oh, yes, indeed, sir! Very much so. I'm really most grateful and my chief super—'

'We'll take his remarks as read, Todhunter, thank you. Petrie-Smith, if you weren't such a damn popinjay yourself, you'd see the truth of all I've said. Now, sir.' Captain Watkiss pushed across the small cabin and planted himself before his Admiral. 'If you fail to come to terms with Villanueva to the extent that he's asked, I shall make representations to Their Lordships and indeed to the Crown immediately upon my return to British waters. You shall not compromise the security of the Kingdom, sir! You shall not, I say! Dammit, I should—' He broke off as a loud knock came on the door, and he swung round. 'Now what is it? Oh, blast you to hell, Mr Perrin, what a time to choose. What do you want, boy?'

'Sir, it's Mr Halfhyde, sir! A word in private, sir.'

Captain Watkiss glared. 'I call that impertinent, coming from a midshipman, Mr Perrin.' Then he remembered the dagoes. 'Oh, very well.' He bustled through the door and shut it behind him. 'Now what is it, for God's sake, Mr Perrin, and why cannot Mr Halfhyde come himself instead of sending a messenger?'

'Sir, Mr Halfhyde was called to the cell flat, sir—'

'Oh, really, by whom?'

'The Master-at-Arms, sir. A Uruguayan officer has been killed, sir. And the prisoner Savory can't be got at, sir, and could die from starvation, sir!'

TEN

'It is one thing after another, Mr Halfhyde, is it not, and I fail to see why I should be singled out for all this blasted bother. Why the devil couldn't you contain your temper, Master-at-Arms, I'd like to know!'

'Yessir.' MAA Pickering, still ceremonious in frock-coat and sword, trembled at attention. Death was death and in the circumstances could perhaps be called murder; certainly the dagoes might look upon it in that light.

'Well? Have you nothing to say, man?'

'Yessir. It were self-defence like, sir. I was facing a drawn revolver, sir. I was at peril o' me life, sir.'

'Possibly. But you've landed me in a pretty pickle now, haven't you?'

'Yessir.'

'You should have thought of that. You're a Master-at-Arms, not some blasted ordinary seaman.'

'Yessir.'

Captain Watkiss fumed irresolutely: this was an impossible situation. He screwed his monocle into his eye and glared at Halfhyde. 'What do you suggest? I value your opinion, Mr Halfhyde.'

'Thank you, sir. It depends on the future action of the Uruguayans, I think.'

'In what way?'

Halfhyde coughed. 'May I know what's been going on in the Admiral's sea-cabin, sir?'

'I don't see why not. Master-at-Arms?'

'Yessir?' The Master-at-Arms saluted.

'Withdraw out of earshot.'

'Yessir.' MAA Pickering gathered up his sword and marched away, leaving traces of rum behind him.

Captain Watkiss gave Halfhyde a summary of the conference to date and added, 'The Admiral is about to agree to a deal involving Savory and the British Ambassador. When he does that, then I believe the Uruguayans will leave the squadron alone.'

'But not totally, sir?'

'No. They'll leave some men behind.'

'I see.' Halfhyde pondered. 'Then I suggest we keep the news of Colonel Oribe's death to ourselves, at least until the deal is settled and the main body of troops withdraws.'

'Hasn't Oribe been missed by any of his own dagoes, Mr Halfhyde?'

'Fortunately, no, sir. That's a situation that may not last for long. I suggest a speedy settlement by Admiral Daintree. After that, we must take things as they come.'

'Yes, there is sense in that,' Watkiss said with a sage nod. 'I shall instil speed into the Admiral, Mr Halfhyde, you may be sure. Now, what about Savory? Blasted man!' The Flag Captain gave a vindictive thrust with his telescope. 'He might just as well die, really, and save everyone a good deal of bother, but I suppose we can't allow that.' He raised his voice. 'Master-at-Arms?'

'Yessir?' MAA Pickering marched back into view.

'Savory. Now you've jettisoned the damn key, how's he to be fed and watered?'

'I just thought o' that, sir. The 'ole, sir.'

'Hole?'

'Spy-'ole, sir. In the cell door, sir—'

'Yes, yes. Well?'

'I shall drive the glass from it, sir, with a utensil. Then food can be pushed through, sir, and water led through a rubber tube, sir.'

'The damn thing's only about an inch in diameter, isn't it?'

'Yessir. Kind o' shredded food, sir. It can be forced through with a marline spike, sir. Then when the dagoes is all gone, sir, beg pardon Uruguayans, the blacksmith can 'ave a go at smashing the lock open, sir.'

'Oh, very well.' Captain Watkiss turned away and bounced up the many ladders that led back to the Admiral's sea-cabin. He was filled with anger, principally against the Master-at-Arms and his confounded complications. The dago would probably not have used his revolver; Pickering had been precipitate, and the affair would have to be further investigated at a more propitious time. Of course, the dead man was only a foreigner, but all this could not have come at a worse time. As he reached the upper deck, the Flag Captain was accosted, rudely, by yet another colonel – Colonel Alonso, third of the boarding trio.

'*Capitan*—'

'I am busy. You must excuse me.' Captain Watkiss tried to push past, but the fellow planted himself in his path and placed a hand on his chest. He was a tallish man and Captain Watkiss was forced to look up at him. 'Kindly move aside!'

'One moment only. I am Colonel Alonso.'

'Yes.'

'I seek Colonel Oribe. He is not seen.'

'Oh, really?' Fear clutched at the Flag Captain's heart. 'You see?'

'No. All da – all Uruguayans look alike to me, as do Chinamen. Perhaps your friend has boarded one of the other ships.' Watkiss waved a hand aft towards the stricken *Cardiff*. 'Why not go and look?'

'Yes.' The fellow went away, but fear did not. Oribe's loss was bound to be discovered at any moment now. The Flag Captain's feet bore him with undignified haste towards his Admiral. Reaching the sea-cabin, he was vastly relieved to find that in his absence Todhunter, together with his own comments uttered earlier, had carried the day with the Admiral and only Petrie-Smith looked mortified, which didn't matter. A ramshackle agreement along the lines of his own submissions had been patched up and the Admiral's servant was pouring gin which Colonel Villanueva was sucking up as though equipped with an elephant's trunk, though as Watkiss entered the Uruguayan belatedly remembered his manners.

He raised his glass and said, 'The health of Your Majesty Queen Victoria.'

'*Her* Majesty,' Watkiss said in a loud voice.

Daintree uttered the next toast. 'The excellent health of President whatsisname.'

Petrie-Smith hissed, 'Barriero.'

'Not Barriero.' Colonel Villanueva, looking angry, lifted his glass and smashed it, gin and all, on the commode beside the Admiral's bunk. 'Barriero *kaput*.' He drew a hand across his throat. 'President Platar.'

'I'm sorry, very sorry,' Petrie-Smith said, his face crimson. It was hard to keep pace with revolutions, but he was supposed to be the expert. The unfortunate lapse seemed to annoy Villanueva beyond its actual importance, and he broke off the gin session by announcing abruptly that he would now honour his word and start withdrawing his soldiers.

'Very good of you,' Watkiss said, anxious to speed the Uruguayans on their way. 'I will render any assistance you wish, Colonel.'

'None is needed. It is you British, with your smashed ships, that need the assistance. So smashed are they that I need leave only a handful of my men to guard.' Villanueva gave an insulting laugh. 'Even the cat would be enough – the good Felix.'

Captain Watkiss ground his teeth; if he caught a sight of the good Felix fouling his decks, there would be another death. However, he gave a painful smirking grimace intended to be a smile appreciative of wit, and called for Mr Perrin to pass the word for the quarterdeck ladder to be manned in honour of the Uruguayans' departure. Then, taking his time about it, Colonel Villanueva descended grandly towards his waiting gunboats. On the quarterdeck he spoke in his own tongue to one of his soldiers who was lounging, a cigar between his teeth, against the guardrail at the head of the ladder. Captain Watkiss caught the names Oribe and Alonso and began to sweat ferociously. He was not going to pull this one off. The soldier brought himself upright and went off with the butt of his rifle banging across the teak planking of the quarterdeck. Watkiss fumed at the sight: just like a dago, no damn backbone, needed a crutch. Perfectly appalling people, not British – what could one expect? Colonel Villanueva, not waiting about for his colleagues, descended the ladder and embarked aboard the gunboat alongside. Captain Watkiss breathed a trifle easier but decided to count no chickens. This was just as well; after a long wait, during which countless Uruguayans streamed down the ladder, the despatched soldier returned with Colonel Alonso and a shouted conversation in Spanish took place with Colonel Villanueva in the gunboat; after which Villanueva called up to Captain Watkiss.

'Colonel Oribe is not found. Why is this, please?'

'I've no idea.'

'I come back aboard.'

'Oh, I'd not do that if I were you.'

'Why not so?'

Captain Watkiss clenched his teeth. What the devil could he say? 'It'll tire you, Colonel. The weather's close.'

'Stupid British.' Villanueva was already on his way back; a moment later he reached the top platform of the ladder, an angry man now, with flashing dark eyes. 'I search all ships. Captain, you will accompany me in my search. I search this ship while Colonel Alonso search next smashed in astern.'

There was nothing for it. Captain Watkiss, fear clutching at his heart, traversed his decks, all of them, in company with Villanueva and a villainous bunch of soldiers. Every part of the ship was poked into – bridge and chartroom, workshops, stores, cabins and offices, wardroom, gunroom, warrant officers' mess, seamen's heads, the lot. No Oribe; Villanueva filled the air with threats, largely against the actual person of Captain Watkiss, whom he plainly suspected of chicanery and double dealing now. The recent agreement seemed a very fragile thing and if Captain Watkiss had his way he would throttle MAA Pickering with his own hands. Down into the ship they went, and just before the double-bottoms, a filthy area of gloom and muck that Villanueva could damn well search on his own if he went that far, they reached the cell flat where, it appeared, lunch was being served. Under the eye of the Master-at-Arms, Ship's Corporal Judd was stuffing salt pork through the spy-hole with the butt-end of a marline spike. Villanueva enquired why this was being done.

'A man in cells,' Watkiss snapped, and held his breath.

'What man? The prisoner Savory, perhaps?'

Watkiss blew out his cheeks. A lie would not help now; when

the spy-hole was pork-free, Villanueva would poke further. 'Yes, Savory,' he said.

'Ah. Savory usually is fed this way?'

'Yes!'

'Strange. He is dangerous?'

'Yes, very.'

'I must search his cell. Also the next one.' Villanueva moved to the second of the two cells and bent his eye to the spy-hole and Watkiss almost collapsed under the strain; but MAA Pickering had foreseen such, and Villanueva's eye was unable to pick up the body placed right against the door just beneath the spy-hole. Villanueva straightened. 'It is empty. And there is no Colonel Oribe. I grow impatient.'

'What a pity.'

'For you, Captain, yes. No Oribe, I take Savory until Oribe is found. When Oribe is found, I return Savory. Open the cell door.'

'Oh, God damn!' Captain Watkiss bounced up and down, feeling his mind coming adrift from its moorings. 'I – I can't! My Master-at-Arms will explain.'

MAA Pickering jerked down the front of his frock-coat and said, 'Yessir. Lorst the key, sir.'

'So?'

'Yessir. Gorn over – don't know where it's gorn, sir.'

'You have spare keys, yes?'

'No spare set, sir, no. Slip-up by our 'ome dockyard, sir, Pompey. Reported like from Valparaiso through the British Consul, sir.' MAA Pickering turned smartly aside towards the ship's corporal. 'Afters, Corporal Judd. Prunes an' custard, best take out the stones or you'll bung up the 'ole. We don't want that.'

It was beautifully done; but it quite failed to impress Colonel Villanueva. Doors, he said, however strong, could be opened *in extremis* by means other than keys. The flagship would no doubt have a blacksmith aboard, and if it hadn't, then Montevideo had. The alternative to a blacksmith, he said, was for his gunboats to open fire upon the British cruisers. His guns might be of small calibre, but the cruisers couldn't move out of their way.

*　　*　　*

Captain Watkiss shook his fist from his quarterdeck, his face purple and furious. Savory had looked happy enough to be free of his blacksmith-blasted cell and on the way to join Admiral von Merkatz; he was smiling as the dago gunboats sailed up river for Montevideo with him safely aboard. Captain Watkiss brandished his telescope towards the one gunboat remaining on guard to maintain contact with the soldiers left behind aboard the cruisers.

'Buggers! I've a good mind to sink that blasted gunboat by way of revenge! This is all too much for a man to bear, Mr Halfhyde. Far too much.'

'I understand, sir, but I would be wary of sinking anything until we see which way the cat jumps—'

'Cat! Don't mention cats to me, Mr Halfhyde.' Before departing with its owners, the good Felix, unable to wait for the earth of Uruguay, had committed an offence; and the Flag Captain had been prevented from kicking it overboard by a dirty dago soldier's arm. 'I tell you one thing: when that bugger von Merkatz steams out with Savory aboard, I'm going to put a broadside into him from all my ships and to hell with any further damage that may be caused to us – at least I'll sink Savory! I regard that as my duty.'

'Mr Petrie-Smith—'

'Oh, balls to Mr Petrie-Smith, Mr Halfhyde, I wish you wouldn't drag him into every conversation. I've no time for the blasted Foreign Office, as you know. They're all pimps and nancy boys, I expect I've said that before.'

'Yes, sir.'

'Well, I say it again now. Foreign Office clerks aboard ships fail to make sense – and then there's that blasted parson and his ridiculous churchwarden or whatever – and that detective fellow – good God, I don't know how I've suffered it all! And now Savory's gone!' Captain Watkiss went on simmering, none too gently. 'Mr Halfhyde, that Master-at-Arms. Pickering. He's to be put in the report and referred to Captain's Defaulters. I'll speak to the Commander shortly and have him charged with murder and treason.'

'I doubt if the charges will stick, sir.'

'Do you, well, I don't. He's killed a man, a foreign national,' Watkiss said, virtuously avoiding the word dago, 'and he's acted directly against the Queen by delivering Savory into the hands of the enemy. I can think of nothing worse. Her Majesty will agree with me!'

'Will that be an order, sir?' Halfhyde enquired blandly.

'Don't be impertinent, Mr Halfhyde, and beware. Your record is not good when it comes to impertinence to senior officers and how I've put up with you for so long is quite beyond me.'

'I ap—'

'Don't argue with me, Mr Halfhyde, I detest argument, *detest* it.'

'Yes, sir.'

Watkiss glared up the river towards Montevideo, falling silent for a moment. Then suddenly he said, 'Can't you think of something, for God's sake? You're not usually backward in coming forward, are you? I'd go as far as to say you've been useful to me in the past, my dear fellow.'

'It's a tricky situation, sir.'

'Oh, goodness gracious me, I'm aware of that, Mr Halfhyde, but we've faced tricky situations before, have we not? Together?'

'Yes, sir.' Halfhyde pulled at his long jaw, his face serious. 'A stratagem may come, sir. I've already had certain thoughts.'

'Confide them in me, my dear fellow.'

'The escorts, sir. *Biddle* and *Delia*. They're in good shape still—'

'Oh, but dammit, the blasted dagoés have put men aboard them, haven't they?'

Halfhyde nodded. 'True enough, sir. Perhaps it won't work after all.'

'You give up too easily, Mr Halfhyde. That's not a sign of a good officer in my view.' Captain Watkiss took Halfhyde's arm in a friendly grip. 'Come, my dear fellow. I'm sure the thought was a good one.'

Halfhyde smiled, shading his eyes across the water to where the two escorts rode to their anchors, farther in towards the great port of Montevideo. The breaking down of the cell door had taken a long time, and already the day was beginning to fade. Quite soon the sun would be down the sky, and long shadows would be spread across the Plate. Ideas were forming fast in Halfhyde's mind, dangerous perhaps, but ones that had to be tried in the line of duty. Savory's expertise, knowledge and overseas contacts must on no account become available to Berlin. Great risks must therefore be accepted. Halfhyde said, 'I suggest we seek audience of the Admiral, sir, the soonest possible.'

ELEVEN

Rear-Admiral Daintree was pottering about his sea-cabin; there was little room, but he was a very small man, and the action helped to soothe his mind, which was in a turmoil thanks to recent events. The loss of Savory had been a most tremendous blow, the possible results of which he found incalculable. Their Lordships, indeed all Whitehall, would be beside themselves; the throne might totter. This latter was a point that the Admiral put to his Flag Captain when Watkiss bustled in with Halfhyde.

'Oh, nonsense, my dear sir, the throne will do no such thing. Why do you think it might?'

'Because the Kaiser is Her Majesty's grandson, Flag Captain, that's why. Surely you can see it for yourself? What will the public think? They'll see chicanery in the very highest places, a ploy by that fellow Gladstone to gain the Queen's favour by – by—'

'By what, sir?'

'Well, by placating her grandson! Family feeling, don't you know.'

'Oh, balls and bang me arse, sir, the Queen detests the blasted Kaiser, so does the Prince of Wales.' Uninvited, Captain Watkiss plumped himself down on the Admiral's settee. 'You may cast such thoughts from your mind, I assure you. Of course, I do not in any sense underestimate the great importance of Savory remaining in our hands—'

'Being returned to them, you mean – thanks to your—'

'Oh, very well, being returned to them, then,' Captain

Watkiss said with dignity. 'Do not cast aspersions at me, sir. Those who live in glass houses—'

'I think you are impertinent, Flag Captain!'

'And I think you've mishandled the whole situation from the start, sir. Firmness was needed, not namby-pambyism and shilly-shallying. In any case, the situation's far from lost, thanks I may say to certain arrangements made by myself.'

Daintree glared. 'What do you mean?'

'I mean, my dear sir, that Savory is to be returned aboard as soon as Colonel Oribe has been discovered.'

'Yes, discovered alive!' The Admiral hopped up and down, bird-like and frail. 'But he's dead as a doornail, is he not, in one of my cells?'

'Yes,' Captain Watkiss said shortly. 'I was coming to that. Colonel Oribe can be circumvented. Mr Halfhyde has a stratagem.'

Daintree looked across at Halfhyde, who was still standing by the door. 'I see. What is this stratagem, Mr Halfhyde?'

'A boldish stroke, sir, but one that has a chance of success.' Halfhyde paused. 'Two birds with one stone, sir – Savory, and Lord Horace Vane, the latter to be removed from gaol by an armed landing-party.'

*　　　*　　　*

Boldish it might be, but complex – thanks to Admiral Daintree – it most certainly was. The involvement of Lord Horace raised vital considerations of state and Mr Petrie-Smith had to be consulted, despite the strongly expressed objections of Captain Watkiss, before any decisions were made. In the event, he might just as well not have been summoned; when he spoke very vehemently against the proposals, he was ignored by all others present. Mr Todhunter, very properly, insisted upon his own right to accompany Halfhyde's suggested landward strike, which would be mounted after the descent of full darkness. Halfhyde accepted this without question, being by now inured to the Detective Inspector's single-mindedness on matters of demarcation: though when Todhunter spoke of the need for himself alone to make the re-arrest in the name of Her Majesty and Chief Superintendent Portlock, Captain Watkiss issued sharp orders that the formal arrest was to be made only aboard a British ship. The conference ended with a search through the Navy List by Admiral Daintree in order to establish the relative seniorities of Halfhyde and Lieutenant Barber, whose ship, *Biddle*, was to be used for the landing. The Flag Captain remarked, loudly, that Barber was not to be found in Burke's *Landed Gentry* and thus was not a gentleman whatever his seniority might be.

'Never mind that, Flag Captain,' Daintree said, and looked up from his perusals. 'All is well, Mr Halfhyde. Mr Barber is two days your junior as a lieutenant, so you may assume the command without my having to refer the matter to the Admiralty—'

'As if you could!' Captain Watkiss snapped huffily; but Daintree took no notice of the interruption. Released from the sea-cabin, Halfhyde lost no time in making his dispositions. A number of petty officers were individually detailed to circulate throughout the ship and pass orders from the corners of their mouths for all hands to be ready, when Halfhyde gave the word later, to mount an attack with marline-spikes on the Uruguayan soldiers left behind as guards. At the same time the chief gunner's mate was told to detail, again by quiet word of mouth, a party of men for landing: twenty hands with two leading-seamen, all of them brawny tars.

When the sun had gone down, Halfhyde passed the word and the shipboard attacks took place. The soldiers were swiftly and silently overpowered by hordes of seamen, denuded of their uniforms, and hustled under their own captured rifles into the boiler-rooms where beefy, grimy stokers stood by with great steel shovels, fire-bars and lumps of coal. The military uniforms were quickly donned by the men of the landing-party. One man dressed as a Uruguayan was left well visible in the after part of the ship so that his reassuring presence could be seen from the decks of the *Cardiff* where more dagoes lurked as sentries. Below, MAA Pickering supervised further work on the part of the blacksmith and the second cell door was smashed open; the corpse of Colonel Oribe was dragged out into the cell flat and divested of its uniform by Ship's Corporal Judd and his mate Ship's Corporal Baines.

'What about the body, Master?' Judd asked.

'Leave it till Mr 'Alf'yde's reported all the other dagoes nabbed, then attach fire-bars to the limbs.'

Judd nodded. 'Going overboard, is 'e?'

'You bet 'e is,' MAA Pickering said. He could scarcely wait to get rid of the evidence, especially as the act had been authorized by the Admiral himself, which cleared his own yardarm good and proper. Afterwards, with no body to produce, that there Captain Watkiss could yell and dance as much as he wanted, it wouldn't get him far along the path of a murder charge once they'd dumped the dago in the mud. For one thing, Watkiss wouldn't be wanting to confess to the Uruguayans that Oribe had been snuffed out aboard his ship. MAA Pickering was on a winner this time. He picked reflectively at his nose; Lieutenant-at-Arms began to look likely again. He told Judd to take the dead man's uniform up to Mr Halfhyde; it would fit where it touched and would look grotesque but Mr Halfhyde intended to wear it ashore and it would have to do. MAA Pickering moved along to his cabin to wet his promotion prospects with a little rum.

Up top a little later, now dressed in Colonel's insignia from the dead Oribe, Halfhyde looked around: the darkness was intense. There was no moon, and the waters of the Plate lay black as pitch; the only relief came from the lights aboard the ships themselves and distantly from Montevideo and from the Argentinian shore opposite. Halfhyde passed the word for his landing-party to muster by the lower boom for'ard where Mr Perrin would be waiting with a cutter under oars. As he reached the lower boom himself, Halfhyde heard footsteps behind him and turned to find Canon Rampling with his churchwarden, Tidy.

'Ah, Mr Halfhyde, I am just in time, am I not?'

'In time for what?'

'I'm coming with you,' Rampling announced.

Halfhyde stared. 'For what purpose, padre?'

'It's my duty. I believe I made the point some days ago. The Ambassador may be in need of my services if he is distressed. I must go to him.'

'Not with—'

'The cloth dictates.' Canon Rampling held up a large hand,

just visible through the gloom. 'Mr Tidy is bringing the communion set, aren't you, Mr Tidy?'

'It's here, like.' Tidy held up a dark squarish box and managed to bang it against a stanchion; there was a tinkling sound. 'Booger! Saving your presence, reverend. I—'

'Oh dear, Mr Tidy, was that the consecrated wine?'

'Reckon it were.'

Rampling clicked his tongue; at that moment Halfhyde heard another sound: a sound of dragging, a clang of metal and a brace of oaths coming forward along the upper deck. Master-at-Arms Pickering was doing his duty as ordered and doing it as far away as possible from any watchful eyes aboard the *Cardiff*, but it was a pity he had chosen this particular moment. Canon Rampling might have a desire to shrive the dead and he could scarcely be expected to connive at such clandestine disposal. For Pickering's benefit Halfhyde raised his voice. 'Very well, padre, you shall come, but embark quickly, if you please.'

'Yes indeed. But the communion wine—'

'There will be more wine and a new bottle aboard the *Biddle*, and I'll allow you time for blessing.'

'Oh, very well. Come along, Mr Tidy.'

Canon Rampling proceeded gingerly out along the lower boom, his cassock making him look like a vast bat upon the bough of a tree. The sounds of corpse disposal, Halfhyde noted, had been suspended: Pickering had taken the hint, evidently. Parson and churchwarden negotiated the boom safely though slowly and descended into the cutter, followed by the landing-party and Halfhyde. Seated in the cutter already was MAA Titmuss, who was too fat to use the lower boom and had been granted a special dispensation to embark from the starboard ladder. MAA Titmuss, dressed now as an Uruguayan soldier, had felt that to volunteer for recovery of his prisoner might compensate in the Flag Captain's mind for his having fallen overboard at sea. He was beginning to regret it now, but the die was cast. As soon as Halfhyde was aboard, he passed the word to Mr Perrin, and the midshipman ordered the boat away.

With muffled rowlocks, and pulling slowly upon the oars so as to keep splashes to the absolute minimum, they made out towards the anchored *Biddle*. They appeared to attract no attention from the decks of the *Cardiff* or the *Hector*, or from the solitary Uruguayan gunboat on station, whence sounds of music and general revelry were coming.

* * *

'Right,' MAA Pickering said, breathing hard. 'Shove. Oh, sod it!' As Colonel Oribe's body vanished over the side, there was a clang.

'What's up, Master?'

'Bugger's got 'is fire-bar round the wrong side o' the bleedin' stanchion and it's 'olding 'im, that's what's up. Oh my God. 'Ere, give us a 'and and look nippy.'

MAA Pickering heaved, with Judd's assistance, on the rope attached to the fire-bar, which was a heavy and awkward object. As he heaved, he became aware of someone approaching from aft; and he looked round. As the heaving stopped, the fire-bar fell on the slack of the rope and banged again on the side plating. The footsteps came up.

'May I ask what you're doing?' Mr Petrie-Smith beamed with interest.

All kinds of answers flashed through the mind of the Master-at-Arms, all except corpse disposal. Fishing? No. The bloke from Whitehall might know about fish, even Uruguayan ones. And you didn't paint ships at night, especially grounded ones and in any case Masters-at-Arms didn't tend boatswain's chairs. All the same, bloody civilians could be fooled easily enough by a little bull. ''Ammering 'ome the golden rivet, sir,' Pickering came up with.

'Really?'

'Yessir.'

'How interesting. What's the function of the golden rivet?'

'Ah!' There was a pause, while MAA Pickering thought harsh things about diplomats. ''Olds the key o' the keelson in place, sir. Very important, that, sir.'

'Yes, I'm sure it must be,' Petrie-Smith said. He moved to the ship's side with the obvious intention of peering down at the work in progress. Quick as a flash, MAA Pickering reached out and laid hold of his leg just above the ankle.

'Good heavens!' Petrie-Smith was much startled. 'Why did you do that?'

'I wouldn't look, sir, not if I was you, sir. That I wouldn't!'

'Why not?'

'Seafarin' superstition, sir. Very strong, sir. If any bl– if any civilian gentleman, or lady come to that, sir, looks at the 'ammerin' 'ome o' the golden rivet, awful tragedy comes about, sir.'

Petrie-Smith appeared amused. 'Really? Comes to whom?'

''Im what looks, sir.'

'Oh, I scarcely feel afraid of that!' Petrie-Smith gave a good-humoured, cultured laugh and leaned over, his leg still in the clutch of the Master-at-Arms until the latter released it and began heaving desperately at the fire-bar so that once it came back round the stanchion the body could be released to oblivion. He was not quite fast enough; Mr Petrie-Smith gave a yelp. 'There's a body there! A naked one!'

'Is there really, sir?'

'Yes!'

'Well, sir, I'll be blowed,' MAA Pickering said unconvincingly.

'The face ... the moustache! It's a Uruguayan, probably Colonel Oribe!'

'Oh, I don't think it can be, sir, beggin' your pardon.' MAA Pickering, cursing the fate that had snarled up the works just when Oribe's face had been hard up against the lip of the deck, heaved mightily and up came the fire-bar. Pickering took the strain of the body for a moment while he flashed the fire-bar and its rope through Petrie-Smith's legs, then let go. Colonel Oribe sped downwards and there was a splash. Pickering got to his feet, dusting his hands together. 'Must be a mistake, sir.'

'It wasn't, I assure you!'

'Oh. Corporal Judd, was you aware o' the presence of a body?'

'Body, Master?'

'Gentleman 'ere says 'e saw one.'

'Oh no, Master.'

'You're both liars!' Petrie-Smith said frenziedly. 'I shall inform the Admiral immediately – I've never known such a dreadful thing in all my life! A ship in foreign waters – a foreign national killed – culpable disposal of evidence – goodness only knows what the Prime Minister's going to say.' His long, thin frame and long, pale face hung like an angry wraith over the two ship's policemen. 'You have been guilty of the most heinous crime imaginable. There will be repercussions, oh yes, there will be repercussions throughout the world. Monstrous!'

Petrie-Smith hastened away aft, muttering to himself as he went. 'Stupid sod,' MAA Pickering said indignantly yet with a fair degree of alarm in his voice. 'Let's 'ope 'e don't make any impression on the Admiral.'

*   *   *

With the party from the flagship embarked and Canon Rampling blessing some red wine in the tiny wardroom, Her Majesty's Ship *Biddle* headed inwards for Montevideo. Half-hyde was on the bridge with *Biddle*'s lieutenant-in-command, the rather common Mr Barber, to whom he outlined his plan of campaign as the little ship moved on at half speed. *Biddle* was to enter the port boldly and openly and go alongside the wharf, where the landing-party would be discharged. The men would form up under Halfhyde and the gunner's mate and march out of the dockyard; if questioned, Halfhyde, who had enough kitchen Spanish to get by, would say that they were soldiers from the guard aboard the British flagship and under orders to report to Colonel Villanueva. They would then make their way to the gaol where Lord Horace Vane was being held, and they would take him over and march him away to safety. Then a message would be sent to the Uruguayan authorities that Savory was at once to be handed back to the British squadron. If he was not, the message would say, then the British Ambassador would suffer; the message would be sent as from Uruguayans of the *ancien régime*, the reactionary counter-revolutionaries anxious to queer the pitch for the new government. No administration, Halfhyde insisted to the dubious Lieutenant Barber, would welcome the world opprobrium that would follow upon any harm coming to an ambassador, let alone the Ambassador of Queen Victoria.

'But,' Barber objected, 'if the harm's done not by the government but by the counter-revolutionaries—'

'Ah, but the government will have it in its own hands to remedy that situation, will it not? They must realize, too, that they have no right to hold Savory. And the sons of the revolution will certainly believe what I tell them – they'll doubtless believe anything of the reactionaries and will certainly not wish to have to admit to permitting harm, even death, to the British Ambassador thus early in their reign. Remember how new to government they are – the situation must still be fluid, in fact. That'll operate in our favour, as you shall see.'

'And von Merkatz?'

'Oh, he'll not interfere with our entry, you may be sure. He won't risk fighting in a Uruguayan port, and if he puts searchlights on to us, he'll see enough natives to keep him happy.'

Barber nodded. 'You can find the gaol, can you?'

'Yes. The Admiralty "Pilot" is very precise and the town is well described.'

*   *   *

'Thank you, Mr Tidy.' Canon Rampling got to his feet and removed the surplice that he had put on for the blessing of the wine, since poured into a rum bottle. Then he saw the look of doubt on the churchwarden's face. 'What is it, Mr Tidy?'

'Just thought, like.' Tidy scratched his head.

'Thought what?'

'T'bottle. T'rum bottle.'

Rampling stared. 'What of it, Mr Tidy?'

'Rum'll be sticking to inside, like. Rum's not been blessed, and congregation—'

'Oh, bother take it, Mr Tidy, yes, I see your point. I shall have to do it all over again.' On once again went the surplice and Canon Rampling knelt and intoned rather sharply: Tidy should have warned him in time. The blessing became something of a gabble as bright light came through the port to indicate the approach to Montevideo and a quick sideways look showed the huge slablike side of a heavy cruiser, which must obviously be the *Kaiser Wilhelm*. Action of a sort was imminent, and Canon Rampling speeded things up further; twice-blessed wine and once-blessed rum dregs were stowed in the communion set by Tidy. Rampling clambered to his feet just as Halfhyde entered the wardroom.

'Are you ready, padre?' Halfhyde asked.

125

'Ready indeed.'

'The surplice off, if you please. The cassock remains. It should act in our favour, since the Uruguayans will respect a man of God.'

Rampling, thrusting a prayer book into some internal stowage of the cassock, asked, 'Are you about to march?'

Halfhyde nodded. 'The men will be fallen in presently.' He turned away and went back to the upper deck. As he did so a searchlight was switched on aboard the German cruiser lying at the opposite wall, and a fat pencil of bright light moved about the *Biddle*'s decks to illuminate a number of apparent Uruguayan soldiers already moving down a brow to the dockyard jetty. The beam penetrated the port into the wardroom and lit upon Canon Rampling before passing on; it was like the eye of the Devil himself. As if by a sudden impulse, the parson crossed himself and then met the accusing eye of Mr Tidy: Wherp-in-Swaledale was very low church, and good Church of England Yorkshire dalesmen didn't cross themselves. Rampling felt a shade guilty, but no matter, this night a blow was to be struck for England and God could surely find no fault with that. Up on deck again the searchlight, now less like the eye of the devil than that of Chief Superintendent Portlock of the Yard, lit sharply and cruelly upon Detective Inspector Todhunter in his idiotic-looking Uruguayan military uniform. He much preferred his bowler hat and he hoped his Gladstone bag with his warrant would be perfectly safe on board ship. Currently, he felt unpolicemanlike and, in a sense, naked; but MAA Titmuss, it seemed, did not regard him as unpolicemanlike in appearance. As the searchlight beamed and dazzled, Titmuss interposed his immense body between the searchlight and the detective inspector and then gave tongue.

'Orf the upper deck, Mr Tod'unter, an' look sharpish or you'll give the game away. *If* you please.'

'Now, look—'

'I'm looking and in my view you 'ave a flatfoot's face what that von Merkatz knows only too well, an' never mind the rig. And don't argue or I'll 'ave you in arrest.'

*   *   *

Daintree sat in his sea-cabin, looking lost in the comparative immensity of his easy chair. 'You're certain it was a body, **Mr Petrie-Smith?**'

'Quite certain.'

'I see. What did it look like?'

'A body! A dead one. Colonel Oribe – as I have already said, Admiral.'

'Ah yes, yes. Well, we know he died, do we not?'

Petrie-Smith breathed hard down his nose. 'I think that's hardly the point, is it? The point is that your Master-at-Arms and his assistants were making a clandestine disposal of evidence such as is not permitted under English law.'

'We're in Uruguayan waters, Mr Petrie-Smith.'

'Or under Uruguayan law either I shouldn't wonder,' Petrie-Smith said acidly. 'It's the Uruguayans I'm worried about. Once they get to know of Oribe's murder—'

'Not murder. Self-defence.'

'An arguable point, Admiral, very arguable.'

'No it isn't!' Captain Watkiss broke in, having by this time decided to change his mind about the action of MAA Pickering. 'It's not arguable at all and you are not to argue about it. It was self-defence and that's fact, I said it. But just to make assurance doubly sure, the order was given for the body to be disposed of—'

'An *order*?' Petrie-Smith appeared flabbergasted.

'That's what I said, wash your ears out—'

Petrie-Smith lifted his arms helplessly. 'Admiral, is this the fact?'

'Oh dear, oh dear, not exactly, no—'

'Come, come, my dear sir!' Watkiss snapped. 'We are men, not mice, and must take the responsibility for orders given, must we not? Of course it's fact! And you gave the blasted order yourself, may I remind you, and it ill becomes you to try to sneak out from under.' The Flag Captain swung round upon Petrie-Smith. 'And as for you – you and your damn drawing-room popinjay's airs and graces – you're about as relevant to naval or military requirements as a fiddler's bitch that's on—'

'Her Majesty shall hear of this!' Mr Petrie-Smith was almost in tears by now.

'Oh, will she. Will she indeed? Well, here's something for her to stuff into her pipe and smoke, and you too: the order was given for the body to be disposed of so that for all the dagoes will ever be able to prove, the bugger damn well *fell in* and was drowned!'

'With iron bars tied to him?' Petrie-Smith asked with a sneer.

Captain Watkiss shook his telescope towards the diplomat. 'They won't know that! The body won't be found, will it? An *assumption* will be made that he fell.' He screwed his monocle into his eye-socket. 'No damn dago has any sea sense, they're all liable to trip over their blasted unhandy feet.' He turned his back, pointedly, in high dudgeon: diplomats were unhandy at sea, too; it was a pity they, like dagoes, didn't fall overboard.

TWELVE

Halfhyde's party formed up under the gunner's mate and once they were all ashore, with Mr Todhunter and Canon Rampling in their midst – without Mr Tidy who had come thus far only to see the reverend safely ashore with his communion set – the *Biddle* cast off fore and aft and proceeded out of the port and back to her anchorage before any interfering Uruguayans could arrive to make enquiries. The seamen marched, or more strictly shambled like a dago army, towards the gate leading out of the dockyard. MAA Titmuss, with his enormously distended stomach and sagging jowls, looked the most genuine of them all even though his uniform was a poor fit. Across the arm of harbour water they could see the great *Kaiser Wilhelm* with her ports and her compass platform ablaze with light; they could see her guns, threatening steel shards of war that in fact were most unlikely to open whilst in harbour, but might well follow them out to sea once Savory was retaken. As the marching men passed behind the lee of a large warehouse, the reminders of German power were removed from sight. At this hour the dockyard was all but deserted; an occasional armed Uruguayan soldier was seen, supposedly on guard but in practice, more often than not, puffing at a cigar in the shadows with his rifle laid upon the ground; and there were scraggy, rangy cats that ran swiftly from their approach towards the more propitious areas of the rat-infested stores and warehouses.

At the guarded gate, they passed through without trouble; Canon Rampling's presence in the bat-like black of his cassock, lent, as Halfhyde had suggested it might, an air of respectability and authority. The soldiery did not query men of God lest God strike back in anger; and Halfhyde was waved through, salutes being exchanged perfunctorily. The men marched out; as they did so several bursts of firing came from the direction of the town, loud and clear and, in the night's awful blackness, frightening to Mr Todhunter.

'Oh dear me,' he said in a high voice. 'What do you suppose that is, Mr Halfhyde?'

'Rifles, but not aimed at us.' The bursts went on. 'The city's not yet settled down after the *coup*.'

'You think it's no more than that, then, Mr Halfhyde?'

'I am sure so.'

'Good.' Mr Todhunter was very much relieved. Once through the gate, Halfhyde took the first turning on his right and after that the seamen were no longer visible from the dockyard. They moved through narrow, smelly streets, between close-set hovels, some of them properly inhabited, some of them in a state of near dereliction but containing, most probably, any number of human dregs, beggars and cripples and prostitutes who knew no other home. It was a depressing scene; the marching footsteps echoed from hard, rutted ground and a dog ran, barking, from their track, to vanish into a side alley filled with garbage. They emerged from the narrow street into a small square, and crossing this entered another constricted thoroughfare. The gaol lay not far ahead; Halfhyde had the route firmly in mind. Finding the target was no worry; but once they got to it, the future would be to a large extent in the hands of fate. So far the signs were propitious enough, but that might not last. Coming to the end of the second street, they emerged into another square: on the far side stood a high wall, with a guarded gate set into it and a guard lantern burning over an armed sentry. This was the gaol, and now had come the time for sharp wits and ready rifles if needed. Halfhyde left his place in the lead of the advance and walked down the line, giving his last-minute orders and warnings.

*   *   *

The recriminations from Mr Petrie-Smith over the disposal of Colonel Oribe's body were still proceeding in the Admiral's sea-cabin when a hurried knocking at the door was followed swiftly by the entry of Lieutenant Lamphorn. The Flag Captain glared at him. 'Well, what is it, Mr Lamphorn? I'm much engaged.'

'Sir, there is firing from the shore!'

Watkiss bounced to his feet. 'Upon us? Have the buggers opened upon us?'

'No, sir, not upon us. Firing has been heard distantly from the direction of Montevideo – rifle fire, I believe. I fear Mr Halfhyde's party has come under attack, sir.'

'Do you, by God!' Captain Watkiss swung round upon the Admiral. 'We shall not stand by and see British seamen shot down, sir. I propose to send reinforcements immediately.'

'We must not be precipitate, Flag Captain.'

'Oh, precipitate my bottom, sir, you are nothing but a recipe for disaster in my opinion and I shall take action immediately in your stead. Mr Lamphorn, have the chief gunner's mate told to make ready another landing-party at once.'

'Aye, aye, sir.'

'Strongly armed and no need for any blasted disguise, we'll go as honest British tars and balls to you, Petrie-Smith, and the ridiculous nonsense you are about to utter about diplomacy. You can hold your tongue. Mr Lamphorn?'

'Sir?'

'Mr Perrin's back from the *Biddle*, I presume?'

'Yes, sir—'

'Then he's to bring the steam picquet-boat alongside the starboard ladder, and further midshipmen will be required at the lower boom for the cutters. I propose to leave the ship myself in the steam picquet-boat, and shall board the *Delia* to proceed inshore. I'm glad it's not the *Biddle*. At least the *Delia* is commanded by a gentleman.'

*   *   *

All had gone remarkably according to plan. Halfhyde had taken his men past the sentry and into the gaol courtyard, indicating to the sergeant of the guard that he was under orders from the new government to take charge of the British Ambassador and remove him from the gaol to an up-country destination where he would be further from any interference by either the British or the Germans. The entry was to some extent helped by Canon Rampling managing to have his cassock impaled upon a bayonet whilst passing through the gate, for the embarrassed sergeant spent so much time offering his humble apologies that he had scarcely time for anything else. He had been persuaded to rouse an official, a man who had come down into the courtyard in his nightshirt to have Halfhyde's revolver thrust into his stomach and Mr Todhunter's handcuffs, British ones from Scotland Yard, snapped over his wrists, which had been hauled behind his back. At the same time the gunner's mate led the main body of the landing-party in a fast swoop upon the guardroom and its occupants. Titmuss seized the sergeant and held him with his face pressed tightly into his stomach so that he was unable to utter a word. Halfhyde pressed harder with his revolver into the awakened official's nightshirt. 'To the British Ambassador, my friend, and quickly. And keep your mouth shut tight, or you'll not live to see the dawn.'

The man was in a state of total fear by now; with four of his seamen, Halfhyde urged him back towards the main gaol building. The nightshirt shook like a leaf in the wind as they went through the door into what seemed to be a reception area for incoming criminals, now deserted except for themselves. There was evidence of recent fighting: bullet-holes in walls and furnishings, and some burning that had left blackened wood-work and ugly patches on the walls. The revolution would no doubt have passed through the prison, and it was likely enough that normal routine was still upset and uncertain. The captured official, with the revolver hard against his spine, indicated a door at the back of the reception area. Going through this, they came to a spiral staircase of metal treads ascending from a stone floor. At the top of this was a gallery running high above the well of the prison. A gaoler armed with a rifle was walking the gallery, around which were set the prison cages, open-barred so that their variegated occupants could be observed clearly.

Halfhyde said, 'Tell the gaoler to bring out the British Ambassador. And remember what I said about the dawn.'

Words were exchanged and the gaoler, though clearly puzzled, came forward and put a key in the lock of a door some half-a-score feet ahead of Halfhyde. Halfhyde thrust with his revolver and his party moved forward to the cell as the door was opened and Lord Horace Vane was brought out. The Ambassador seemed a sick man, unable to walk without the assistance of the warder's arm. His face was grey and drawn, his eyes hollow. He stared from one to the other without speaking. Halfhyde addressed him, still using his Spanish.

'You will come with us. There will be no questions. It is for your own good.'

Vane's lips moved and a tongue came out to lick at them. He said, 'I am tired and unwell.'

'Perhaps, but you will do as I say. My men have guns and will use them if I give the order. Come quickly.' Halfhyde gestured to two of his seamen and they moved to the gaoler and disarmed him. With Vane, both the gaoler and the night-shirted official were pushed towards the staircase, surrounded by the British guns. They hastened down the stairs, through the reception area, still deserted, and across the courtyard: MAA Titmuss emerged from the guardroom, looking as if he were about to salute and make a nautical-style report; Halfhyde forestalled him by running ahead to take the report in closer company.

'Well, Master?'

'All correct, sir. Dagoes all tied up an' gagged, sir. Used their socks. As gags, like, sir.'

'Good! I'm taking the gaoler and the man in the nightshirt, just in case my Spanish is seen through in retrospect – it's important we're not known to be British.' Halfhyde paused; Titmuss had confessed to a knowledge of some Spanish, picked up in Gibraltar's brothels and bars. 'You managed to keep the deception going, I hope?'

Titmuss nodded. 'Yessir.'

'Good! Where's the gunner's mate?'

'Here, sir,' a low and cautious voice said. 'I didn't utter a syllable, sir.'

'Right. March out, if you please, gunner's mate, prisoners in the centre, and all hands to be ready for action.'

'Aye, aye, sir. Where to, sir?'

'Well, the river's the nearest way out of the town, and I'm confident no alarm's been raised. I've a strong instinct we should make back for the dockyard.'

'But the *Biddle*'s gone back out to the anchorage, sir.'

Halfhyde gave a grim laugh. 'I know, but it was never my intention to take Lord Horace out to the flagship. I shall steal a boat from the dockyard, and may perhaps head for the Argentine coast. It usually helps if one can confuse the issue.'

Within the minute the British seamen were clear of the gaol and moving at the double towards the dockyard with their prisoners; for Halfhyde's money they would have a clear run at least until it was discovered that the gaol gates lacked a sentry, and that might not be until the whole guard was changed, probably next morning. At the moment Halfhyde's chief worry was the Ambassador: he was having to be carried by two seamen, and he had the look of needing a doctor badly. Canon Rampling, bounding along the streets of Montevideo like a bullock at Halfhyde's side, breathlessly suggested communion before it was too late.

'I'm sorry, padre, but we can't stop now.'

'God should come first, my dear fellow.'

'I hardly think He would agree in the circumstances.'

'Then you're quite wrong.' Rampling puffed and blew; a cassock was not the best garment for hard physical exercise and the communion set was heavy. 'He is always insistent that He—'

'I think,' Halfhyde snapped, 'that it is not God but the church that is insistent. I have never believed God to be as self-centred as the church teaches.'

Rampling's mouth opened but no words came; this was partly due to sheer lack of breath but mostly to shock. He had listened to heresy and did not like it. The Lord thy God is a jealous God. Shutting his mind to what he had heard, Rampling plunged on, sweating profusely into his cassock and clutching the communion set tightly to his chest so that its contents did not rattle about and shatter. The dockyard was not far ahead now, and a minute later, as they rounded the last corner, the gates were seen and possible danger loomed; Canon Rampling uttered a prayer for the deliverance of all – generously, he felt. The prayer was answered; the gate sentry, a good son of the revolution, was drunk. He sprawled in the roadway smelling strongly and with a nearly empty bottle still in his grip. The British party passed through unremarked, and Halfhyde made towards the wharves and jetties, heading away from the wall where the *Kaiser Wilhelm* lay. An instinct bred of a long experience of dockyards and their layout led him in the right direction for the boatyard, where the small craft would be found, and almost certainly unguarded. It was when he had found a suitable boat that Halfhyde's plan was revealed to Detective Inspector Todhunter.

* * *

'You are blasted *slow*, Mr Perrin, and I will not have it.'

'Sir—'

'Oh, don't argue, I never heard of such a thing as midshipmen opening their mouths, Mr Perrin, and I won't have that either.' Captain Watkiss pulled out his turnip-shaped watch and studied it under the light from the quartermaster's lobby. 'Two damn minutes since the steam picquet-boat was called away, I ask you! When I was a damn snotty, Mr Perrin, my Captain would have had my balls for breakfast had I not been alongside for him in *sixty seconds*! What have you to say to that, Mr Perrin?'

Mr Perrin had nothing to say, and shuffled uneasily.

'Mr Perrin, kindly answer when spoken to by a senior officer, I dislike uncouthness and dumb insolence in a midshipman.'

'Y-y-yessir. I'm sorry, sir.' It was impossible to get it right with Captain Watkiss. Mr Perrin saluted as being the best thing to do and was told angrily to improve the appearance of the quarterdeck by leaving it at once to return to the steam picquet-boat. This he did; and once he had embarked all ready to salute again, the tub-shaped Flag Captain went down the ladder importantly and stepped into the sternsheets. As he did so there was a reaction from the direction of the *Cardiff*: a number of yells swept for'ard, and Captain Watkiss frowned.

'Very mannerless.'

'Yes, sir.'

'But what can one expect from foreigners?'

The question had been rhetorical, but Mr Perrin still had his last lesson in mind. 'It depends upon the particular foreigner, I suppose, sir—'

'No it damn well doesn't!'

135

'No, sir.' Mr Perrin jumped in alarm as the crack of a rifle came and a bullet, the wind of which he could feel as it passed him by, clanged off the bell-mouthed funnel. 'They're firing, sir!'

'Yes. Exactly! What did I say about foreigners?' Captain Watkiss said in disgust. 'Well, what are you waiting for? Get your boat away at once!'

'Yes, sir.' Perrin paused as a disturbance was heard from the quarterdeck and an angry figure began to shout down towards the boat. 'Sir, the Admiral, sir!'

'What about the Admiral, Mr Perrin?'

'He is ordering you to return aboard, sir.'

'Disregard the Admiral, Mr Perrin.'

'But sir—'

'Do as you're damn well told!' the Flag Captain snapped. 'You will take your orders from me, not the Admiral. Get me away from those blasted dago bullets!' Two more had come, somewhat perilously close to Captain Watkiss even though he sat concealed beneath the wood of the canopy. Mr Perrin gave the orders and the picquet-boat left the ladder to head towards the *Delia*; some way ahead of them, thanks to Mr Perrin's dilatoriness earlier and to consequent delays caused by Captain Watkiss' reprimand, sped the two cutters under oars carrying the additional landing-party commanded by a lieutenant with the chief gunner's mate in attendance. The steam picquet-boat, under the coal-shovelling of Leading-Stoker Bustard, was fast and had soon not only overtaken the pulling cutters but had gone beyond the range of the Uruguayan rifles aboard the *Cardiff*. By this time Captain Watkiss had emerged from the canopy and was standing in the sternsheets, looking back towards the squadron through his telescope. He cried out with much pleasure when the telescope picked out a blaze of light near the *Cardiff*'s port after davits and he saw a cutter – its after fall held fast whilst the for'ard one ran away – tip its occupants, dagoes he hoped and believed, willy-nilly into the sea.

'Mr Perrin, the stupid buggers have no idea of how to lower a boat!'

Perrin turned to look.

'Face for'ard and look where you're going, if you please, Mr

Perrin, you are in charge of the blasted boat and are not to hazard your Captain's life.'

'No, sir, sorry, sir.'

'And go alongside the *Delia* carefully. If the other damn midshipmen had not been on the sick list or otherwise employed, I'd never have allowed you in the steam picquet-boat at all.'

'No, sir.' Perrin wondered once again why he had ever come to sea. Captain Watkiss didn't give a man confidence, but perhaps not all captains were quite like Captain Watkiss. Time would tell; but at present time was bearing him towards the ordeal of touching Captain Watkiss very gently against the side of the *Delia*, and this required all his concentration. In the event he did it efficiently and was rewarded by a grunt as Captain Watkiss climbed aboard and ordered the picquet-boat back to the flagship. Met ceremoniously by the gentlemanly Lieutenant Forbes-Forrester, Captain Watkiss returned his salute.

'Delighted to have you aboard, sir,' Forbes-Forrester toadied.

'Thank you, Mr Forbes-Forrester,' Watkiss said, casting an eye around. 'I see you run a smart ship, as one would expect, of course. I trust she's tautly run as well?'

'Yes, indeed, sir.'

'Good. The two normally go hand-in-hand, do they not?' Watkiss paused. 'Tonight your decks may run with blood, Mr Forbes-Forrester. Blood! I wish you to take me into the dock-yard, and to man and arm your guns.'

'Aye, aye, sir.'

'Upon arrival I am to be landed with my seamen. Then I shall storm the – the—' Captain Watkiss waved his telescope and began hissing with furious mortification. He had no idea what he was going to storm; this must be left to on-the-spot decision.

'Sir?' Forbes-Forrester enquired politely.

'I prefer not to reveal what I shall storm, Mr Forbes-Forrester, such things are better kept secret even from one's own officers.'

'Quite, sir.' Forbes-Forrester was very smooth. 'I understand fully, sir.'

'Do you?' Watkiss asked, a shade blankly.

'Yes, sir. The first principle of warfare, I'd call it.'

'Oh.'

'What a man does not know, sir, cannot be forced from him by enemy torture if such should occur.'

'Yes, quite. Quite.'

*   *   *

Mr Todhunter was shattered: Mr Halfhyde must have taken leave of his senses. Having found a nice boat to take them all safely from Uruguayan soil, if not Uruguayan waters, Mr Halfhyde had proposed leaving him, Mr Todhunter, behind. There was a job for him to do, it appeared, but Todhunter didn't want to do it. The assignment involved becoming Mr Halfhyde's emissary to the upstart Uruguayan government. He would bear the tidings that the British Ambassador was in hostile hands and if he was to live then Savory must be handed over to the British squadron to which assistance must be rendered so that they might sail away to England.

Todhunter wrung his hands. 'It's not consistent, Mr Halfhyde, it's not consistent at all.'

'In what way?'

'Why, sir, I'm a police officer and my duty is to my chief super. I've no experience of this sort of carry-on!' Todhunter added indignantly, thrashing about for any excuse to get out of it. 'It's stupid, that's what it is, bloody stupid if you don't mind the word. Anyway, I'm dressed as a native soldier and they'll go and shoot me as a spy when they find out I'm British.'

'I doubt it, Mr Todhunter, when you produce your warrant—'

'It's aboard ship.'

'Well, never mind, you have an honest face, Todhunter. You shall say you were captured by what you took to be a band of brigands who have seized Lord Horace Vane and will shoot him if the terms are not met by noon tomorrow. You broke away, very bravely, and have come to report what you know. You will say you are willing to return to your captors with messages – and I've no objection to your asking for a military escort under a flag of truce if you think that would add authenticity to your story. I have already had words with Lord Horace, who knows that he is in British hands by now – he has advised me of a safe place in which to hold him. Now, what do you say?'

'I say no,' Mr Todhunter stated firmly. 'Look, how do I explain how I came to be ashore in order to get captured by brigands in the first place, Mr Halfhyde? I'd be barmy, wouldn't I?'

'Not in the least. You were put ashore from the *Biddle* in disguise and on duty. You were pursuing Savory, as is your duty ... your duty to your chief super, Mr Todhunter.'

'Oh, dear!'

'Not to mention the Queen.' Halfhyde wagged a finger in the policeman's worried face. 'Duty is a small word but a large concept, Mr Todhunter. You'll not fail in yours, will you?'

'No, I'll not do that, but it's not my duty, Mr Halfhyde, to indulge in jiggery-pokery and that sort of lark, it's not proper.' Todhunter returned to his original plea. 'It's not *consistent*.'

Halfhyde nodded. 'Very well, Mr Todhunter, it's not consistent. Other things are.'

'Such as what?' Mr Todhunter asked in alarm.

'Reports to be made to Whitehall – and to Scotland Yard. I understand Chief Superintendent Portlock to be a stickler for duty, and a harsh superior to boot. If one of his juniors refuses to assist the naval power of Britain in the apprehension of a traitor to the Queen, then something tells me Chief Superintendent Portlock would catch fire, Mr Todhunter. I would think very carefully about that, if I were you.'

'Oh dear, oh dear...'

'And quickly as well, for time is short.'

* * *

As Captain Watkiss, aboard the *Delia*, reached the berth earlier occupied by the *Biddle*, Detective Inspector Todhunter, having been apprised of where he was to rejoin Halfhyde, sneaked fearfully back past the drunken sentry who had now finished his bottle and looked dead. Mr Todhunter went along the street where he had gone before, casting glances everywhere. He was much worried: how, unless he really was a spy, was he to explain to the Uruguayan government the fact that, having come ashore purely to hunt Savory, he happened to be dressed in one of their own bloody uniforms, whether or not he called it a disguise? That would need thought, but he was in no fit state to think properly; all he could think about, his own safety apart, was Chief Superintendent Portlock, the man who would catch fire. Mr Halfhyde had not exaggerated in that, not at all he hadn't ... Mr Todhunter plodded on, following a route to the local government building given him by Halfhyde from the Admiralty's bloody book. Mr Todhunter, not normally given to thinking swear words, was much aggrieved. Being aggrieved, he managed to get lost; and he fetched up where he had been earlier – outside the prison. He sweated: this was the scene of the crime, the crime in which he had taken part. One of the wise saws of Chief Superintendent Portlock was that the dog always returns to its vomit, by which he meant the criminal always returns to the scene of his crime, which was not a nice situation for a detective inspector of the Metropolitan Police to be in, not nice at all.

Mr Todhunter dithered, wondering what to do next. The gaol could of course put him in touch with the blokes he was supposed to talk to, the men of government. At the very least they would know the way, and Mr Halfhyde had made the point that time was short. Also, Mr Todhunter did very badly wish to re-arrest the traitor Savory. That was indeed his whole purpose.

He squared his shoulders and marched forward as much like a policeman as possible in his scruffy foreign uniform, all tabs and tassels and of what rank he really had no idea, and entered the still unguarded gates. It was dark yet; not a lot of time had passed in fact, and never mind Mr Halfhyde. Mr Todhunter tapped at the door of the guardroom, then, when there was no response, he opened the door and put his head in.

'Beg pardon,' he said.

No answer; he went right in. A light was burning and in its beams he saw the members of the guard, all tied up and gagged as they had been left when last he had been here. Dark eyes stared and glared balefully. Mr Todhunter fingered his chin: should he, or should he not, release them? Yes, if he wished their assistance, of course he must. That might get him off on a better foot, anyway.

He stepped forward: sergeants first. Mr Todhunter was tugging at the bonds around the sergeant's arms when noise came from outside and very suddenly an important-looking person, all red and gold and sky-blue, entered behind a drawn revolver and rushed towards the miscreant whose finger was upon the ropes. Mr Todhunter nearly fainted; he had been caught redhanded at his own crime. Talk about dog vomit.

THIRTEEN

Captain Watkiss aboard *Delia* addressed the lieutenant in charge of the storming party. 'Mr Hillman, form up my men on the jetty.'

'Aye, aye, sir.'

'And lose no time about it. Report when ready, and I shall join you. Mr Forbes-Forrester, I have changed my mind and shall now inform you where I intend to march, and this information is to be passed back to the flagship – you will return to the anchorage for that purpose, and then come back to stand by for me, do you understand?'

'Yes, sir,' Forbes-Forrester said. 'Shall I pass it by signal, sir?'

'Most certainly not,' Watkiss said promptly. 'It is secret and will be passed by hand of officer in a boat. I would have thought any fool would have realized that.' He paused, bouncing up and down on the balls of his feet. 'I intend to strike at the heart of local power. There is no point in dealing with underlings. I shall march upon the government offices and present my case.'

'I see, sir. Do you intend to march immediately?' Forbes-Forrester asked.

The Flag Captain stared superciliously. Even gentlemen could be idiots. 'You don't expect me to hang about on the jetty like a lout at a street corner, do you?'

'I was merely about to say that the dawn is still some way off, sir, and the offices are unlikely to be manned. Except perhaps by duty underlings,' Forbes-Forrester added.

'Oh, nonsense, it'll take my party some while to get there and someone of importance will be in early attendance. They start

work early in these dago countries where they spend the afternoon in siesta. You should learn some geography, Mr Forbes-
Forrester.' Captain Watkiss pointed with his telescope. 'What's
that line doing, hanging judas over the fo'c'sle? Have it brought
inboard, it's a disgrace to the squadron.'

*   *   *

'I am a detective inspector of the Metropolitan Police,' Mr
Todhunter said, wishing desperately that he had never been
talked into wearing his tabs and tassels. 'I have an important
message to deliver to whoever might be in civil charge of the
city. The mayor, perhaps.'

The uniformed person spoke Spanish, which was no doubt
natural, but Mr Todhunter didn't understand a word of it.
When hands were laid upon him, roughly, by the released
soldiers, he protested but it made no difference and he was
hustled inside the gaol, being almost swept off his feet in the
rush. Within fifteen minutes of his arrival at the gates, he was
facing the ultimate indignity for a policeman: he was locked
into a cell. It was not a cell such as was used in London, but was
more like those he had been given to understand were used in
the United States of America: all bars and no privacy. There
was a raised plank for use as a bed and Mr Todhunter sat upon
this with his head in his hands after the gaolers, refusing to
listen to his pleas, had departed. His surroundings were
horrible and filled with different noises; there were snores, there
was the sound of vomiting, there was a clunk of very heavy
metal as though somewhere in his vicinity men were tethered
by ball and chain, and from the neighbouring cell another
sustained sound indicated that its occupant was using the
chamber-pot after having spent the previous hours in a bar.
When the man had finished his task, he began rattling at the
intervening bars and trying to attract Mr Todhunter's attention. Mr Todhunter rapidly developed a nasty headache, and
was forced to look up and remonstrate.

'That noise. Do please stop, I am unwell.'

There was an intake of breath from the man, a huge man with
a vast chest and shoulders, hairy as an ape, much tattooed in
the less hairy parts. 'So? Englees, no?'

'Yes.'

'Ze uniform! Spy, now caught, yes?'

'No!' Mr Todhunter felt quite frenzied; this was precisely what he had mentioned to Mr Halfhyde as being only too likely to happen. 'I'm a—'

'Spy! Shoot, bang.' The man lifted his arms and squinted along an imaginary rifle.

'Oh, dear!'

'Eight o'clock, zey shoot spies. You will know when is eight o'clock every day.' Having said this, the man appeared to lose interest; buttoning his flies, he turned about and dropped like a sack on his plank bed. Mr Todhunter put his head back in his hands and trembled. South America was a dreadful place; he had not had a happy time in Chile and he didn't want to die in Uruguay. Most probably they didn't issue casualty lists or whatever and he would simply vanish for good and Chief Superintendent Portlock might never know what had happened to him and would think he had deserted or something, and the name of Todhunter would be mud in the Metropolitan Police. The shame of it! But surely it wouldn't really come to that; they'd never dare, not in the case of a British subject, why, for one thing, the Ambassador ... but the Ambassador had his own problems, Mr Todhunter suddenly remembered. However, even that aspect could possibly redound to his salvation, provided the Uruguayans were not precipitate: if no word reached Whitehall through the British Embassy's cable link as to the Ambassador's release, Whitehall must surely conclude that Admiral Daintree's squadron had failed in its purpose and then they would send an expeditionary force, possibly from the garrison at Bermuda which might not take too long to sail south.

There was really no need for despair, and the eight o'clock shoot was only hearsay after all.

Mr Todhunter couldn't sleep even though he was dead tired, and his watch had been removed before his incarceration so he couldn't tell how much longer the night had to go; but go it did and somehow or other the gaol inmates seemed to know the time, and they all began banging and rattling at the same instant, creating proper bedlam, and quietened only when gaolers came along with rifles and used the butts to beat at bar-gripping knuckles. Very soon after this Mr Todhunter's stomach turned to water: hearsay had become fact. From outside came the sound of rifle-fire, a number of distinct and separate volleys. It was eight o'clock.

*　　*　　*

Halfhyde and his party were well up-river now, some miles west of Montevideo. Odd boats passed them, but no notice was taken as what appeared to be local soldiers rowed on with Canon Rampling sitting coxswain-like in the stern, his great size and capacious cassock almost acting as a sail as the dawn came up splendidly from seaward, bringing a fair breeze from aft.

'How much farther?' Halfhyde asked the Ambassador.

'We're close now. A mile or two only.' Lord Horace was keeping going manfully, but was sadly weak. There was, however, more than a spark of continuing life and Halfhyde believed he would rally when his ordeal was over; and because of this had again, more than once, deflected the parson from use of his communion set. Such could prove depressing and Lord Horace was in need of a more optimistic approach. 'There is a landing stage...'

'Yes. Take it easy now. A watch is being kept.'

They rowed on, passing flat, muddy banks with farms on undulating land, crops growing and cows chewing rich grass. Men were moving in the fields and occasionally there was a wave towards the boat. Halfhyde returned these greetings punctiliously. Soon the landing stage was seen ahead on the northern bank; the boat was brought alongside and made fast and the men disembarked quickly. Around the stage there was cover – trees and bushes growing thickly, extending northwards from the bank.

The Ambassador, carried again by two seamen, said that this would take them all the way to the hide-out, which he had described as being a disused military fort, and they should be able to reach it unseen. Before moving out, Halfhyde ordered the boat to be dragged ashore and concealed in the bushes; then, following the Ambassador's directions, they started on the trek for the fort. They reached it within the hour. Small and now derelict, it was still defensible with rifles if it should become necessary, and Halfhyde lost no time in concealing all hands behind the thick walls and picking out the best defensive positions if action should come. The cellars were still usable, as he found when the rubble had been cleared away to reveal the entry, and could be lived in at least as long as they could forage for food and water to sustain life.

Halfhyde brought out his watch: a little after seven o'clock. Soon now, Todhunter should be in contact with the Uruguayan authorities. Halfhyde could only hope the policeman had managed to lie low somewhere in safety during the night hours.

*　　*　　*

Captain Watkiss had come well equipped: his monkey-jacket was criss-crossed with leather belts from shoulders to waist, one of them bearing revolver ammunition and the other supporting a water-bottle, a dirk for hand-to-hand fighting, a tin containing chocolate and cheese, a sustaining mixture according to the Fleet Surgeon, and a map case empty of maps but well filled with such handy goods as quinine in case he should catch malaria in a swampy land, malted milk tablets, a flask of whisky, an onion and some plugs of chewing tobacco, a habit unfit for officers but useful to have for barter. In addition to all this he had his revolver holster and his telescope. He bounced along the dockyard stones in front of his men like a mobile bargain basement, clattering and chinking. Passing through the gate as Halfhyde and then Todhunter had done before him, he espied the grounded sentry, still drunk.

He clicked his tongue at Mr Hillman. 'What a country.'

'Yes, indeed, sir.'

'Disgusting. Can you imagine this kind of thing at Portsmouth Dockyard, Mr Hillman? *I* can't. I detest foreigners, detest 'em. What was that?' He shied like a horse as a dark object scurried across his path, and his tin of chocolate banged against his medicine chest.

'I believe it was a cat, sir.'

'Oh. More like a blasted rat, I thought.'

On they marched, through the night. There was just a hint of dawn rising in the east. Captain Watkiss, thinking of the east where the squadron lay, reflected bitterly on the ships' predicament. That was another thing he intended to protest about most strongly: the blasted dagoes should have offered assistance without being asked – the ships were British, it was unthinkable to leave them there all rammed together, it just showed what base minds foreigners had, no damn respect for their betters was what it amounted to. Foreigners had no respect for themselves even, as witness the drunk sentry. Captain Watkiss simmered, then started violently. '*What was that?*' It was no cat this time, and the sound had come from his rear. 'Mr Hillman, I believe that was a bugle!'

'So do I, sir.'

'Whose, that's the point! It wouldn't be the *Delia*, she doesn't possess a bugler and she should be on her way to pass my message in any case.' Watkiss brandished his telescope furiously. 'It's the damn Hun! It's that bugger von Merkatz! He must have noticed me landing and he's giving chase!'

Lieutenant Hillman nodded. 'Have you fresh orders, sir? Should we—'

'Nothing of the sort, Mr Hillman, if you were about to suggest retreat you shall think again. You may be lily-livered, I am not. Advance at the double, if you please, holding our present course.'

The order was passed back by the chief gunner's mate and the men picked up the double, cursing their heavy equipment that was the very devil to run with, especially after slothful weeks at sea. Captain Watkiss sounded like an orchestra. By sheer good fortune they took the right track with Captain Watkiss issuing the directions, and in due course reached their target, the centre of the local administration, newly formed but housed in well-weathered buildings. Watkiss ordered the halt, and the men, sweating and out of breath, were stood at ease.

'Mr Hillman!'

'Sir?'

'Rouse someone out.'

Hillman looked dubious. 'How shall I do that, sir?'

'How? How my bottom, Mr Hillman, you're an officer and you should know how. *Go and ring the blasted bell!* Or bang, if there's no bell.'

Mr Hillman saluted and advanced upon the building, going

up a flight of steps to a massive door. He found a bell-pull, and tugged. Melodious ringing came from within, faintly. Mr Hillman waited.

'*Mr Hillman!*'

The lieutenant turned. 'Yes, sir?'

'Don't wait about like a blasted tradesman! Come back here at once, and stand to your men like a naval officer under arms.'

'Yes, sir.' Hillman returned.

'That's better. I'm not to be trifled with, as they shall find out,' Watkiss announced importantly. 'If none of the buggers are yet at their work, then they shall find me here when they are. Form a guard across the bottom of the steps, Mr Hillman, then stand the men easy again.'

* * *

'Come,' a gaoler said, unlocking Mr Todhunter's cell door. Todhunter felt quite faint and wished he had some sal volatile. It was just past eight as indicated by those dreadful volleys, just past execution time. Possibly they wished to fit one more into today's list ... his knees felt like jelly as he emerged from the cell. His last sight of the world, and it had to be in a filthy dirty foreign gaol, like a common criminal, the very people he had spent his life fighting. It was too bad and it was all Mr Halfhyde's fault, his own too of course for weakly agreeing. But once out on the gallery, a thoroughly noisy place since the banging and rattling had started up again, he straightened his shoulders. He must face what was to come and face it like a policeman, a British policeman at that, and even more import- antly, a *London* policeman. In his time Mr Todhunter had faced Plaistow, Poplar, Bermondsey and the Commercial Road on a Saturday night, likewise the Mile End Road and the East India Dock Road. He hadn't funked it then and although his old mother had spent her nights praying for his safety from vicious men, she had been proud of him. Now she was up there some- where through the roof and would be looking down and expect- ing him to be brave so she could go on being proud of him. He would die with a smile on his lips.

With his armed escort, Mr Todhunter reached the spiral staircase and was urged down. In the reception area were many men, Uruguayans yelling at each other excitedly and waving their arms. Two came towards him, and they were actually smiling and bowing. Mr Todhunter was amazed, really amazed. Unless these people actually enjoyed seeing other people being shot, and Mr Todhunter found it hard to believe that, then death seemed perhaps unlikely. Just yet, anyway.

One of the advancing Uruguayans spoke quite good English. He said, 'You are English policeman?'

'Yes, that's quite right, I am.'

'High one, no?'

'Detective Inspector. Highish, yes.' He added, 'Señor.'

'Detective Inspector! Important, I think?'

Mr Todhunter nodded. 'Well, yes,' he agreed. 'Important, yes, señor.'

Hands were clasped together. 'Good, good! In England, zee civil power, eet ees superior to the military, no?'

'Oh, yes. Yes, it is. Definitely.'

'Aha! A peaceful solution, my friend! Our new government, eet does not wish for war and fightings. You rank with general, perhaps, or admiral?'

'Well, not quite I would say,' Mr Todhunter answered cautiously.

'With *capitan* of four gold rings in British Navy?'

'Perhaps, yes.' It was a lie, but not such a big lie as claiming parity with an admiral or general, and the man seemed to expect a yes.

Again the hands were clasped. 'Outside our building of government is a *capitan* from your British ships, with many men and rifles. You will tell him to go away?'

Mr Todhunter's heart sank to his boots again. 'What if he doesn't?'

'You will give police order, order of civil power to military. Then he will go. Zee British are law-abiding.' There was a pause, a rather nasty one Mr Todhunter thought, and he was right. The man went on, 'You will not fail, officer of British police. Failing brings death by firing squad tomorrow.'

FOURTEEN

Mr Todhunter knew that he was as good as dead. It seemed that in Uruguay they had an exaggerated idea of British police powers, and he had gone and encouraged them in this view, imagining, foolishly as it had turned out, that to heighten his importance might lead in a more propitious direction. Now it had headed him smack into the firing squad. It must; for Captain Watkiss of all captains was never going to take orders from a detective inspector.

Mr Todhunter licked at his lips and sweated into his military uniform. He looked at his tormentors; some of them seemed decent, kindly men. Not many, but some. They, at least, might listen, and he still had to get Mr Halfhyde's vital message delivered to high authority. No one had listened so far, but it was worth a try.

'Half a tick,' he said.

'Please?'

'There's something else. I've a message for the mayor. Or the military governor, I don't know. It's about the British Ambassador, Lord Horace Vane.'

Talk about attention! They were all ears and flashing eyes. Mr Todhunter proceeded. Certain brigands, he said, from whose hands he had fled successfully, were going to shoot the Ambassador and blame it on the newly-formed Uruguayan government. This would cause a furore and it wouldn't be confined to Uruguay. People didn't kill Ambassadors without bringing about wars, Mr Todhunter said. He waved an arm in what he believed to be a seaward direction. Out there were three British cruisers. No matter that they were all fast aground; Britain had a tremendous number more, plus bigger ships – battleships with immensely heavy guns – and they might all set sail for the Plate if the Ambassador was killed.

'You threaten?' asked a dark and savage-looking man.

Mr Todhunter jumped. 'Oh, good gracious me, no! Not me. Those bandits.' He swallowed, then went on, 'They won't kill the Ambassador if you do what they ask, of course.'

'And this is?'

Mr Todhunter explained at some length; only one of the Uruguayans appeared to know about the traitor Savory and he seemed unwilling to commit himself. No doubt, Todhunter thought, he was not important enough to act on his own initiative. Todhunter said diffidently, 'If you'd be so kind as to inform the mayor, or the military governor ... I don't suppose they would mind handing the man Savory over to justice. Savory was removed from my custody only as a hostage, after all. And I would venture to say, even Colonel Oribe is probably not worth a bombardment.'

This was a mistake; everyone spoke, shouted rather, at once. Mr Todhunter brought out a handkerchief to mop at his face; in the heat of the moment he had imagined the handkerchief to be his own, but it wasn't, it was the uniform's former owner's and it was filthy. Mr Todhunter dropped it like a hot bun, fearing disease. The atmosphere was threatening; perhaps Colonel Oribe was, or had been rather, a popular man. Thinking of Colonel Oribe, Mr Todhunter suddenly remembered all those Uruguayans who had been overpowered aboard the flagship and were still being held. My goodness, that would mean trouble too, and here he was, all handy to take the rap for Captain Watkiss! Meanwhile, the Uruguayans were in a real tizzy; half of them suddenly left the gaol's reception area and ran down the steps, making for the gate. Possibly they meant to pass the message on, and if they did, then that part of his task could be considered complete.

There was still the matter of giving Captain Watkiss an order to go away. And it was very plain that Mr Todhunter was to be allowed no option on that.

* * *

Captain Watkiss tugged at his many pieces of equipment and removed his gold-peaked cap to mop his brow. The sun was up now and the day was hot. Also, by this time, the British seamen were not alone. A crowd had gathered, men and women and children and their dogs, mangy beasts with long yellow teeth and snarls. Like wolves. The children were the worst of all. Some were scared, which meant that the parents shot baleful looks at the British, while others laughed and jeered and catcalled in Spanish. One of these others now advanced on the cluttered Captain Watkiss and made a rude gesture before skipping back and away from the English sailor's advance, threateningly made.

'Blasted brat! Needs a whipping.' Watkiss turned his back and craned his neck. 'Mr Hillman, where are you? Oh, there you are. Do you speak Spanish?'

'I'm afraid not, sir.'

'Some officers are quite useless,' Watkiss said distantly. 'Do it in English, then.'

Hillman seemed puzzled. 'Do what, sir?'

'God give me strength.' Captain Watkiss stamped a foot, which caused more laughter. *Get rid of those blasted children!*'

'Aye, aye, sir.' Hillman paused uncertainly, fingering his chin. 'I wonder if that's wise, sir?'

'Oh, balls to wisdom, Mr Hillman, what are you, a sea-lawyer? Do as I say.'

'But I don't see how, sir, short of sending a volley over their heads, which might be misconstrued by the Admiralty as well as by the populace—'

'Oh, hold your tongue!' Watkiss snapped, having sensed a certain truth in what the lieutenant had said. He made shooing motions with his arms. 'Go away, Mr Hillman, for God's sake, go over there and be laughed at by yourself.' As Lieutenant Hillman marched obediently away to draw the catcalls, Captain Watkiss inadvertently turned his eyes towards the other side of the square and saw something he had been trying to avoid looking at ever since it had appeared: a strong detachment of German sailors from the *Kaiser Wilhelm*, rifled and bayoneted, sensibly and coolly clad in white uniforms, wearing gaiters, with a proliferation of petty officers and lieutenants, and commanded by a tall, bearded officer wearing the shoulder-straps of a commander in the Imperial Navy. Overcome with rage, Captain Watkiss shook a fist in their direction. He had no idea as yet what they intended to do; soon after their arrival, not far behind his own, he had despatched Mr Hillman to parley, but the result had been inconclusive. Mr Hillman had been rudely received and the Germans had refused to answer his questions. The Flag Captain, the bearded Commander had said, must come himself. Of course, Captain Watkiss wouldn't do that. What was equally annoying was the fact that no one was laughing or jeering at the Germans. Either von Merkatz had suborned the local population, or the Huns looked more dangerous, more nasty. That was probably it. Huns *were* nasty, and untrustworthy buggers to boot, men who might lash out at some unfortunate child. British tars, his tars, would never do that. Children always responded to the British tar. (Nearly always.) They were kindly men till roused.

Captain Watkiss turned his eyes from the German line; it was stronger numerically than his own, and even though one British serviceman was equal to ten of any other nationality, he wished he had brought more. There could well be bloodshed if tempers got out of hand, and of course he was out of contact with his squadron and there would be no reinforcements. However, he would cope – and he would win, by jove! Captain Watkiss thought of Her Majesty Queen Victoria, crowned, robed and enthroned, a splendid vision of power that enveloped a quarter of the world's earth surface and all the seas that mattered. Heart and stomach swelled and Watkiss' eyes misted over a trifle. A splendid woman ... when his eyes cleared again Captain Watkiss saw a familiar face but it was not Queen Victoria; it was Detective Inspector Todhunter.

That damn policeman! *With the enemy!* Captain Watkiss screwed in his monocle to make sure. He was not mistaken. The fellow was flanked by dagoes and was standing slap in front of the door to the government offices, shifting about as though he wished to make water. Ashamed, no doubt. Watkiss' face went puce. He bounced along, away from the Germans towards the building, rattling and clanking, and drew his revolver whilst on the march. He flourished the revolver at Detective Inspector Todhunter as he halted.

'What's the meaning of this?' he called out.

Todhunter opened his mouth; but no words came. Watkiss saw one of the dagoes nudge Todhunter, who then uttered with obvious reluctance. He said, 'The Uruguayans would like you to go away, sir.'

'No doubt. I'm not going to go away.'

'But if you don't—'

'There are no buts, Todhunter, no buts at all, thank you. Kindly cease giving succour to the enemy or you shall be branded as a traitor the moment I reach Portsmouth. What the Uruguayans wish has nothing to do with me. I, for my part, have wishes and they are to be obeyed, and since you are there with the blasted dagoes you shall be my spokesman. Now then. Mr Hillman?'

'Yes, sir?'

'The men are to load and stand-to. And fix bayonets.'

'Aye, aye, sir.'

Captain Watkiss clanked impatiently. 'See to it, then.'

'Aye, aye, sir.' Lieutenant Hillman turned and marched away to pass the order. There was a rattle as the shining bayonets were clamped to the muzzles of the rifles, and a snick of bolts as the cartridges were driven home. Captain Watkiss waited a moment, then cleared his throat importantly.

'Now, Todhunter. You already know my wishes, but I shall restate them so that no one present remains in any doubt. The man Savory is to be returned aboard the flagship, or better still handed over to me here, and the dockyard is to render assistance to the squadron.' As an afterthought he added, 'And I shall take delivery of the British Ambassador, Lord Horace Vane. There is to be no more jiggery-pokery. Tell them all that, Todhunter.'

'I have, sir.'

'What?'

'The position has been made clear, Captain,' Todhunter shouted desperately. 'And I—'

'If it's been made clear, why the devil have they not done as they were told, Todhunter?'

'Well, it seems to be because their wishes run counter to yours, and—'

'Oh, balls and bang me arse, Todhunter, I don't want excuses, I want action!'

154

'If you would allow me to finish, sir.'

'What is it now?'

'Savory's under another threat, sir. Another person's wish,' Todhunter said, with total obscurity so far as Captain Watkiss was concerned. 'And Lord Horace Vane has disappeared.'

'Disappeared?'

'That's right, yes. He was taken by brigands.'

'*Brigands?*'

'Yes.' Todhunter sweated. How could he make his meaning clear, how could he penetrate the naval mind? Inspiration came, and he called down, 'Tar brigands.'

'*Tar brigands?*' Captain Watkiss made darting motions with his revolver. 'For God's sake ...' Then something stirred in his mind and he began to get the drift of the policeman's utterances. 'Ah. Yes, I see, or I think I do. *Half* tar brigands, perhaps? Men who *hide*?'

Todhunter let out a long breath of relief; at least he'd got something across. 'That's right, sir. That's perfectly right. Now, I—'

'One moment, Todhunter. Mr Hillman?'

'Yes, sir?' Lieutenant Hillman once again marched up and saluted; as Captain Watkiss returned the salute one of his cross-belts came adrift and the chocolate tin fell to the cobbles of the square and rolled away. Lieutenant Hillman ran after it and brought it back, and there was renewed laughter from the watching children as it was reconnected to the British sailor.

'Damn those children. Mr Hillman, a word in your ear.' Captain Watkiss thereafter whispered. 'From what Todhunter says, I deduce that Mr Halfhyde has succeeded in cutting out the Ambassador, and has secreted him away somewhere. Now he will be bargaining for Savory's release.'

'As planned, sir.'

'Precisely! All seems well so far. My presence will prove an additional lever upon the dagoes, bound to. Now is the time to press, and press hard, for what I've asked for. Success is within my grasp, Mr Hillman.'

'Yes, sir.'

'Tenacity never fails to pay off, Mr Hillman, as you will discover if ever you reach the rank of post captain. You may return to your men, and await my next order.'

'Aye, aye, sir.'

As Lieutenant Hillman marched back to the rear, Captain Watkiss addressed Todhunter again. 'You will tell the Uruguayans to produce Savory instantly.'

'I can't do that, Captain!'

Watkiss glared. 'Can't? What d'you mean, can't? Napoleon said there was no such word as can't and he was right. Do as I say at once!'

Todhunter blew out his cheeks in despair as the dreadful moment was reached at last. He glanced sideways, fearfully, at the Uruguayan faces. They were beginning to look angry, though Mr Todhunter believed they had not understood everything Captain Watkiss had said. They'd have taken some of it in, all the same, they weren't daft and one at least had some English. Mr Todhunter saw quite clearly that if he didn't obey them soon, he would be in great danger. He grasped his courage firmly, putting heart and soul into his tones.

'I have to order you, sir, if you don't mind and it's for the best I do assure you, to leave the square.'

'Leave the square, you—'

'That's right, sir, and go back aboard ship. Peacefully.'

Watkiss yelled, 'Traitor! Turncoat! Go back my bottom. Have you taken leave of your senses, man?'

'No, sir. It's not that, sir. My chief super, he'd say the same thing if he was here. I am the civil power acting superior to the military, sir, in the best interests of all if you take my meaning. I do hope you'll do as I say, I do indeed.'

Watkiss' voice was icy. 'You are the civil power, my good Todhunter, are you?'

'Yes, and—'

'You are the law. But I represent Her Majesty the Queen, Todhunter, and you know her position, do you not?' Watkiss was almost purple. 'She is above the law! As her representative upon this spot, so am I above the blasted law! Mr Hillman?'

Once again, Lieutenant Hillman marched back to his Captain's side. 'Yes, sir?'

'Mr Hillman, you will order your men to take aim upon the top of the steps, and fire together the moment I pass the order.'

'Aye, aye, sir.' Away went Lieutenant Hillman, right arm

swinging, left hand upon his sword-hilt. After he had reached the ranks, the snick of the bolts in the rifles, a nasty sound, told Mr Todhunter that rounds were now going up the spouts. He felt that death was now one hundred per cent certain, if not from the Uruguayan bullets, then from the British.

FIFTEEN

Aboard the *Delia*, now back in the dockyard at Montevideo after her message-passing duty, Rear-Admiral Daintree munched breakfast gloomily. His Flag Captain's tidings had reached him in the dead of night and he had been woken again from the slumber to which he had returned angrily after failing to prevent Watkiss' expedition leaving the flagship. That had been an act of defiant disobedience that would be reported in due course, but in the meantime Daintree had felt unable to do anything about it. It had been a *fait accompli* and it would have been an act of defiant disobedience that would be reported in the waters of the Plate in an attempt to get his orders obeyed. But all that could wait; when the message had come back that the Flag Captain intended marching upon the seat of power, then Daintree had felt his own presence to be required ashore, and he had ordered Mr Forbes-Forrester to take him into the dockyard.

Breakfast, taken early, was poor: the *Delia*'s galley was not so good as the flagship's. Admiral Daintree prodded at under-done, fatty bacon and sipped at gritty coffee together with his Flag Lieutenant, one Mr Porteous. Since Admiral Daintree did not speak at breakfast, Mr Porteous, on the occasions when he breakfasted with his Admiral, had learned not to speak either. But today was to be different: at the door of Forbes-Forrester's cabin, given over for the Admiral's use, knocked churchwarden Tidy.

'Beg pardon.' Tidy came right in, unceremoniously. Forelocks were seldom touched in Yorkshire. 'I'm worried about parson.'

'Parson?' Daintree asked crossly.

'Canon Rampling, like.'

'Yes, yes, why are you worried, Tidy?'

'He went on shore, like—'

'I know that. With Mr Halfhyde, as I understand. He's in good hands, Tidy.'

'Ah, but then along comes that there Captain Watkiss, see, and—'

Something struck Admiral Daintree and he said, 'I thought you and Canon Rampling came in aboard the *Biddle*, did you not?'

'Aye. But when there were all that rumpus like, when we went back out to the anchorage, and that there Captain Watkiss got on the *Delia*, I came over in a boat to go back *in* again.' Tidy produced a chalice; it came from behind his back, like a conjuror's rabbit. 'Chalice, see? Reverend'll miss that. Got left out of t'communion set. I was wondering if you'd take it to him, like. But it's not just that.'

'What is it, then?'

'It's that there Captain Watkiss. He always stirs things up,' Tidy said complainingly. 'If parson's in danger it'll be his fault. I thought I'd put it to you.'

'Yes, yes, but I'm sure you needn't worry.'

'I'm *not* so sure. There.' Mr Tidy dumped the chalice on the Admiral's breakfast table, catching the end of Daintree's coffee spoon and shooting it up into the air. It fell back into a pot of marmalade. Mr Porteous was about to remonstrate on his Admiral's behalf when a volley of distant rifle fire was heard through the open port.

Daintree started. 'What was that, Porteous?'

Porteous identified the sound and added, 'It might be Halfhyde, sir.'

'More likely my Flag Captain, I fear.' Daintree rose to his feet. 'We must go ashore, Porteous.'

'Yes, sir. I still think we should have brought armed seamen, sir—'

'No, no, no! That was my whole point! I am the Admiral – I at least must go in peace and not seek provocation.' Daintree's gaze rested upon the chalice. 'We shall take this chalice, Porteous – I know how much store Rampling sets by his ability to administer Holy Communion at appropriate moments. Besides, there's another point and an important one: The Uruguayans are most religious people – Roman Catholics, of course, but still. The chalice may be seen as an emblem of a peaceful mission, so you shall carry it, Porteous.'

*　　　*　　　*

The stench of gunsmoke swept across the square, and a haze of blue drifted in the air. Captain Watkiss spun like a top, unable to believe his ears, unable to trust his vision. The blasted Huns had opened all of a sudden, without warning, sending no less than three rapid volleys crashing over the British heads to thud into a blank brick wall on their right flank. The crowds dispersed like magic, and that at least was something. The official dagoes, too, had gone, darting backwards into the Town Hall or whatever it was, and Captain Watkiss, from the corner of his eye, had seen a hand come out and grab the detective inspector's military uniform and yank him within just when he had looked as if he might be about to join the British. Perhaps the fellow wasn't a traitor after all, but there was no time to ponder upon that at the moment. Mr Hillman was dashing hither and thither and looking uncontrolled, indeed panic-stricken, and Captain Watkiss called out to him.

'Are you a lunatic, Mr Hillman, or a naval officer? *Answer the buggers' fire!*' He took over himself. 'Ranks about face!' he yelled.

'It's too late, sir!'

'Oh, nonsense, Mr Hillman, am I never to expect support from my blasted officers? Oh.' It was, indeed, too late, as Watkiss now saw; the German line had extended in a half moon and were converging upon the British seamen, who were virtually surrounded and were greatly out-numbered as Watkiss had noted earlier. 'Well, never mind, I shall go to meet the Germans after all, and parley rather than allow useless bloodshed.'

'Sir, I—'

'Don't argue, Mr Hillman, it's an insubordinate habit and I won't have it. The men are to order arms and stand at ease. We must show some dignity. We are not a rabble.' Captain Watkiss marched forward towards the German officer-in-charge, a hand clutching his equipment to prevent it rattling. 'Now then,

Commander, do you speak English? I expect you do, since all Germans are potential spies and infiltrators. Well?'

'I speak English, yes. I—'

'Good. Because I don't speak German, I don't need to. Kindly explain why you opened fire upon my men, an act that I regard as hostile to Her Majesty Queen Victoria.'

'To prevent a serious situation, Captain. I overheard your order to aim.'

'You'd no damn business to!' Watkiss snapped.

'My hearing is good, and your voice is loud.'

'Be that as it may, you'll not get away with opening fire like a damn bandit. I require to know your purpose in coming here at all.'

The German Commander shrugged. 'To act as a buffer, Captain, between the Uruguayans, who are the friends of Germany, and yourself.'

'That's not all, is it? I think you know what I'm talking about, and I'm here to see that you don't get away with it, by God!' Watkiss half turned. 'Mr Hillman, where the devil are you?'

'Here, sir.' Lieutenant Hillman appeared from Watkiss' other side.

'Oh, there you are, you're like a blasted jack-in-the-box, do try to remain in one place for two minutes together. Mount the steps and demand a parley with the Uruguayans on my behalf—inside the Town Hall, not out here.'

'I thought you intended parleying with the Germans, sir?'

'I did, and I have. I've said all I had to say. There's no more to be gained by talking to Huns, Mr Hillman, so go and do as I told you.' Lieutenant Hillman saluted smartly and went off towards the steps. Captain Watkiss glared angrily towards the German landing-party but refused further conversation with the Commander, who had a stone wall look about him and would only infuriate him more. Captain Watkiss was thinking of Todhunter's frustrated dash for freedom: it was perhaps just possible that Todhunter knew something that he, Watkiss, did not. He would be worth rescuing, even though the risk was great; and Captain Watkiss intended to get him out and then face another risk – that of fighting his way through the German line, which would probably collapse when it recognized the implacable British intentions. Foreigners were like that, no real stomach, no staying power. As Captain Watkiss planned his moves, time passed. After a while he brought out his turnip-shaped watch, not without difficulty owing to his array of tins, and looked at it irritably. Another ten minutes and Mr Hillman had still not returned from his mission; Captain Watkiss grew more and more restive and began parading up and down. Like all his officers, Hillman was a fool, and unreliable. Most likely he was allowing himself to be browbeaten by the dagoes – he might even have been captured and would be turned against his Captain like a boomerang. Watkiss decided to give him another ten minutes and then, by God, he would act. He would go up the steps himself and make his demands in no un-certain manner and that would teach the dagoes a thing or two.

It was blasted hot – blasted hot! Captain Watkiss, fuming, mopped at his forehead again. He scowled across the square: once again, the crowds were gathering, a little more distantly than before to be sure, but the buggers were coming back and Watkiss didn't like it. A crowd could turn very quickly into a mob, and he had the distinct feeling that they would side with the Hun if that should happen. And damn Mr Hillman, who had very likely fainted with terror once he was inside the Town Hall.

Captain Watkiss made a trumpeting noise indicating sheer frustration and anger, and, waving his telescope, strutted towards the steps. But half-way up something – a vague move-ment from the crowd – made him look round. At first he saw nothing of note, then he heard his name, or rather his designa-tion, being called aloud in a high, urgent voice: 'Flag Captain! Flag Captain, I say!'

Into full view through the crowd came Rear-Admiral Dain-tree and his Flag Lieutenant, the latter bearing in his hand some kind of pot as though it were a talisman. Captain Watkiss breathed out through his nose, angrily.

'My dear sir,' he shouted, 'this is no place for you!'

'On the contrary, Flag Captain. Quite the opposite. It is you who should not be where you are. Come down the steps immediately.'

'May I enquire why, sir?'

'An order from your Admiral is not to be questioned, Flag Captain.' Daintree, who had moved with astonishing speed towards the steps, was now at their bottom. He stared up, bright-eyed like a sparrow. His next words held overtones of the bird kingdom as well. 'I come bearing an olive branch, Flag Captain, whereas you come with rifles.' He wagged a finger reprovingly. 'That is not the way. Come down the steps.'

Captain Watkiss came down angrily. 'Kindly explain what *is* the way, then!' he snapped.

'A peaceful approach—'

'Oh, peaceful approach my bottom! All the buggers understand is strength, and if I'd had more men with me I'd have swept both the dagoes and the Huns into the blasted river—'

'You had no orders—'

'You *gave* none that had any damn sense behind them—'

'I tried to prevent your leaving my flagship—'

'Bah!'

Daintree's face grew scarlet. 'Flag Captain, if you say bah to me once more I shall place you under arrest. Mr Porteous and Mr Hillman—' He broke off. 'Where is Mr Hillman, Flag Captain?'

Watkiss lifted his telescope and pointed it towards the great doors into the building behind. 'In there. Either making a balls of it or at the mercy of the enemy. I was about to find out when you interrupted me, my dear sir. If anything has gone wrong, on your head be it! I shall most certainly ensure that blame falls in the proper place. However, you are the senior officer, and you're here.' Watkiss folded his arms across his stomach, ostentatiously if figuratively sitting back. 'I await your next order.'

'Yes, yes.' Admiral Daintree turned and gazed all around the square, at the British seamen, at the Germans, at the crowd of Uruguayans who seemed to be waiting with bated breath for the next move. Then he looked up the steps at the doors, which were still firmly closed. 'You believe that untoward events may be taking place, Flag Captain?'

Watkiss snorted. 'That is a way of putting it, sir. At this moment the fate of your squadron, and of Savory, is in the hands of a mere lieutenant, as are Her Majesty's wider interests in South America. All are withering, while you talk of peace!'

'I shall knock upon the door,' Daintree said in a distant tone, and set foot upon the lower step. 'I shall ask for admittance, and then—' He stopped suddenly, looking surprised. The Town Hall door had opened. Captain Watkiss swung round to see Detective Inspector Todhunter standing in full view. Daintree said, 'Bless my soul!'

'Eureka!' Mr Todhunter said in an excited voice.

'What?'

'Eureka, sir!'

'What the devil are you talking about?' Watkiss demanded.

'The Uruguayan high command has acceded to Mr – to the brigands' request. I am to lead a delegation to the brigands' place of hiding ... and I am to be accompanied by the prisoner Savory!'

'Oh. Where's Mr Hillman? I wish—'

'He's being held in my place, just till I get back.' Mr Todhunter was cock-a-hoop; his execution was delayed, to say the least.

*   *   *

There was a general retreat now, away from the square and back to the dockyard. Rear-Admiral Daintree marched with Captain Watkiss, and behind them, still with the chalice, Lieutenant Porteous took the place of the temporarily absent Lieutenant Hillman. On Daintree's insistence, overtures of peace and goodwill had been made to the Uruguayans and a measure of agreement had been obtained over vital repairs to the British squadron upon Daintree's apology, abject in Watkiss' opinion, for his violation of Uruguayan territorial waters. The Uruguayans had agreed to withdraw their soldiers from the British cruisers, a conciliatory act that raised its own problems.

'What about Colonel Oribe?' Captain Watkiss asked sourly whilst marching back to board the *Delia*.

'Yes, yes, a difficulty. Also the Uruguayans imprisoned in my boiler-rooms. They must be released at once, of course.'

'To tell the tale,' Watkiss snapped.

'True, but that is inevitable—'

'So's Oribe.'

Daintree shrugged. 'War is war, Flag Captain.'

'In the mouth of a man of peace, that is a remarkably stupid thing to say – in the circumstances.' The march continued, harassed by flies as the day's heat struck full. Smells arose from the hovels and the dockland streets, which were littered with refuse. When they reached the *Delia* it was little better: the river stench assailed the nostrils. Later, gazing through his telescope at the *Kaiser Wilhelm*, Watkiss witnessed the return of the German landing-party. Removing the telescope from his eye, he shook it towards the German flag. The buggers hadn't got what they wanted, which was Savory. Not yet, anyway. It was up to Todhunter and Halfhyde now.

*　　*　　*

Mr Todhunter was being extremely polite; the Uruguayans had behaved well in his opinion and he had no wish to anger them by discourtesy, though the bonds on his wrists and the knife in his back were in fact neither friendly nor trusting. The journey was uncomfortable; it was being made on mules, with Mr Todhunter seated on the front of a saddle with a Uruguayan rider on the back part, very close and strong-armed. What would happen upon arrival at Mr Halfhyde's fort was a thought that made Mr Todhunter sweat with fear. There were all kinds of imponderables: since the Uruguayans had known the fort's situation once he had mentioned it, they really didn't need him as a guide at all, so it was quite possible they meant to use him as some sort of cat's-paw – how, he didn't know. Also, it was possible they were sending in another force to strike from another direction, so that Mr Halfhyde would be over-whelmed. Another thing: they had told a lie. Savory was not with them, as they had promised he would be. Mr Todhunter didn't like that; it boded, in his view, ill. Liars were not to be trusted, ever. Mr Todhunter began to have a sinking feeling, a feeling that he could have been hoodwinked all along the line. No harm in trying to find out a little more if he could – as a detective inspector of experience he knew how to formulate the right questions and even liars, which criminals always were, sometimes revealed the truth under interrogation.

Mr Todhunter turned his head as far as he was able and spoke to his personal guard.

'Pardon me.'

'*Si?*'

'I don't want to pry, *señor*, but might I ask where the man Savory is now?'

'Ees not 'ere.'

'No, indeed, I realize that.'

There was a laugh. 'Soon you will see.'

It was all very puzzling. The mules jogged on; they didn't seem to be hurrying, but then South Americans never did and not much could be read into that. The saddle was very uncomfortable, especially as his fundamental part was jogging up and down on the upturned bit at the front end. 'When we arrive...'

'*Si?*'

'When we reach the brigands' hide-out, what will you do?'

Another laugh; nothing else. Well, of course, it stood to reason really. There was going to be a fight. All the Uruguayans were heavily armed and he was going to be helpless, right in the line of fire between the two sides. He might just as well have gone to the eight o'clock execution, really.

* * *

Accompanied by Canon Rampling, Halfhyde strode up and down in front of the crumbling walls of the old fort. With the eye of a seaman, he studied the weather: the day was fine and hot, but cloud was starting to form over the Argentine coast, and the wind, such as it was, came from that direction also. Halfhyde had a feeling the wind was going to freshen, and it would bring rain with it. Not that it mattered much; his interest was no more than an instinctive professional one. Halfhyde's worries concerned the Ambassador and the outcome of Todhunter's mission.

'We're in need of a medical man,' he said, not for the first time. 'I wish now I'd told Todhunter to bring one.'

'Water under the bridge, my dear Halfhyde.' Rampling spoke irritably. By now he had discovered the loss of the chalice from his communion set, and with his guns spiked, he felt somewhat superfluous. The tin mugs carried by the seamen as part of their landing equipment had been too close to profanity to be suitable substitutes for an unsullied chalice, but if Lord Horace should approach death closely, then one might have to be blessed. God would probably forgive that. Canon Rampling's cassock swept extremely dusty ground, and he gathered it up. 'Todhunter has had ample time now, surely? Should we read failure into his non-appearance, do you think?'

'Your guess is as good as mine, padre.'

'A gallant fellow. I have prayed for his success and safety.'

'Good.'

'Perhaps we should scout for his approach?'

'I've already posted picquets. They'll return as soon as anyone's seen.'

'Ah.' The clergyman swatted at a fly, a persistent one, and wondered how the monks of Tibet, who abused no living creature, managed about flies. Conversation languished; Halfhyde seemed preoccupied, and Canon Rampling left him to his thoughts and went off to minister to the sick man, quartered in the fort's underground strongrooms. He found the Ambassador's condition, to the non-medical eye at all events, unchanged. He might live if help was obtained speedily; Canon Rampling settled down to read to him from the Bible, selecting stirring messages of hope. He was in the middle of a passage from Zechariah when hell appeared to break loose up above: there were running footsteps and shouts from the gunner's mate for the men to stand-to, followed by a thud and a shower of loose stones down the steps. Canon Rampling shut his Bible with a snap, and felt the excitement creep up his spine. Men of God should hold themselves aloof from combat, of course, but on occasions even the cloth could suffer a touch of forgetfulness. Canon Rampling seized a handy piece of timber and charged up the steps to strike a blow for the Queen.

SIXTEEN

Aboard the flagship, MAA Pickering faced a problem. Rear-Admiral Daintree, seeing the fate of the shipboard Uruguayan soldiers as important, indeed central, to any continuing co-operation on the part of the shore authorities, had taken the *Delia* back at full power to the anchorage to pass verbal orders to the flagship's executive officer; and had then steamed back to the dockyard to await developments, leaving a degree of con-sternation in his wake.

MAA Pickering, closeted with Ship's Corporal Judd, put his finger on the vital point. 'That Oribe,' he said, sounding acutely anxious. 'The rest – they don't signify. We can just get the buggers up from the boiler-rooms and 'ose 'em down on deck. That Captain Watkiss, 'e'll dream up something to satisfy the shore dagoes as to why we shoved 'em down there. It's that bloody Oribe, and I reckon I've got an idea.'

'Yes, Master?'

'When I went down to look at that lot in the boiler-rooms, see? One of the buggers, 'e's the spit image of Oribe.' MAA Pickering drew a hand across his nose, reflectively. 'When Mr 'Alf'yde gets back aboard with Oribe's uniform, we can dress this bloke up as Oribe as well. Right?'

'I don't see—'

'Well, 'ang on an' I'll tell you. We says this bloke *is* Oribe.'

Judd looked bewildered. 'What does the bloke say 'e is, then?'

'Ah – 'e don't! We *clobbers* him, see. First we gets 'im drunk on rum, then we clobbers him 'ard and puts 'im out till 'e's safe ashore. I reckon that does it, eh?'

'Maybe. Only for a short time, though, as long as it takes 'im to come round. Then 'e says 'oo 'e is, don't 'e?'

'Yes,' MAA Pickering agreed judicially. ''E does, but we don't. *We* say, that is the Captain says, that 'e said 'e was Colonel Oribe. That's what 'e told us, like. An' *we* say, to account for the fact 'e was missing, that 'e was at the rum from the moment 'e come aboard.'

Judd blinked; the Master-at-Arms was a fast talker, hard to keep up with at times – more educated than Judd, full of book-learning. Judd said, 'Well, I dunno, Master.'

'Why not?'

'What about 'is mates? They'll know 'e's not Oribe, won't they?'

MAA Pickering jeered that one out of court. 'Wouldn't bet on it. Don't matter anyway, it's what we said 'e said, see? Them dagoes, they're all bloody liars at the best o' times, an' thick as collision-mats. They'll confuse each other like as not. I reckon it's the way. Can't think of anything else, any'ow. Can you?'

'Well – no.'

'There you are, then! I'll put it to the Captain when 'e comes back aboard.' MAA Pickering pulled out his watch. 'Six bells, Judd. Up spirits . . . and stand fast the 'Oly Ghost.' He got to his feet to prepare for the daily issue of rum to the lower deck. He felt rather more at peace now that he'd come up with a workable idea. Colonel Oribe – possibly somewhere beneath his cabin unless the shifting waters had lifted the body, fire-bars and all, farther out to sea – had been on his mind and causing him some loss of sleep. But on his way to the rum store to break out the spirit ration MAA Pickering was visited by a very disturbing thought: suppose the shifting waters shifted the corpse the other way, back in towards Montevideo? What then, for heaven's sake? But of course he wouldn't shift anywhere, not really. The fire-bars were too heavy.

*   *   *

'Gunner's mate?'

'Yessir?'

'I've picked out Mr Todhunter,' Halfhyde said, looking intently through his telescope. 'He's on the last but one mule.

Pass the word at once, that mule's to be shot wide of if we have to open fire.'

'Aye, aye, sir.' The gunner's mate went off at the double, making sure all hands understood about Mr Todhunter. Half-hyde brought down his telescope and looked round as Canon Rampling approached.

'How's the Ambassador, padre?' he asked.

'Holding his own, I fancy.'

'And that club you have? Do you intend to use it?'

Rampling said, 'Only in defence of the sick.' All at once there was a heave and a swirl of black cloth and Canon Rampling stood clear of his cassock. Though not naked, he looked it by contrast: his ample body was clad in long underpants and a white shirt topped by his starched clerical collar and ending in a long tail for tucking in – enough for decency, but an unusual and surprising sight in Halfhyde's eyes. Rampling said, 'The Lord's servant shall take part, but not His garments. Besides, the day is warm.' The clerical collar was next pulled free of its retaining studs. Rampling picked up the wooden stave which he had laid against the stone of the fort and swiped it in the air. It made a satisfactory whistling sound.

Halfhyde said, 'I'm not sure you wouldn't have more effect as a priest. As has been said before, the South Americans respect the cloth.' Rampling smiled but made no answer; he swiped again. In the meantime, the Uruguayan soldiers were advancing with ready rifles and Mr Todhunter was clearly to be seen, jogging up and down on his uncomfortable saddle with his captor's arm clasping him tight. Halfhyde cast a look backwards in the direction of his seamen, all of them in good cover and all still dressed as Uruguayan soldiers. As the genuine Uruguayans' advance slowed cautiously Halfhyde moved forward into the no-man's-land beyond the fort's perimeter, hoping that Todhunter would keep his wits about him. When he was some twenty feet clear of the fort, a loud voice called on him to halt.

He did so.

'You are the counter-revolutionaries?' the voice, that of a large fat officer in the van, asked hoarsely. The man spoke, properly enough, in Spanish; Halfhyde answered in the same tongue.

170

'We are,' he confirmed. 'Do you bring the Englishman, Savory?'

'We do not.' There was a nasty pause. 'You do not sound Uruguayan. Why is this, please?'

'I'm from Mexico,' Halfhyde said.

'Mexico? So. Why do you interfere in our affairs, if you are from Mexico? I tell you: because like all Mexicans you interfere from the bottom of your black natures, seeking riches. We do not bring Savory, no. We bring an important person, a police-man from London.'

'Who escaped from us.'

The man laughed. 'Yes, and has told the revolutionary authorities what you mean to do to the British Ambassador—'

'Unless you bring Savory, yes.'

'Why do you wish Savory? I will tell you why you wish Savory.' The man seemed bent upon answering his own questions. 'You believe that if you present Savory back to the British Admiral, the British government will show its gratitude by giving your forces support to regain power. You believe the British Ambassador to be of less value than the person Savory ... yet of enough value to our new Uruguayan regime to make us hand over Savory to you.'

'That's right,' Halfhyde said with a grin.

'Perhaps, but it is not quite so.'

'I think it is! If the Ambassador dies, it will be represented as the act of the new regime. You can understand that, *señor*!'

There was an oath, and the fat man turned away. There was as yet no Savory and every moment lost meant another moment available for the transfer of Savory to German custody. That must not happen; yet there was a strong possibility that in fact it had happened already. Something decisive had to be done, and quickly. A risk must be taken, and Halfhyde made up his mind to do it. He bowed ironically in the direction of the large fat man, who was conferring with his henchmen and gesticulating violently. 'I go now,' Halfhyde said. 'I go to place the Ambassador ready to be shot, where you can see him. You will send men to bring Savory here. If they have not returned by the time the sun goes down, the Ambassador dies.'

*   *   *

Rear-Admiral Daintree, with his Flag Captain, was upon the small bridge of Her Majesty's sloop *Delia* as she left the wharf in the dockyard once again and proceeded down-river towards the anchorage; Daintree had felt a sudden need to return to his squadron in order to ensure personally, ahead of the event, an orderly hand-over of the Uruguayan guards to their own people, and to satisfy himself that the story that would be told to them was consistent, watertight and foolproof. Daintree stood in a corner of the bridge while Captain Watkiss strutted from one side to the other, getting in the way of the Officer of the Watch and the Lieutenant-in-Command. After a while he halted, his gaze caught by something drifting up river from the direction of the open sea. A heap of debris, probably, yet he fancied it was not quite that.

He levelled his telescope and studied the object closely. 'Mr Forbes-Forrester, use your telescope and tell me what that is.'

'Aye, aye, sir.' Forbes-Forrester looked, then said, 'I believe it's a body, sir.'

'Exactly! A dead one. Naked, I fancy. And I think I recognize it.' Watkiss called across the bridge to the Rear-Admiral, in much excitement. 'I believe Colonel Oribe has broken adrift from his blasted moorings, sir!'

'What?'

With forbearance, Captain Watkiss said it all over again. 'I suggest we confirm, sir.'

'How?'

'Alter towards him, of course, and have him grappled alongside.' Without further ado, Watkiss requested Mr Forbes-Forrester to take the necessary action. While this was being taken, Watkiss reflected that all dagoes looked alike but there might well be clues on the body and if it was Oribe then it was vitally important to stop him floating into the dockyard at Montevideo, or even up river to lodge with incriminating effect upon the bank. Captain Watkiss bounced about the bridge in anxiety and a consuming impatience. The blasted hands were too slow, and what about the fire-bars? Fish, most probably. Dago waters held very vicious fish, predatory brutes with immensely sharp teeth that could easily cut through quite heavy rope in their attacks upon corpses. Some fool should have thought of that and used wire rather than rope to secure the fire-bars, and if anything should now go wrong, some fool was going to suffer for his sins.

The naked heap closed as the sloop altered course; from the vessel's after deck men reached down and trapped the thing with grappling irons and hauled it close to the side. Down went Captain Watkiss for inspection. Certainly fish were responsible, no doubt about that. A goodly portion of the body itself had been eaten, though not the face. Watkiss gazed down at the face and pondered: a thin black moustache, but they all had that. A dago without doubt – the face looked evil and was sallow even for a corpse. Then came the clincher: a seaman heaved a little upon his grappling iron and a limb – a leg – rose free of the filthy water, for just long enough to enable Captain Watkiss to see the bitten-off length of rope attached to the ankle: good, 21-thread ratline with the distinctive coloured identification of Portsmouth Dockyard's ropewalk woven into it. What could possibly be more certain? Nothing, obviously. Captain Watkiss ordered the corpse to be cast adrift and then climbed back to the bridge as fast as he could go.

'It's Oribe,' he reported briefly. 'He must be disposed of quickly.'

'But—'

'*Quickly*, sir! There is no time to argue the matter. I propose—'

'The fish'll do it,' Daintree said dismissingly.

Watkiss bounced up and down. 'Fish are too blasted slow and unreliable, and the current's swift. Mr Forbes-Forrester?'

'Sir?'

'Man and arm your gun, Mr Forbes-Forrester, as fast as is humanly possible. Aim and fire the moment your sights come on. And if you fail to blow the bugger up, I shall have your balls for breakfast.'

*   *   *

Sorry tidings reached Halfhyde on his return within the fort's defences. They came from Canon Rampling, incongruously reporting tragedy in his shirt and pants. 'I'm afraid he's gone, my dear fellow.'

Halfhyde blew out his cheeks. 'The Ambassador, padre?'

173

'Yes.' Rampling lowered his eyes. 'I'm afraid so. Poor fellow. A sad ending.'

'It can yet be made useful. I believe he would have wished that.'

'I don't follow you,' Rampling said.

'Then I'll explain, and you must accept it. He's not to be known to have died, and he's to be exposed to the Uruguayans out there.' Halfhyde waved a hand towards the armed party, plus Mr Todhunter, on their mules, and told Rampling of his recent threat to shoot the Ambassador. 'I'm sorry – this is hard for your cloth to accept, I know – but the dead must now help the still living.' He turned away abruptly and strode across the sun-baked earth of the fort's courtyard, calling for the gunner's mate.

'Here, sir.'

'The Ambassador,' Halfhyde said without preamble. 'The body's to be set on a high point of the walls, in a sitting posture, well propped from behind and below. See to it at once, and make the effect as life-like as possible.'

'Aye, aye, sir.' The gunner's mate went off at the double calling for hands to assist him. The job was speedily done; wood, such as the stave found by Canon Rampling, was produced and a long plank-like piece was inserted up the Ambassador's trouser-leg and behind the cover of the wall he was hoisted like a spare spar being sent aloft, while more men stood ready to make the body fast. It was hove into a sitting position, with the legs, after the plank had been removed from the trousers, dangling down the broken stonework; and more props set into position behind would give, Halfhyde hoped, reasonable stability and verisimilitude, at least when seen from afar. The Uruguayans would be well aware of Lord Horace's state of health, and would be unlikely to query the rendering of physical assistance to a sick man.

With the corpse in position, Halfhyde watched the reaction of the Uruguayans. He was puzzled; there was in fact no precise reaction other than what seemed to be another conference and much arm-waving. No riders left the party; no one was being sent to bring Savory. Halfhyde swore roundly. Time was vital; and now time held another threat: time and strong sunlight would have a poor effect upon the British Ambassador. Already there was a great black swarm of flies about the body, which might have been expected to swat them away. Cursing again, Halfhyde was about to order a remote-controlled swatting party when there was a sudden flurry from before the fort and a desperate-looking figure hurtled from the ranks of the mule-borne Uruguayans and dashed towards the fort. It was Detective Inspector Todhunter, complete with attached guard. Half-hyde roared out to the gunner's mate to give the policeman covering fire over the Uruguayans' heads; and in the same instant Uruguayan bullets began pecking the ground around the hurtling mule's hooves. One of them struck Mr Todhunter's captor in the back and he slumped sideways, pouring blood. But Mr Todhunter made it to safety, falling off the animal's back in a heap immediately after reaching the fort.

Halfhyde picked him up; he seemed unhurt though dusty. 'Well done,' Halfhyde said. 'That was a brave thing to do, Mr Todhunter.'

'Not really, Mr Halfhyde. I can't claim it as that. The bloody mule bolted ... I believe it was stung on its behind by one of those flies. Nevertheless, Mr Halfhyde, here I am, safe and sound.'

Halfhyde nodded. 'Duty nobly done, Mr Todhunter, as befits the Metropolitan Police, however far flung. Chief Superintendent Portlock will be proud—' He broke off, very suddenly, and swung round. From the fort's rear, from the direction of the river, shots were coming. There was a sound of shouting – guttural shouting, loud with the promise of victory. From up above there came a clatter of sliding masonry and a number of stones fell, as did the dead Ambassador. The body toppled to the ground with an almighty crash, and when he had landed Halfhyde saw the bullet hole in the back of his head.

Round both flanks of the fort stormed Admiral von Merkatz' seamen, with bayonets fixed.

SEVENTEEN

As the Germans stormed in and more bullets flew, Halfhyde's seamen fought with their backs to the wall, heavily outnumbered and taken by surprise. While the fighting went on the Uruguayans took their chance to advance bravely from the front behind the fat man; but their advance did not last long. The Germans turned their fire upon them. The fat man, wearing an expression of much surprise, crashed heavily from his mule – he was weighed down with an arsenal of cartridge belts – and the rest turned and fled. German bullets pursued them till they were out of range, and then the firing stopped.

The German Commander lifted a hand at Halfhyde and smiled. 'Pax, my friend!' he said. He looked round: all the British were held at the point of the bayonets. 'A bloodless victory, I think!'

Halfhyde asked coolly, 'What are you here for?'

'I think you know why,' the German said.

'Then you have the advantage of me. I do not know.'

'I find it hard to believe you, my friend.' The German's smile was pleasant, but his tone was hard and supercilious. Looking away to Halfhyde's right, he said, 'One of your men appears to be trying to attract your attention. I wonder why. You may speak to him – you have my permission.'

Halfhyde turned; on his flank, just inside the broken wall, stood MAA Titmuss looking full of portent. Halfhyde asked, 'What is it, Titmuss?'

'Hard to say, sir.'

'What d'you mean by that?'

'Hard to say, sir, what I mean.' Something curious was

happening to MAA Titmuss' eyes: they were swivelling back and forth from Halfhyde to the German officer and each swivel was followed by a backward jerk of the head. Halfhyde understood: what Titmuss had to report was not for German ears, but he was making the fact rather obvious. With a touch of desperation Titmuss became more explicit. 'The person, sir.'

'Thank you, Titmuss—'

'Yessir. Figgy duff, sir. Below, sir. *Here*, sir.'

Halfhyde opened his mouth, then shut it again. The Master-at-Arms had been obscure, but ... figgy duff, the seamen's oft-served second course, or pudding. In the wardroom the officers would be served – *savoury*, no less! Halfhyde caught his breath. It sounded impossible that Savory could be present, but Titmuss was unlikely either to be mistaken in his prisoner's identity or to play games with his officer. Halfhyde glanced at the German, standing before him with drawn revolver. The fellow was smiling still, just as though he, too, had understood; and then something else hit Halfhyde like a blow in the face. The Germans knew – and Savory was the reason for their presence. And a moment later Halfhyde's suspicions were confirmed. The German officer said, 'Summon your man, and let him tell you what I know already, that Sir Russell Savory lies concealed in the dungeons.'

Stony-faced, Halfhyde turned. 'All right, Titmuss. You can speak.'

'Yessir.' Sweating and eager, MAA Titmuss saluted – twice, one for Mr Halfhyde, one for the German. 'Savory, sir. In the cells like the German gentleman's just said, sir. Tied an' gagged, sir, with 'is socks and underpants.'

'Why,' Halfhyde asked wearily, 'was he not discovered sooner, Titmuss?'

'Yessir. Sorry, sir. Some rubble's only just fallen away from the door, sir. I 'eard a sound, sir, what proved to be the prisoner Savory being sick. 'E'd managed to remove 'is socks, see. I lifted a socketed bar, sir, and entered, and I see—'

'Yes, thank you, Titmuss. Where is Savory now?'

'Still tied up, sir. I thought—'

'Quite right.' Halfhyde turned back to the German. 'I understand you knew this. Will you be good enough to explain?'

'But of course,' the German said easily. 'My Admiral was informed by the new government of Uruguay, as represented by the military governor of Montevideo, as to where Savory was being held—'

'A somewhat cruel imprisonment, and unnecessary. Why not hold him in Montevideo?'

The German shrugged. 'It is a matter for the Uruguayans, who are primitive people. Perhaps this place was regarded as safer than Montevideo – against you British, you understand. However, my Admiral was further informed that a British force was known to have occupied the fort subsequently – I believe a policeman from London brought word of this to Montevideo—'

'And so you were ordered to extract Savory, and take him back to the *Kaiser Wilhelm*?'

The German brought his heels together and gave an ironic bow. 'Yes. Which is what I shall now do. My Admiral will be much pleased, which yours, I think, will not.'

'Possibly. But there's something about which your Admiral will be far from pleased – your Kaiser likewise.'

'And this is?'

'The killing of Her Britannic Majesty's Ambassador,' Halfhyde said with his tongue in his cheek. He went on to give the undoubted facts. 'A bullet entered the back of Lord Horace's head whilst he was facing the Uruguayan soldiers. When extracted, that bullet will be found to be of German origin.'

'I do not believe this!' The officer had gone as white as a sheet. 'You tell lies—'

'Come and you shall see the body for yourself.' Halfhyde started to turn aside, then very suddenly flung himself at the much rattled German, seized his arm and twisted it up cruelly. The officer gasped with agony. Halfhyde removed his revolver and thrust it into the German's side, pressing hard. He called out to the German ratings, not doubting that his meaning would be understood. 'Drop your arms or your officer will suffer!' He paused. 'Master-at-Arms?'

'Yessir?'

'See to the disarming of the German party, if you please. Where is Mr Todhunter?'

'Here I am, Mr Halfhyde,' Todhunter said from behind a hefty German seaman.

'Divest yourself of your guard, Mr Todhunter, and arrest your prisoner before he removes his underpants and escapes us.'

In an aggrieved voice Todhunter said, 'Easier said than done, I fear, Mr Halfhyde. If I make the arrest on foreign soil, Captain Watkiss will—'

'Captain Watkiss is not here, Mr Todhunter, but I am. Act as though I were Chief Superintendent Portlock, and execute your warrant immediately.' Halfhyde pressed again into his prisoner with the captured revolver. 'Call off your men, or it'll be the worse for you,' he ordered. 'I have no doubt that Queen Victoria will ask for your head, but I may be able to assuage her wrath with certain reports if you cease from hostile acts.'

*   *   *

Captain Watkiss had reached the flagship now; he lost no time in sending for MAA Pickering in regard to Colonel Oribe. 'You need have no further fear, Pickering,' he said. 'Colonel Oribe's body no longer exists. I myself witnessed its total destruction with my own eyes.'

'Yessir, thank you, sir, much obliged I'm sure, sir.' MAA Pickering touched his cap peak and then felt another twinge of fear in regard to the man who looked like Colonel Oribe, already clobbered before approval had been sought from the Flag Captain. He explained, with reluctance.

Watkiss clicked his tongue. 'You're a blasted fool, Pickering.'

'Yessir.'

'This will complicate matters with the damn dagoes just when everything was set fair! How, precisely, was this man struck?'

'Clobbered over the 'ead, sir, with a piece 'o timber.'

Watkiss found the solution. 'Fell down through a hatch, Pickering. Produce witnesses in case they're needed. That's all and you may go.' As the grateful Master-at-Arms touched his cap again and left the flagship's compass platform, Captain Watkiss, scanning the now dusk-shadowed seas, hummed

'Rule Britannia' to himself in much satisfaction. He steadied his telescope upon a cloud of smoke proceeding outwards from the direction of Montevideo; then as it came closer, the Flag Captain let out an expletive at the yeoman of the watch.

'God damn, it's the blasted Hun!'

'Hun, sir?'

'Yes! A steam picquet-boat from the *Kaiser Wilhelm* – I can see the blasted Hun ensign quite clearly. Where's the Officer of the Watch for God's sake?'

'On the quarterdeck, sir—'

'I know that, you fool. Get him.'

'Aye, aye, sir.' The yeoman padded away to the voice-pipe that connected with the quartermaster's lobby aft. Captain Watkiss vibrated like a spinning-top, shaking his telescope. Within two minutes Lieutenant Lamphorn hastened up and saluted.

'Sir—'

'Oh, it's you. Sound for action, Mr Lamphorn.'

Lamphorn stared in consternation. 'Action, sir?'

'Yes! Kindly do not repeat my orders at me! Von Merkatz' blasted barge is approaching and I'm going to damn well keep him at arms' length. Go and do as I say at once.'

'Aye, aye, sir.' Lieutenant Lamphorn, shaking his head in astonishment even though he was becoming accustomed to Captain Watkiss and his peccadilloes, summoned the bugler who obediently sounded for action. Disturbed in his sea-cabin, Rear-Admiral Daintree emerged and hastened to the compass platform.

'Flag Captain, what for heaven's sake is it now?'

Watkiss turned irritably. 'My dear sir, you behave as though you were a cuckoo-clock. The Huns are approaching and I won't have it.'

'You are certainly not opening upon them with my—'

'I don't intend to. I shall threaten only. I suspect it's Oribe.'

'Oribe's disintegrated,' Daintree said disagreeably.

'I'm aware of that, sir. I refer to the gunfire that *caused* him to disintegrate. Von Merkatz may have been disturbed by that, don't you see! I'm not having him aboard and that's that.'

'I doubt if you will,' Daintree said. He had been studying the approaching boat through his telescope. 'I suggest you fall out from general quarters, Flag Captain, and point my guns somewhere else.'

'But good God above—'

'Mr Halfhyde is in the picquet-boat, Flag Captain, and appears to be fully in command.' Daintree spoke vengefully: he was at the end of his patience and the prospect of a long repair in the company of Captain Watkiss was an appalling one. 'I think you need glasses. I have a mind to make a report to that effect and have you before a medical board—'

'Oh, balls and—'

'Which may well,' Daintree went on, raising his voice, 'decide you're insane to boot and recommend that you finish your service in a strait-jacket.' He vanished down the ladder; extended argument tended nowadays to bring on an attack of indigestion.

* * *

'I commandeered the Germans' boat,' Halfhyde reported soon after, and added, 'Admiral von Merkatz' landing-party will be found, if you care to make him a signal, at the fort.'

'Yes, I see. Will they not have marched back to the dockyard by now, Mr Halfhyde?' Watkiss asked.

'I doubt it, sir. I left them well tied up, to ponder on the shooting of Lord Horace Vane.'

'Where's Lord Horace now?'

'In the picquet-boat's cabin, sir.'

Watkiss nodded. 'We must bring him inboard. He can go in the cold store.'

'Not as far as Portsmouth, sir. We shall be many weeks in dockyard hands before we can leave the Plate. Canon Rampling is anxious to arrange a ceremonial funeral ashore.'

'And leave a British Ambassador upon foreign soil, Mr Halfhyde?'

'It's inevitable, sir.'

Watkiss gave a heavy nod; important, well-bred death was a serious affair and made him lugubrious. 'I think I shall keep up the fiction of death by a German bullet until that blasted von Merkatz takes his damn ship to sea and leaves me in peace. The knowledge of it will be keeping the bugger fixed to his lavatory

seat all the way to his blasted Fatherland I shouldn't wonder.'
Captain Watkiss dwelt his inward eye upon the scene with
much satisfaction; things had worked out well, and he
remarked as much. 'I feel I've brought things to an excellent
conclusion, Mr Halfhyde. I fear Admiral Daintree would not
have done. It was obvious from the start that a forceful
approach was needed – the threat of my guns, by God! That's
what's done it.' He lunged in various directions with his telescope and thrust out jaw and stomach in warlike fashion. 'It's
no use being namby-pamby with blasted foreigners, Mr
Halfhyde.'

'Indeed not, sir. Mr Hillman,' Halfhyde added, 'might not
agree, perhaps.'

'Mr Hillman? What about Mr Hillman, pray?'

'He's still being held in the town, sir, as a hostage against the
return of Todhunter.'

'Oh, blast the fellow, so he is, I'd forgotten about him, he's
not important.' Watkiss clicked his tongue in annoyance. 'I'll
ask the dagoes to send him back. The buggers who were put
aboard as guards ... they'll be going ashore shortly and Mr
Hillman can come back in exchange, I suppose.' He paused.
'That fellow from the Foreign Office – Petrie-Smith.'

'Yes, sir?'

'Blasted nuisance as usual. He's insisted in advance that if
the Ambassador should be killed by the dagoes the Admiral's to
order mourning bands to be worn throughout the squadron,
and how the hell do we find material to make blasted mourning
bands I'd like to know!' Captain Watkiss simmered. 'I've a
damn good mind to get the Admiral to insist Petrie-Smith takes
over in the room of Lord Horace, then with any luck he'll be
kidnapped too!'

*   *   *

The cell door shut upon Savory by hand of MAA Pickering gave
a very satisfactory clang, and Detective Inspector Todhunter
sighed with great relief and mopped his brow, which was about
to be topped once again by his bowler hat. He couldn't wait to
get out of his military uniform, but first the prisoner Savory
had had to be put under lock and key. And next there was a

little ceremony; MAA Pickering, who was thirsty, prevailed upon Mr Todhunter to join him, with MAA Titmuss and Ship's Corporal Judd, in his gloomy cabin to partake of rum.

Mr Todhunter lifted his glass. 'Your very good health, Mr Pickering.'

'Likewise.' A large tot went down, gulp. 'An' 'Er Majesty . . . seein' as 'ow it's 'er booze.'

'Her Majesty,' Mr Todhunter said loyally, and coughed in some embarrassment. Stolen government property . . . but let it pass, he thought, the chief super won't ever know of any connivance. However, Mr Todhunter refused more rum; the others did not, and Mr Todhunter listened somewhat agog to several tales of drink and women in half the world's ports where the ship's police had obtained oats beyond the ken of the Metropolitan Police. The party was interrupted after a while by the sound of bugles, and they all rushed up on deck and stared from the fo'c'sle.

Great shapes were stealing through the twilight, and MAA Pickering identified them as the *Nürnberg*, the *Königsberg* and the *Friedrich der Grosse*, the latter evidently drawn with success from the Staten Island rocks. As the bugles ceased a sound of hearty laughter from very many men came clear across the waters of the Plate, and a German searchlight played rudely upon the British flagship's shattered stern and the embedded bows of Her Majesty's cruiser *Cardiff*, with the *Hector* behind again. From the compass platform the *Friedrich der Grosse* a signal came, to be reported by *Halcyon*'s chief yeoman to the Admiral and Captain Watkiss.

'*Cardiff* is in a rudely suggestive position,' the chief yeoman read out. 'Like lucky Alphonse in the famous joke – in the middle again.'